SUMMER AT THE CHÂTEAU

JENNIFER BOHNET

Boldwood

First published in Great Britain in 2021 by Boldwood Books Ltd.

Copyright © Jennifer Bohnet, 2021

Cover Design by Debbie Clement Design

Cover Photography: Shutterstock

A CIP catalogue record for this book is available from the British Library.

Paperback ISBN 978-1-83889-090-2

Large Print ISBN 978-1-80162-900-3

Hardback ISBN 978-1-80162-899-0

Ebook ISBN 978-1-83889-091-9

Kindle ISBN 978-1-83889-092-6

Audio CD ISBN 978-1-80162-717-7

MP3 CD ISBN 978-1-83889-089-6

Digital audio download ISBN 978-1-80162-718-4

Boldwood Books Ltd
23 Bowerdean Street
London SW6 3TN
www.boldwoodbooks.com

This one is for Bianca with love.

'Oh time, thou must untangle this, not I
It is too hard a knot for me t'untie!'

— *TWELFTH NIGHT. SHAKESPEARE.*

PROLOGUE
TEN YEARS AGO

'Perchance to Dream'

— *Hamlet. Shakespeare.*

A Notaire's Office in the town of Carhaix Plouger, Brittany, France.

The notaire's office Pixie Sampson and her husband, Frank, were ushered into was a bright modern space, typical of office complexes the world over. But as she looked around, Pixie realised that, despite the twenty-first century setting, the room was quintessentially old French. Perhaps it was the combination of the subdued cream of the walls and the pale green of the woodwork; the gallery wall of portraits of past partners in antique gilt frames; or maybe the opulent chandelier hanging from the ceiling adding a certain *je ne sais quoi*. Antique-style chairs were placed in front of the painted French desk with its curved lines and gilded edges, a sleek gold coloured laptop placed exactly in the centre of its surface.

Jean-Yves Ropars, the notaire, solemnly shook their hands as he wished them 'Bonjour', first Frank and then Pixie, before indicating for them to sit as he placed the file of papers he'd brought into the room with him on the desk. They both declined the offer of coffee and Jean-Yves opened the file and began to explain exactly what they were signing. Three quarters of an hour later, when Pixie personally was beginning to lose the will to live, having struggled to understand Jean-Yves with his fragmented English and wishing that they had asked for a translator to be present, it came to an end.

'And now, is the final one,' Jean-Yves said, pushing the paper across the desk with a flourish and smiling as they both sighed with relief at the same time.

Pixie rubbed her right hand, trying to relieve the ache that had developed from signing and countersigning after Frank so many pieces of legal paper. She'd stopped counting after fifteen.

Jean-Yves gathered up all the papers, placing them in a neat pile before looking at them both, standing up and holding out his hand for them to shake. 'Felicitations, Monsieur and Madame Sampson, you are now the proud owners of un petit château Français. Bonne chance.'

PART I

'We are such stuff as dreams are made on.'

— *THE TEMPEST. SHAKESPEARE*

1

Pixie Sampson's thoughts were all over the place as she lay in bed at nine o'clock on the Wednesday morning after the funeral, trying to summon the energy to get up and face the world.

She'd spent the three weeks since her husband Frank's death in a kind of stupor, more dead than alive herself. Married for thirty-five years, the shock of Frank's accident had thrown all the known certainties of her life up in the air, leaving her struggling to accept the inevitable changes his death had brought. Becoming a widow at fifty-nine because of some teenage joy-driver had never featured in her life plan.

Widow. How she disliked that word. But she had no option other than to accept it. To, 'Keep Calm and Carry On' as the faded poster pinned to the kitchen wall of her grandparents' Devonshire home had urged her as she was growing up. She'd learnt that lesson well. So well in fact, her friends called her stoical in the face of a crisis, which made her smile. If they only knew how hard she had to work to keep showing that face to the world. To keep the pretence up.

Her name, Pixie, alone had given her more opportunities than she wanted to learn stoicism in the face of torment. Why her mother had thought it a good idea to christen her daughter with such a childish name was beyond her. Her twin brother had rebelled against his name, Augustus, which he'd shortened to Gus by the time he arrived at secondary school and proceeded to thump any boy who dared to call him anything else. All her mother had ever said when Pixie complained bitterly about her name and ask 'why' was, 'You were so tiny when you were born, you looked like you'd jumped out of one of the illustrations from the Flower Fairy books.'

'But you could have given me a sensible proper name to fall back on and call me Pixie as a nickname.'

Gwen had just smiled at her. 'Didn't want to,' and had wafted away to her pottery studio in the garden, to make and paint more Devonshire gnomes and pixies that the tourists seemingly couldn't get enough of.

Pixie sighed. She wished Gus and his family hadn't re-located to Wales a few years ago, she missed them all so much, especially her godchildren, Charlie and Annabelle. At least her mother still lived reasonably close.

Five years ago, Gwen had finally been persuaded by the twins to move from her isolated house on Dartmoor and live nearer Pixie and Frank. Protesting loudly, she'd finally decided on a cottage down near the coast in the South Hams, situated on the outskirts of a large village with lots of amenities like a doctor, supermarket, bank, cafe, post office, et cetera, all within walking distance.

It had taken just six months for Gwen to become a part of the community: she'd joined the WI, was welcomed into the church choir, went Old Tyme Dancing once a week and had even started to paint again. She told people that moving to the village was one of the best decisions she'd ever made, never mentioning how anti the move she'd been when Pixie and Gus had first suggested it.

Eighty-four next birthday, she was still as irrepressible and independent as ever, but Pixie had sensed her mother was beginning to struggle with certain things. Not that Gwen would ever admit it. Maybe the time was coming when another move was needed? Not to a home, Gwen had made the twins promise years ago that they would never put her 'out to pasture' as she put it. With her brother and his wife living with their family too far away in Carmarthenshire, Pixie knew helping Gwen would be her responsibility, which, loving her mother as she did, was something she willingly accepted. Would daily visits be enough or should she invite Gwen to live with her now that she was a widow?

Maybe she should downsize – another word Pixie hated – and buy something suitable for her and Gwen to live in together. A bungalow perhaps? The thought flashed through her mind, while she'd happily take on the role of carer for her mum, who would do the same for her? The longed for family she and Frank had planned for had never happened. Life had thrown the curveball of infertility in her direction and after years of tests and treatment both she and Frank had given up on their dream of having a family, accepted the fact that it would never happen and got on with life and growing older together. Frank had seemed more accepting of things than Pixie, who, whilst never admitting it to anyone, never quite got over her inability to do the one thing a woman was supposedly on earth to do, produce babies.

For over thirty years, though, they'd been happy together. It was only recently, in the last year, that Pixie had begun to feel that everything had slipped into becoming a habit. They never seemed to talk any more. She'd tried to console herself with the thought that this was what happened to people in long, successful marriages. Frank still loved her and was as attentive as always, but there was a sort of hesitation in the air sometimes in the way he regarded her, as if he wanted to say something before changing his mind. She didn't think for one moment he was having an affair, he was incapable of hurting her like that, but there was definitely something on his mind. When, some weeks ago, Frank suggested a 'city break' weekend away in Bath, Pixie had happily agreed, promising herself she'd do her best to get Frank to talk to her properly, like they always had. Then, the accident that changed everything happened, a week before the booked break.

Pixie didn't think the memory of the events of that Friday, the first week in March, would ever leave her. She'd spent the day in her study doing the final read through and tweaking of her next book before pressing the button to send it to her editor. It was early evening when she stood up, stretching her arms above her head and giving a sigh of relief. It was done. Hopefully her editor would like – no, love it, and the edits when they arrived in a couple of weeks wouldn't be too harsh. In the meantime, she'd enjoy some downtime, especially the coming weekend in Bath. To think, this time next week they would be on their way there. Frank had reserved a room at one of their favourite hotels, booked tickets for the theatre and was talking about dinner afterwards at one of the five-star restaurants the city boasted.

As she'd turned to leave the study, her mobile rang. Frank.

'I'm sorry, but I'll be later than I thought getting back this evening. The traffic coming out of Exeter is horrendous and it's pouring with rain so I've stopped in the motorway services and I'm going to have a coffee and something to eat until everything settles down.'

'Sounds a sensible idea,' Pixie had said. 'You take care and drive safely. Love you.'

'See you soon. Love you too.' And the connection had died.

Pixie had mooched around for the next couple of hours. She'd opened a bottle of wine, made a cheese and cranberry sandwich (a combination she loved and Frank hated), tidied the kitchen, flicked through the TV channels, before slipping one of her favourite DVDs into the player, *Midnight in Paris*, and settling down to watch it.

When the door knocker banged at ten minutes past ten, Pixie's first thought was Frank had forgotten his keys again, before remembering they'd agreed on a secret hiding place for the spare key. So who was visiting at this time of night? She had cautiously opened the door and came face to face with two policemen. She'd slammed the door shut again. Policemen on your doorstep meant bad news. News she didn't want to hear.

'Mrs Sampson, please open the door,' a quiet, concerned voice had said.

Numbly, she had loosened the chain and let them in to confirm what she had known the instant she'd seen the two of them standing there. Road traffic accident on the A38 Expressway. Joy riders in a stolen car. Lost control. Frank dead at the scene. The police had stayed with her for some time before reluctantly leaving. They had offered to drive her to Gwen's, but Pixie had refused. Gwen was too old to be visited by police officers at midnight. She told them she'd drive over in the morning and break the news and stay with her. After they'd left, Pixie had collapsed on the settee, shaking with the enormity of the tragedy.

Pixie sighed, remembering the awful days, now weeks, that followed before managing to switch her thoughts back to the current day. Gwen had suggested lunch at the pub in her village and Pixie, still lacking the energy to either cook anything or to challenge the hidden agenda she guessed was behind her mother's invite, had agreed. This afternoon she had a three o'clock appointment with the bank manager to organise the financial side of her life from here on in. Perhaps over lunch she'd gently probe Gwen on how she felt about the two of them living together.

Right, there was a bit of a purpose to this day so she'd better get up and get on with it. Maybe after the bank this afternoon, she'd come home and make a start on sorting out Frank's things. Maybe.

2

Ten miles away from Pixie, Gwen Ellis was eating her breakfast sitting in the gazebo-shaped shed in the corner of her garden, breathing in the fresh air and watching the never-ending convoy of tiny blue tits, blackbirds, sparrows and other birds devouring the seeds and fat balls she'd put out earlier for them. She adored this corner of her garden and often sat out here thinking about everything and nothing., even in winter when she wrapped herself in an old duvet. This spring morning though she'd simply zipped up her warm fleece and her thoughts were all about Pixie.

The last few weeks had been hard on Pixie and it would, of course, take time for her to recover, but, in the meantime, Gwen promised herself she'd do her best to help her face the rest of her life. Life was too short to stagnate; it seemed to disappear in a flash. Look at her – surely it was only five minutes ago she was thirty-nine and now suddenly she was eighty-three. The forty-odd years between had disappeared like a puff of smoke from one of the cigarettes she used to enjoy and was denied these days. Still, she'd been lucky, those years had been mainly good and she reckoned she still had a fair few left in her. There was time to set Pixie

on the right path now that she was on her own. Not the she'd
interfere – she could do subtle nudges as well as the next woman
if she had to.

Over lunch today, she'd offer to help Pixie sort through
Frank's clothes ready to go to the charity shop. It was coming up
to a month since he'd died and things like that needed to be dealt
with. The longer they were in the house, the harder it would
become to stop the place morphing into a shrine to his memory.
Once that had been dealt with, she'd gently probe Pixie about
her plans for the future. Thankfully, there had been no unexpected bequests in Frank's will for Pixie to deal with. As his wife,
she inherited everything. Gwen had heaved a huge silent sigh of
relief over that. These days, so many people, knowing they would
be beyond questioning, seemed to take delight in disclosing
secrets from the past in their wills, which only served to hurt
those left behind. Gwen was of the opinion that the majority of
secrets were better taken to the grave than left to grieving rela-
tives and she planned on taking hers with her. Not that there
were any scandalous revelations to be made. The skeleton in her
cupboard was a personal regret, not a major drama involving
other people.

Gwen was ready and waiting for Pixie when she arrived and
together they walked the short distance to the village pub, The
Rose and Lion. Once Gwen was settled at her favourite table,
close, but not too close, to the log burner in the corner, Pixie went
up to the bar to order the food and to get their drinks. Gwen
looked at her pensive face as she returned with a gin and tonic for
Gwen and a glass of non-alcoholic wine for herself as she was
driving.

'What's on your mind, Pixie?' Gwen asked gently. 'Anything I can help with?'

Pixie shook her head. 'Not unless you can magically bring Frank to life again and make this nightmare go away.' She took a sip of her drink before placing it on the table. 'The house feels so empty. I keep expecting to find him in the kitchen banging saucepans around starting to fix dinner, a large glass of red on the work surface.' She glanced at her mother. 'Do you remember how you felt all those years ago when…' she hesitated, 'when Dad left? Did you miss having him around?'

'I remember only too well. And no, to be truthful, I didn't miss having him around at all. It was a huge relief when he left,' Gwen answered. 'I had you and Gus to bring up, and as far as I was concerned, Colin leaving was one less mouth to feed.' Gwen reached out and touched Pixie's hand. 'I've told you all this before, I love you and Gus. Giving birth to you two was the best thing I've ever done in my life, but I was never in love with Colin like you and Frank were with each other. That makes a big difference.'

Pixie nodded. 'It does.' She hesitated. 'I was wondering, how do you feel about moving in with me?'

'Why? You afraid of being alone?' Gwen looked at her sharply.

Pixie let out a deep sigh. 'No, of course not. I was thinking we could both sell up and buy a bungalow for the two of us, somewhere like Torquay or maybe Dartmouth? Be company for each other.' She gave her mother a quick glance.

Gwen knew that the underlying, unspoken message was 'you're getting older, you're going to need help soon'.

Gwen took a slow drink of her gin and tonic, gathering her thoughts at this unexpected conversation. Carefully, she replaced the glass on the table.

'Stairs are good – not too steep or too many, I grant you – but they're good exercise. Keep the legs moving, the heart pumping. Bungalow indeed,' Gwen snorted, before looking at Pixie. 'Darling, I'm certainly not ready for the quiet life,' she shrugged, 'and you're twenty-four years behind me. You don't need a bungalow or a quiet life. You need to get yourself together and live a bit. Spend some of that insurance money Frank left you. I know,' Gwen said, her eyes lighting up. 'You could buy a berth on that "The World" yacht and sail the Seven Seas, or, at least, the Med, for a few years. I'd join you on that venture. Probably cheaper than living on shore with everything all found,' she mused. 'Burial at sea is always a possibility too.'

'Mum, what are you on about? I could no more do that than book a flight on a rocket to the moon.'

'Now there's a thought,' Gwen said. 'I quite fancy a trip there,' and she hummed 'Fly me to the moon' while smiling across at Sam, widower and owner of The Rose and Lion, who was currently manning the bar.

'Mum, behave. You'll embarrass the poor man.'

'Nonsense,' Gwen said, raising her glass and acknowledging the wink Sam gave her. 'He knows I'm only being friendly.'

'So a bungalow is out then, but how about buying something else suitable for the two of us?' Pixie asked.

'I'm not sure. You'd have to promise not to cramp my style,' Gwen answered, a twinkle in her eye.

'Oh, you're impossible,' Pixie laughed.

Their food arrived at that moment and they tucked into the chef's special of the day, a delicious home-made steak and kidney pie. As she ate her own meal, Gwen watched as Pixie pushed food around the plate rather than eating with enjoyment.

'Not long to Easter,' she said. 'Maybe you should think about going away for a break. How about France? I quite fancy a trip there myself.' She glanced across at Pixie. 'Are you any nearer taking possession of that place in Brittany you bought, what, must be ten years ago? Always seemed a bit naive on your parts to me, buying a place you couldn't move in to until the owner either moved out to give you vacant possession or died.'

Pixie sighed. 'Frank explained at the time, Mum. It's a well-known system in France called viager. They calculate the value of the property based on various things, including the age of the vendor. We made a down payment, which the French call a bouquet, and then a monthly payment while the vendor is alive. Once he dies or moves out, the property is ours. It's a bit of an investment gamble, but it does mean you can eventually end up owning a really nice property for a bargain price.'

'What happens now that Frank's died and not the seller?'

'We bought it jointly, my name is on the deeds, so I will be the sole owner now I guess, when the time comes. I'll have to talk to someone in France about selling it on. I won't go and live there now without Frank, so there's no point in keeping it.

Gwen looked at her. 'Why can't you live there? When you bought the place, you planned to move over – you talked about running writers' retreats, didn't you? You could still do that. You're as free as a bird now.' Seeing the look on Pixie's face, she added, 'Even keep it as a second home.'

'Living in France was something we were going to do together. It was our dream – what's the point without Frank?' Pixie sighed. 'And it's too big to be a holiday home. Anyway, I know Madame Quiltu died a several years ago, but Monsieur Quiltu is still alive and in residence. Besides, I can't leave you. Gus lives too far away to be any help in an emergency.'

Gwen wagged her finger. 'Do not use me as an excuse, my girl. If you want to go and live in France, you jolly well go. I could probably be persuaded to accompany you – a last adventure. Would beat a bungalow, that's for sure.'

'Not going to happen,' Pixie shrugged. 'I need to start reorganising my life and...' she hesitated. 'And, I was thinking I might make a start sorting out Frank's clothes and things this evening, but I'm not sure I'm up to it yet.' Her voice faded away.

'I can give you a hand if you want,' Gwen said gently, glad that Pixie had raised the subject. 'Always better to have company for things like that. But not this evening. That's a thought – you should come OldTyme Dancing with me tonight.'

Pixie looked at her. 'Seriously? Have you forgotten I've got two left feet and can't keep to a basic rhythm?'

Gwen laughed. 'I admit I had forgotten about your lack of co-ordination. We'll find something else for you to get involved with.'

'Once everything has settled back down, I'll have plenty to do. I'm still under contract for two more books. My editor sent me a gentle email only yesterday wanting to know if I was up to coping with the edits for my latest book,' Pixie said. 'I'll be back in a writing routine before you know it.'

'All work and no play,' Gwen muttered. She ignored Pixie's shake of her head and the pained expression on her face.

'Do you want to come with me into town?' Pixie asked. 'I shouldn't be too long at the bank. You could have a look round the shops. Do some window shopping, if nothing else.'

Gwen shook her head. 'No thanks. I've got an appointment with Emma at Nailed It. I'm thinking of having dark blue varnish with silver question marks on alternate nails. What d'you think? Pink is so boring.'

The way Pixie shook her head at her with a look of disbelief on her face told her the answer, and Gwen gave her daughter a mischievous smirk.

3

There was a fly trapped behind the vertical Venetian blinds of the bank manager's office and Pixie found herself watching it rather than concentrating on what the man sitting opposite her was saying for his quiet voice threatened to send her to sleep. Frank had always laughed at her when she quoted the old saying '*why keep a dog and bark yourself,* you're the financial expert in this family.' She and Frank each had their own bank accounts and a joint one for all household expenses and holidays to which they both contributed the same amount by monthly direct debit. The arrangement had always worked well. Now she hated the thought of having to get to grips with everything herself.

'Now that all payments to France have ceased, we've switched the monies into a savings account,' the bank manager said, looking at his computer screen. 'One that—'

'I'm sorry,' Pixie interrupted, suddenly on high alert. 'But that can't be right. Those payments should not have stopped. If we default on that agreement, we stand to lose the not inconsiderable amount of money we've already paid in the last nine years.

You had no business stopping those payments.' She glared at the manager.

'Mrs Sampson, your husband instructed us to stop paying out the monies on...' he glanced at the screen again and told her the date. 'I remember the reason he gave was the viager agreement had come to an end when the owner died the week previously.'

'What?' Pixie felt herself slump in her seat. 'You mean we have wholly owned the property for the last...' she did a quick calculation in her head. 'The last sixteen months.'

'Correct.'

'I'm sorry – but why didn't I know?'

The bank manager gave her a sympathetic look. 'I'm sorry too, but I can't answer that question. Your husband is the one to have told you and, for some unknown reason, he chose not to.'

* * *

Pixie drove home from her meeting at the bank on autopilot, her mind whirring with unanswerable questions. Why had Frank not told her? Why hadn't they visited? What state was the place in, having been empty for over a year? What did she do now? The questions kept coming and coming.

Once home, she abandoned the car on the driveway and made straight for Frank's study. Frank had always kept the room meticulous; everything filed away, with a laptop and an old-fashioned Filofax placed on the desk.

Pixie sank onto the wooden ship's chair with its padded leather seat and curved arms that Frank had always used in preference to a regular office chair. The bottom left-hand drawer of the desk was deep with space for hanging files and she pulled it open. Half a dozen files were all titled and placed alphabetically behind each other in the drawer, the contents stacked neatly inside: Bank, Household, Investments, Insurances/Personal, Tax, Work. Pixie's fingers hovered over the drawer before pushing the last three files to the back and flicking through the contents of the Investment file. She pulled out an envelope marked 'French Château' and sat back, looking at it thoughtfully, remembering their excitement all those years ago.

They'd talked about buying a holiday home in France for years. Not in the more popular areas like Provence, the Dordogne or the Cote d'Azur because neither of them could take the summer heat of those places. Besides, Frank had said, what's the point of moving somewhere and joining a bunch of ex-pats? 'No, authentic France is what we want.' Pixie had agreed. Together they'd decided on the western side of France, in particular the ruggedness of Finistère in Brittany appealed and they'd spent holiday after holiday annoying estate agents and looking for their dream home but had been unable to find anything that ticked all their boxes and inspired them to take the plunge. Until they'd both fallen in love with Château Quiltu on sight. It was, they decided, the perfect buy to celebrate their joint fiftieth birthdays and look forward to their eventual retirement.

Although a smaller property than the word château usually conjured up, it was bigger than they'd envisaged buying, with its six large bedrooms, four bathrooms, two salons, a kitchen twice the size of their current one, a floored attic area, four hectares of land, complete with a small cottage, a couple of barn-like buildings, a lake and woods. There was even a dilapidated orangery on the back of the property.

Situated in Finistère but close to the borders of both Morbihan and Côte d'Armor, Château Quiltu was ideally situated about an hour from both the west coast and the north coast, which included the ferry port of Roscoff. With its easy access to the towns of Carhaix Plouger and Châteauneuf-du-Faou, as well as Huelgoat with its ancient forest and mystic atmosphere, the château was located in the middle of a perfect French triangle.

Château Quiltu, Pixie had fleetingly thought, would make a wonderful writers' retreat. The fact that it was for sale under the viager system – a system they had never heard of before – complicated things. It was an investment gamble, albeit a legal one drawn up by notaires.

They met the current owners, Monsieur and Madame Quiltu, both in their eighties and neither in the best of health. The château had been in Monsieur Quiltu's family since the Revolution and they were both sad they were the last generation to live in it as they didn't have any children to inherit.

Frank had pored for days, weeks really, over the pages and pages of bureaucratic paperwork, working out which particular viager deal to go with before deciding to go with the lump sum, known as the bouquet, and a smaller monthly payment to the current owners, who would live in the château until they either moved out or died, when Frank and Pixie could take possession of it.

For over eight years, regular monthly payments were made and they'd waited patiently, planning their French retirement and dreaming of the day it would become a reality. Except when the day had finally arrived and they could take possession Frank hadn't even mentioned going to France. Sixteen months ago, he'd been alive. Busy working with business trips all over Europe. If only Frank had told her the château was theirs, they could have made the long-awaited move to France then – and Frank would still be alive.

Pixie bit her bottom lip as she took the papers out of the envelope. It didn't make sense. She was going to have to go to France, talk to the notaire there and instruct him to put the château on the market.

She picked up the phone and rang Gwen.

'Mum, how do you fancy going to France with me for Easter?'

4

Pixie had decided when booking their tickets on the Pont Aven for the overnight ferry crossing from Plymouth to Roscoff that she'd treat them both to a Commodore Cabin as it was supposed to be a holiday break after all. And besides, they were both too old for bunk beds. But unlike Gwen, who was asleep the moment her head hit the pillow, Pixie tossed and turned, unable to settle. In the past, she and Frank had always taken a daytime ferry and enjoyed the six or seven hours it took to cross the hundred miles of Channel separating England from France.

A meal in the restaurant, a drink at the bar, time up on deck at both ends of the journey watching the coastline disappearing or getting closer. Usually there was even time for her to open her laptop and do some plotting, if not actual writing, for her next book. This time though, confined to the cabin, with several enforced hours of night-time solitude and thinking time, Pixie's thoughts were as choppy as the waves the boat was powering through.

She'd spent the ten days since the bank manager had dropped

the bombshell news that Château Quiltu was now hers wrestling with two unanswerable questions. Firstly, why had Frank kept it secret from her for so many months and, secondly, when had he planned to tell her, if fate in the form of a joy-rider hadn't intervened? Try as she might, Pixie had failed to arrive at an answer for either question. The envelope she'd found in the file in the desk drawer contained the original papers they'd both signed, plus a letter from the notaire informing them of the death of Monsieur Quiltu, and a large bunch of keys that were now like a lead weight in the bottom of her tote. But there were no clues to explain Frank's uncharacteristically secretive behaviour.

When Gwen had jumped enthusiastically at the idea of Easter in France, Pixie hadn't told her that the viager scheme had finished and the château now belonged to her. She'd simply said, Gwen was right and the break would be good for both of them; she'd tell her the truth once they were in France. Her mother, she knew, would be unable to stop trying to dissect the reason Frank had kept the news to himself. Pixie had simply told her that she needed to go and sort things out with the notaire face to face and to instruct an estate agent. 'You know how the French love their bureaucracy, there are sure to be papers for me to sign before I can put the place on the market.'

Pixie reached an arm out and picked up her phone from the small shelf where she'd placed it and sighed – 4 a.m. Another two hours before she needed to get up. She couldn't even concentrate on thinking about the storyline for her new book. The deadline for which her publishers had compassionately pushed back a few months because of Frank dying, but she still had to think of a name for her main character, not to mention some sort of plot, and to actually write the thing. Maybe if she wrote mysteries or crime stories, she'd be better at solving the puzzle in her own life, but she didn't, she wrote women's fiction dealing with relationships between the whole spectrum of human beings: brothers and sisters, friends, aunts, cousins and uncles, as well as married couples.

But even with her expertise at solving the problems of fictional characters, she hadn't been able to figure out what had been happening in her own marriage. She knew, though, that both of them had become increasingly busy with their own careers in recent years. Frank, headhunted a few years ago because of his expertise in the fight against the piracy of DVDs and other consumer goods, had found himself in the role of roving European ambassador for several major companies. Weekly business trips to Europe had become the norm in his life and Pixie had become used to spending more and more time at home by herself. Which, coincidentally, had helped her to achieve her own dream.

A freelance journalist for most of their married life, she'd always wanted to write fiction and the year she turned fifty, with Frank's encouragement, she'd taken the plunge, given up journalism and written a novel. Unable to land either an agent or a publisher, she'd gone the independent route, which was a steep learning curve to say the least. When her third book hit the bestseller list, it had been her turn to be headhunted and she now had both an agent and a publisher. Her latest novel was winning accolades and was on the shortlist for an international prize and she'd agreed to start the edits for the next one after Easter. And then, writer's block permitting, she needed to start a new one.

Lying there listening to the water slapping against the sides as the ferry cut its way through the water, Pixie vowed she'd get her act together, once Easter was over and she was back home, with the château on the market.

Inevitably, her thoughts turned to the way things between

herself and Frank had seemed to change in the last year. How she'd planned to tackle him about it on that never taken city break. How things would have panned out between them if Frank hadn't been killed was another of those unanswerable questions. The last time they'd spent any real 'quality' time together had been their summer holiday last year. They'd gone to the eastern side of France, a first for them both, staying in Isla 2000 in the Mercantour Park, close to the Italian border. A ski resort in winter, during the summer months it was full of beautiful countryside to explore with quaint mountain-side villages. Both Nice, an hour away down on the coast, and several small Italian villages were easily accessible. It had been a good holiday. Almost like a second honeymoon, Pixie had felt, but once home again nothing had really changed as they both slipped back seamlessly into their individual routines. She could only wish now that she'd asked Frank about whatever was bothering him on that holiday. If wishes were fishes...

Pixie knew from the date the bank manager had told her and the date on the final completion paper in the envelope, the château had been theirs then: they could have gone there together for the first time as owners. So why hadn't they? The only explanation Pixie could think of was the holiday had already been booked and paid for and Frank hadn't wanted to change their plans and lose either the deposit or the airfare. Although that still didn't answer the question why he hadn't told her about Monsieur Quiltu dying and the château finally becoming theirs. They could certainly have visited in the months since. Had he lost interest in the place? Wanted to put it on the market and didn't like to broach the subject, knowing that living in France was a dream of hers that he no longer shared? The unanswerable questions went round and round in her head.

Pixie turned despondently onto her side, pulling the cover

over her, trying to get comfortable in the hope she would drift off. She had a rendezvous with the notaire tomorrow, she could only hope he would be able to throw some light on things. And today she would once again be seeing the château that she'd fallen in love with the first time she'd set eyes on it. And with that happier thought, she finally drifted to sleep.

5

In the morning as they sat in the car waiting for the man to wave the queue they were in off the ferry, Gwen's tummy rumbled and Pixie glanced at her, smiling. 'Sorry I couldn't face breakfast on the boat, but I thought we'd drive into Roscoff and treat ourselves to crêpes and coffee at a little cafe Frank and I went to occasionally.' She didn't mention the need to psych herself up to driving on the 'wrong' side of the road for the seventy kilometres she faced to reach Château Quiltu.

Quarter of an hour later, Pixie had parked the car and they were sitting at a pavement cafe with steaming bowls of coffee in front of them, waiting for their ham and egg crêpes.

'Good coffee,' Gwen said, swallowing another mouthful.

'I need to tell you something,' Pixie said, deciding now was as good a time as any to tell her mother the truth about their visit. 'Monsieur Quiltu died sixteen months ago, so Frank and I have owned the château since then. Frank instructed the bank to stop the viager payments but neglected to tell me the château belonged to us.' She held up her hands in a placatory gesture. 'I have no idea why he didn't tell me, or why we haven't visited since, so please, no questions. I'm hoping the notaire tomorrow will be able to tell me more.'

Gwen placed her coffee bowl on the table. 'I did wonder about the sudden decision to come to France.'

Pixie shrugged. 'I fancied seeing the place for one last time before I instruct the notaire to sell. Besides, the break will do us both good. I hope you like the auberge I've booked us into for a couple of nights. It's in a village close to the château. Frank and I stayed there when we first found the château and it was lovely. Fern is a wonderful cook.'

'Not staying at the château then?'

'Not sure what state it will be in – I did contact the electricity people to check it was still connected,' Pixie said. 'We'll suss it out first and decide.' She didn't mention the bed sheets and the towels she'd packed in the car boot just in case.

The waitress arrived with their breakfast crêpes at that moment and wished them 'Bon appétit' before leaving them to tuck in.

'That was delicious,' Pixie said five minutes later, placing her cutlery on the empty plate. 'Another coffee?'

'A small one this time, please. Give us a bit more time to sit and watch the town wake up,' Gwen said, watching a shopkeeper on the corner rolling up the security shutters of his art gallery windows. Across the road, a woman was positioning a postcard display stand near the shop door of a touristy gift shop.

By the time they'd drunk their coffees and paid the bill, the streets of Roscoff were alive with early-morning activity.

'Shall we walk around town and the harbour before leaving?' Pixie asked. 'Have a proper sniff of the sea air?'

The first holiday weekend of the year would begin on Saturday and there was a definite buzz of happy anticipation in the air as the two of them strolled through the town with its ancient stone buildings towards the harbour. Several shop windows had displays with an exuberant Easter theme – lots of yellow chicks, daffodils and Easter eggs.

Standing by the harbour breakwater looking out to sea, Pixie took a deep breath, smelling the tangy air drifting across from a couple of fishing boats unloading their night-time catch of crabs.

'I know it's bigger, but it always reminds me of Brixham harbour,' she said, watching several seagulls swooping and diving over another fishing boat making its way in.

Gwen nodded. 'Very similar. Did you and Frank ever go over to the Île de Batz?' she asked, looking out to sea. 'When I was here back in the fifties, there was an abandoned tropical garden over there which has been restored since.'

Pixie stared at her. 'You never mentioned you've been here before.'

Gwen shrugged. 'Haven't I? I know I've told you about being a childminder when I was about twenty – more of an au pair really as I had to do the domestic stuff too – because both you and Gus laughed and said you couldn't imagine me doing other people's housework when I barely did my own.'

'Yes, you told us that, but I thought it was Paris you went to.'

'The family had a second home in Brittany. We spent August here. It was wonderful.'

'Did you ever go over to the island?'

'No. We planned to, but then...' Gwen shrugged. 'It didn't happen.'

'We?' Pixie looked at her mum, who was still staring out to sea, but Gwen didn't answer. 'We could take the ferry over one day if you'd like to?' Pixie offered.

'Maybe,' Gwen answered, staring out to sea again.

'Well, think about it. Right now, though, I think we'd better make tracks. It will take us over an hour to reach Château Quiltu.'

The smell of freshly baked pastries drifted out of the boulangerie as they walked back through town to the car park and Pixie quickly nipped in and bought a couple of still warm pains au chocolat.

'Elevenses,' she said, tucking them carefully on the top of her tote, trying not to squash them.

Twenty minutes later, Pixie had set the satnav with the postcode for the château and they were navigating the narrow streets of Roscoff, heading for the main road south. The road was relatively free of traffic and they sped past field after field where the artichokes were beginning to sprout at the start of a new growing season. They reached the road that crossed the Parc d'Armorique within half an hour and soon the tall telecommunications mast that dominated this side of the moor was in view. A few kilometres later, the satnav instructed Pixie to turn left at a large roundabout, direction Huelgoat and Carhaix.

'Another half an hour and we should be there,' she said, glancing across at Gwen. 'The château is in the countryside between the two towns. A few country lanes to negotiate before we get there.' Driving through the nearest village to Château Quiltu, Pixie pointed to a small road down the side of the église. 'Auberge de Campagne, where we're staying tonight, is just down there.'

At the crossroads outside the village, Pixie turned right and five minutes later the entrance to the château appeared.

'You were right when you told me it was in the depths of the countryside,' Gwen said.

Pixie turned onto the drive and the tyres scrunched on the gravel. 'Monsieur Quiltu told us that the lime trees here on either side of the drive were planted in the eighteenth century at the end of the revolution. Apparently, the French regard them as a symbol of liberty. Imagine – the five or six that are left are over two hundred years old. It must have been a wonderful sight arriving here in a horse-drawn carriage when the whole drive was lined by them.'

Gwen caught her breath as Château Quiltu came into view as they drove further up the driveway. 'Oh my,' she said. 'What a place.'

Pixie smiled to herself. Gwen had had the same reaction as herself the first time she and Frank had seen the château. Built from a mixture of the coloured granite stone that Brittany was famous for, it stood proudly at the end of the driveway. With its round towers at either side, one castellated and the other with a steep conical roof, it looked like a perfectly proportioned fairy-tale castle.

Pixie stopped the car and they both sat looking at the front facade for several moments. Three storeys high, on the ground floor shutters painted in a faded Bretagne red hid the tall windows on that level. In front of them was a terrace with a stone balustrade running the length of it, separating the property from the drive. On either side of the centrally placed heavy oak front door were classic stone urns standing on stone plinths. Windows on the first floor were rectangular and placed immediately above the windows and the entrance below, while the third floor had arched dormer windows set into the roof. Fifty metres away to the right was the cottage that years ago had housed the housekeeper and the gardener.

'Come on,' Pixie said. 'Let's show you the inside,' and taking the large bunch of keys out of her tote, she opened the car door and got out. She glanced across at the cottage, noticing a display of primroses and daffodils in its neat front garden with not a weed in sight and the closed shutters. If it hadn't been for the closed shutters and the general locked-up appearance of the cottage that mirrored the château itself, she'd have suspected the place was occupied.

The lock on the thick oak door turned with a satisfactory clunk when Pixie inserted the key, but it took a hard push to get the door to open. Inside it was much as Pixie remembered. The doors to the large rooms on either side of the hallway were open and she walked in and switched on the lights in the left-hand side one.

Gwen gasped at her first sight of the room. Old-fashioned brown chunky leather furniture, a large chandelier and a huge granite fireplace with a shield carved into the main beam, thick rugs on the wooden floor. 'It's beautiful,' she said. 'It's like a film set for *Downton Abbey*.'

Pixie smiled. 'The other downstairs room is very similar. Come and see the kitchen.'

Walking through the hallway past the sweeping stone staircase that dominated the space towards the kitchen, she pointed out another door. 'That leads to the cellars, no need to go down there right now.' The lovely wooden floors throughout the ground floor were in desperate need of a polish and the whole place could do with an airing.

Pixie flicked a switch in the kitchen and the lights came on as she moved across to open the French doors and push the shutters back against the outside wall. A large knife-scarred pine table stood in the middle, a mixture of chairs placed around it, an ancient refrigerator stood against one wall, a range and a sink were situated at the back. An elaborately carved Breton dresser dominated the remaining wall space. The wooden floors in here had given way to hexagonal terracotta tiles and there was a sad-looking wicker cat or dog basket pushed into a corner. It looked exactly as Pixie remembered it, even down to the faded paintwork.

'You could feed a lot of people in here,' Gwen said as she followed Pixie and stepped out through the doors onto the terrace at the rear of the château. A round wrought-iron table and four chairs were placed there for easy access from the kitchen. 'Imagine sitting out here to eat with that view,' Gwen continued, looking out over the lawn in front of them to a small copse in the distance, where a lake was shimmering in the sunlight. 'Beautiful. The orangery looks in need of some TLC,' she noted, taking in the neglected structure with its shabby paintwork and cracked glass in places.

'Not sure it's worth saving,' Pixie said, following her gaze. 'Come and see the upstairs.'

On the half-landing at the top of the first flight of stairs where the staircase curved to the left before continuing to the next level, a large suit of armour stood guard to one side in a pool of sunshine pouring in through the large arched window that looked out over the grounds at the rear of the château.

Opening doors and switching on lights, pointing out the original claw-footed baths in the four bathrooms, the four-poster bed in the main bedroom, the candelabra on the hallway walls, Pixie smiled as Gwen enthused about the château.

'I understand now why you and Frank fell in love with this place.'

'The next floor was originally the servants' quarters, I think,' Pixie said, leading the way up the plain wooden functional staircase that served the third floor. 'I planned on having my office up here in this room,' she added, opening the door to a large room with two dormer windows that looked out over the drive at the front of the château. Standing there talking to Gwen she remembered how excited she'd felt the day she had stood in the same spot with Frank's arms around her. She could hear his voice now, urging her to follow her dream. 'We'll buy this place, and when we go home, you will start writing that novel you've always wanted to so that when we do move over here in a few years, you'll be established. And this room will be your library-cum-office, where you'll find more inspiration for bestsellers and organise writers' retreats to which other authors will flock.' He'd had it all planned out.

Pixie smothered a sigh. She'd worked hard and established herself as a novelist, so that part of her dream had come true, but as for the rest of it – moving to France and running a writer's retreat – that wasn't going to happen now. At least she'd fulfilled half her dream, she'd have to be content with that.

A large pile of new wooden planks in the far corner caught her eye. Had they been there before? The rest of the château was as she remembered from their original visit and from the photographs they'd taken and looked at so often. Pixie shrugged; it didn't matter.

'Pixie, are you all right? You've gone very quiet,' Gwen's voice broke into her reverie.

'We were going to turn this room into an office-cum-library for me,' she answered. 'Come on, let's go back downstairs. So what d'you think? One night at the auberge and then camp out here?'

'Definitely,' Gwen answered. 'Which bedroom are you having? The master bedroom with its four-poster? I'd like this one,' she said, walking towards a room in one of the round towers. 'I shall feel like a queen lying under that beautiful scarlet canopy.'

'Consider it yours. Tomorrow, after the notaire, we'll go shopping for food and supplies,' Pixie said.

Wandering back down through the house, the strong feelings she'd felt when they'd first viewed it came back. *I could be happy living here.*

Pixie pushed that thought away. It was another dream that would never happen.

'Did you know you would get all this furniture too when you bought the house?' Gwen asked, stopping to examine the grandfather clock that stood in a nook to the side of the stairs in the main hallway.

'Monsieur Quiltu assured us that everything we saw on the day we bought would still be here. No family, he said, to squabble over who got what. Sad really. Right, I'll just get the bedding out of the car and dump it in the hall for now, and then we'd better go and check in to the auberge and find somewhere for a spot of lunch.'

Once she'd locked the house up again, Pixie walked over to the cottage to show Gwen around.

'Funny, I don't seem to have a key that fits,' she muttered as she tried all the keys on the ring. 'I'll ask the notaire tomorrow if he has one, otherwise I'll have to find a locksmith from somewhere.'

6

Although it was several years since Pixie and Frank had stayed at the Auberge de Campagne, she received a warm welcome when she arrived with Gwen and knocked on the door.

'Bonjour and welcome back,' Fern said, ushering them both in and showing them to their rooms, Gwen's on the ground floor overlooking the garden and Pixie's on the first floor.

'You have a good memory for your guests,' Pixie said as they climbed the stairs, surprised that Fern had remembered her.

Fern nodded. 'I do actually, but in your case it was the fact that you were buying Château Quiltu and I've been hoping to see you again for years. Not that I wished Monsieur Quiltu dead, but you know what I mean.'

Pixie smiled and nodded. 'We're going to camp out at the château for a few days so it will be just the one night here.'

'That's fine. Will your husband be joining you over Easter? He was full of plans when he stayed here last year.'

Pixie swallowed hard. 'He died a few weeks ago.'

Fern was instantly contrite. 'I'm so sorry for your loss. I know how hard that is to cope with.'

'You weren't to know,' Pixie said, her mind reeling from Fern's words earlier. Frank had stayed here without her knowledge? Before she could say any more, a tall good-looking man appeared in the doorway, and acknowledged them with a nod and a smile.

'Fern darling, I'm just going to walk the dogs. Back in about half an hour,' he said, his American accent surprising Pixie.

'Okay, Scott,' Fern said as he disappeared. 'I married Scott a couple of years ago,' she said, looking at Pixie. 'My first husband died shortly after your first stay here.' She shook her head as Pixie went to speak. 'I'm very lucky to have Scott in my life now. I hope you'll find happiness again in due course.

There was a short silence before Fern spoke again, changing the subject. 'Would you like dinner here this evening?'

'Please. I seem to remember 7.30 being the time?' Pixie answered, pulling herself together.

'I'll see you then.' And Fern left her to settle in.

Pixie closed the door behind her and sank down on the bed. Why had Frank come here last year? And why hadn't he told her about the visit?

* * *

The next morning at breakfast, Pixie and Gwen declined the offer of a full English, settling for Fern's home-made hot cross buns, offered instead of croissants as it was Good Friday, and delicious coffee. Fern placed everything on the table and left them to enjoy their breakfast. A breakfast Pixie found she had no appetite for after another night of tossing and turning, thinking about unanswerable questions.

She watched as Gwen cut open her hot cross bun and slathered it with butter. 'You do know that's not good for you, don't you?'

Gwen shrugged. 'I'm on holiday. You should try one.'

Pixie shook her head. 'Not hungry. Coffee will do me.'

She sighed and Gwen glanced at her sharply. 'Guess you didn't sleep very well.'

'There are so many unanswerable questions in my life right now that keep me awake. And one of the biggest is why did Frank come here a year ago without telling me?'

Gwen sighed. 'No idea. Problem with the château? Hopefully the notaire will be able to shed some light on your questions this morning. I'm sure there will be a perfectly reasonable explanation.'

'I bloody well hope so,' Pixie muttered. 'I'm beginning to get a bad feeling about things.'

'Language!' Gwen admonished.

'Sorry,' Pixie said, feeling despairing, not apologetic. What on earth had Frank been up to? And was she ever likely to learn the whole truth now that he was dead?

* * *

The notaire's office was opposite a large supermarket with a cafe and Pixie parked in the car park and told Gwen she'd see her in about half an hour in the cafe.

The memory of walking into the modern building all those years ago when she and Frank had been excited about buying Château Quiltu threatened to overwhelm her as she entered the office foyer. They'd felt so upbeat that day, full of plans for the future. Well, that planned future was in the past now and she had to deal with the present without Frank.

Jean-Yves Ropars, the notaire, greeted her with a handshake and ushered her into his office. Pixie smiled to herself as she sat on one of the antique-style chairs in front of the painted French desk. Nothing had changed in here over the years. Jean-Yves himself looked no different either, apart from a few grey hairs sprinkled through his hair. His English had improved though, she noticed. He was fluent now.

'I was so sorry to hear about your husband, Madame Sampson,' Jean-Yves said quietly.

'Thank you,' Pixie replied.

'How can I 'elp you today?'

'Frank neglected to tell me that the viager scheme had finished sometime ago and that we now owned the property, so I have a few questions I'd like to ask you,' Pixie said. 'Did my husband have a rendezvous with you in the months after Monsieur Quiltu moved out?'

'Yes. Twice. The first time he came alone. The second time a few weeks later, he came with a woman.'

Pixie stared at him. 'Did he say who she was?'

'No. He simply said that she would be living in the cottage for the foreseeable future and he wanted to introduce her to me,' Jean-Yves paused. 'And that if she ever approached me for legal advice, I was to 'elp and send my invoice to him for payment.'

That could only mean one thing, Pixie thought. The woman was important to him.

She took a breath. 'The cottage is currently shuttered and locked, is she simply away for the Easter holiday or has she moved out?'

'As far as I am aware, she still lives there, so she has probably gone away for the holiday.'

'Do you have a key for the cottage? None of the ones I have fit and I'd like to look around it.'

'Désolé, I don't 'ave a key and I'm duty-bound to tell you that, legally, you shouldn't enter the cottage without the tenant's knowledge, even though it is your property,' he added as Pixie went to protest.

'Does the tenant pay rent?'

'No. That is something I discussed with your husband. With no rent book or formal agreement, neither party is protected and it would be difficult to evict the woman if necessary. Monsieur Sampson just said it was a purely private arrangement and thanked me for my advice, which he declined to take.'

'Will having somebody living in the cottage affect things when I put the château on the market, which I intend to do in the near future?' Pixie asked.

Jean-Yves nodded. 'Maybe. The law would regard the woman as a squatter and you would need to evict her during the summer months. If she is still in residence in November, she will be able to stay there until the following March.'

Pixie stared at him. 'I see.'

'Perhaps you will be lucky and when you ask the woman to leave, she will go without protest.'

'I certainly hope that is the case,' Pixie said.

'So, you do not intend to move here?' Jean-Yves asked. 'Didn't you think about running retreats for writers?'

'The plans we made were for us,' Pixie replied, surprised that he'd remembered her mentioning retreats. 'Things are different now. I can't possibly move here and do the things we planned on my own. It wouldn't be the same.'

Jean-Yves regarded her steadily before nodding thoughtfully. 'I don't suppose it would. How long are you here for this time?'

'Six days,' Pixie answered, standing up. 'Thank you for your time. You will handle the sale of the château, won't you, when I'm ready? Thank you,' she said when he nodded.

'Before you leave, I have a question for you,' Jean-Yves said. 'That first visit when he came alone, your husband brought the papers I'd sent him for the two of you to sign regarding the final transfer of the château. Your signature appeared to be genuine and yet you say you didn't know about the end of the agreement?' He looked at her, puzzled. 'I do hope your husband didn't forge your signature. That would be highly irregular.'

Pixie was lost for words and stared at him as the implication sank into her brain.

Opening the door of the office to show her out, Jean-Yves said, 'Enjoy your stay and happy Easter.'

'Thank you. And the same to you,' Pixie replied, her mind reeling. Surely Frank wouldn't have forged her signature?

It wasn't until she was crossing the road to reach the super-market that she realised she'd hadn't asked the name of the woman who was living in the cottage. Blast. Too late now to go back in and ask, there had been a couple waiting for their meeting with Jean-Yves. She'd have to wait and find out from the women herself when she returned.

* * *

In his office, a pensive Jean-Yves stood by the window watching as Pixie Sampson crossed the road. Should he have said something? Warned her? She seemed to be a lovely woman. Finding out the truth was bound to be hurtful. He rubbed his chin before taking a deep breath. He'd never broken a client's confidentiality and he wouldn't now. But he made up his mind that if Pixie, he suppressed a smile at her name, ever asked for his personal help, he would give it to her wholeheartedly and without question.

7

Gwen enjoyed herself in the supermarket waiting for Pixie. She'd taken a trolley and loaded it up with all sorts of delicious things. Things that she wasn't supposed to indulge in, but what the heck, she was on holiday and it was a long time since she'd been to France. Several blocks of different cheeses, a couple of bottles of Bordeaux wine, a bottle of champagne, baguettes, a still-warm Kouign-amann from the patisserie counter, a roasted chicken, butter, tomatoes, milk, some cold meats, coffee, two luxury Easter eggs, one each, all that and more found its way into the trolley.

As Gwen wandered around, the memory of yesterday's conversation about the Île de Batz with Pixie slipped into her mind. Seeing the island out there in the Channel had brought all the old dreams back and she'd spoken without thinking. She hoped Pixie would forget her words and not start asking probing questions about a past she'd never mentioned to anyone. That long-ago magical summer had been one of the best in her life. A turning point. Of course, it hadn't been really magical, otherwise it would have been the beginning of the rest of her life with...

'Excuse-moi, madame,' a quiet voice behind her said.

Gwen jumped. She was blocking the fish counter. 'Désole. Pardonnez-moi,' the polite words she'd learned over half a century ago sprang instantly from her lips and she pushed her trolley to one side. This wouldn't do; there was absolutely no point in thinking about what might have been. She needed to get a grip, and a coffee once she'd paid for the shopping in the trolley.

She'd barely sat down at a table in the cafe, a coffee in front of her, before Pixie arrived.

'Gosh, Mum, you've been busy. I thought we were going to do the shopping together,' she said, looking at the trolley. 'Champagne? What are we celebrating?'

'Nothing in particular. Everything in general. We're in France, what's not to celebrate? Besides, it's the national drink,' Gwen said, her heart sinking at the look on Pixie's face. 'How did it go with the notaire? Was he able to answer your questions?'

Pixie nodded. 'Most of them, but the answers have opened up a whole lot more, including the fact that Frank has let the cottage to some mysterious woman. I'll just get a coffee and I'll tell you all I know.'

Stunned, Gwen watched her go to the counter. Frank had another woman? Ever since Pixie had discovered his secrecy over the château, Gwen had wondered if there was another woman behind it. Initially she'd dismissed the idea, because, unlike her own ex-husband, Frank wasn't the type to play away from home. Personally, she was going to take convincing that he was guilty of what Pixie clearly thought he was.

Pixie came back with her coffee and sat down heavily. 'She's living in the cottage rent-free.'

'Was the notaire sure?' Silly question, notaires didn't make mistakes over things like that.

'Frank had been to see him twice. The second time, he took

this woman with him.' Pixie took a long drink of her coffee. 'I knew something was bothering him over the last year. I kept asking what was wrong. He kept brushing me off, saying he was just tired from work and travelling.' Pixie replaced her cup on its saucer. 'And all the time he was having a classic midlife crisis ten years late.'

'You don't know that for certain,' Gwen ventured quietly. 'Maybe he was just giving someone a helping hand in life?'

Pixie threw her an angry look. 'Then why all the secrecy? He would have told me if that had been the case. I thought the cottage looked too neat and tidy not to be occupied.' She looked at Gwen, disconcerted by another thought. 'Do you think whoever she is knows about Frank? The notaire didn't until I phoned him this week to make the appointment. Perhaps she knows and has left.' Pixie took a deep breath and stood up. 'Come on, let's get this lot back to the château and settle in. At least it seems we've got the place to ourselves for Easter. Next week, and the possible return of that woman, will get here soon enough.' And Pixie grabbed the trolley and started to wheel it towards the exit.

Gwen stayed silent on the journey back to the château, letting Pixie concentrate on her driving, but her thoughts were all about how she could help her daughter, what advice she should give her. As Pixie turned into the château driveway, Gwen came to the conclusion that until they'd met this woman and sussed out what had really been going on, it would be better to forget all about it. As Pixie parked the car, Gwen prepared to get out and help carry the shopping in.

Pixie handed her the bag containing the two Easter eggs. 'The rest is too heavy for you. Take these and have a search in the kitchen for plates and things. And a kettle. I'll bring the shopping in and then I'll take the cases and the bedding stuff up.'

Gwen crossed the fingers of her free hand as she accepted the bag. 'Pixie darling, please don't spend the next few days worrying about this mysterious woman and spoil your holiday. I'm sure there will be a simple explanation.'

* * *

After she'd carried all the shopping into the kitchen, Pixie apprehensively plugged in the ancient fridge, which, to her relief, responded with a satisfactory hum.

'It will take time to cool down, but we can put stuff in there anyway,' she said, as she left Gwen to unpack the shopping. For the next half-hour, Pixie concentrated on getting the cases upstairs, making the beds, putting towels in the bathrooms and locating the switch for the hot water boiler. She lifted Gwen's suitcase up on to the top of a chest of drawers to make it easier for her to unpack later before making for her own bedroom.

She'd adored this master bedroom the moment she'd opened the door and walked in for the first time. It was a real French boudoir with its toile de jouy curtains and matching bed linen, thick cream wool rugs on either side of the four-poster bed, an ottoman at its foot and a velvet bedroom chair in front of the carved dressing table. Today, though, the bed was unmade.

Pixie picked up the bedding she'd placed on the chair and concentrated on making the bed. Bottom sheet, pillowcases, duvet. As she moved around the bed, tucking in and smoothing things down, she caught her reflection from time to time in the gold-framed free-standing mirror placed to the side of the large wardrobe. Once the bed was made up, she crossed over to and opened the wardrobe, hoping to find some hangers there for the few clothes she'd packed. There were half a dozen or so empty hangers, alongside ones with clothes already hanging on them.

Men's new clothes. A pair of chinos, jeans, a couple of shirts, a jacket. On the shelves to the side of the hanging space, carefully folded, were a couple of jumpers, a sweatshirt or two and, importantly, three scarves. Seeing the scarves, Pixie knew without any doubt that she was looking at a collection of Frank's clothes. By the time they'd met and married, Frank, who hated wearing a tie, had already adopted the habit of wearing and tying a scarf like a true Frenchman. He was always adding to his collection.

Pixie reached out and picked up the dark midnight-blue and cashmere scarf. It was one she'd bought for him as a present on a visit to Paris about five years ago. She bunched it up and held it in front of her face and sniffed the soft material. Definitely Frank's. There was still a hint of the spicy cologne he always wore.

Pixie took a deep breath and replaced the scarf on the shelf before closing the wardrobe door. She'd finish her unpacking later.

Gwen was busy investigating the cupboards of the Breton dresser when Pixie ran downstairs and went into the kitchen.

'There's some lovely crockery in here and I found a kettle,' Gwen said, glancing up. 'And there's an old-fashioned built-in larder with marble shelves and some kitchen basics, like rice, chickpeas, tins of peas, et cetera, all within date too. There's masses of cutlery and table linen in the table drawers. What's up?' she added as she registered the unhappy expression on Pixie's face.

'I found three of Frank's scarves in the wardrobe and some new clothes I've never seen before,' Pixie said, a catch in her voice as she looked at Gwen. 'I wasn't expecting that.'

'You sure they're Frank's?' Gwen asked. 'Not Monsieur Quiltu's?'

'I'm sure. I bought him all three scarves – including a cashmere one that he always swore was his favourite.'

Gwen looked at her. 'I'll go up later and pack them away if you like. There must be a charity shop somewhere we can drop them off after Easter.'

Pixie shook her head. 'Thanks, Mum, but no. I'll do it myself later. Right now I'm going to open a bottle of that red wine and organise lunch. Baguette, cheese and cold meats okay? Save the chicken for dinner tonight? Shall we eat on the terrace?' she asked, glancing out through the French doors. 'The sun is shining, it should be warm enough.'

The terrace proved to be a suntrap and Pixie went in search of a parasol, opening a door off the kitchen, which she vaguely remembered leading to a boot room and storage area. With a bit of luck, she'd find a parasol or two to keep them cooler in the direct midday sun. There were a number of boots and weather-proof coats hanging in the room, along with extra outdoor chairs and tables. Pixie smiled as she saw several parasols leaning against the wall, as well as a pile of chair cushions. The big cream parasol would be perfect and she dragged its heavy, sand-filled base out to the terrace. By the time she'd opened the parasol and put cushions on two of the chairs, Gwen had placed everything for lunch on the table, poured two glasses of wine and handed one to Pixie.

'Santé,' Pixie said as they clinked glasses. 'Despite all the unanswered questions – here's to a good Easter.'

Over lunch, Pixie did her best to push all thoughts of Frank out of her mind and relax. 'I thought we'd spend the rest of the day here and settle in, maybe go for a walk this afternoon, dinner this evening under the stars and then tomorrow we'll go out for a couple of hours and I'll show you around. Unless there is somewhere in particular you'd like to go?' she said, remembering Gwen's words in Roscoff.

Gwen didn't rise to the bait. 'That sounds like a plan,' she answered with a smile.

Sitting there, glass of wine in hand, Pixie finally relaxed. The Easter weekend had barely begun, so whoever this woman was, living in the cottage, she was unlikely to return before Tuesday at the earliest. In the meantime, Pixie determined that she and Gwen would enjoy living in the château and being in France on holiday. She'd take lots of photographs to remind her of their time here once she had sold the château.

'Fancy a wander down to the lake?' she said, standing up. 'It's right on the edge of my land – the château land,' she corrected herself hastily. It wouldn't be hers for long, no point in claiming ownership. 'We'll clear the table afterwards.'

Together they walked past the two small barns and a lean-to without bothering to glance inside and wandered along a gravel pathway that led them down to the lake. Lots of rhododendron bushes and azalea shrubs had been planted in a haphazard manner in the grounds and some were already showing signs of flowering.

'These are going to be glorious in just a few weeks,' Pixie said, stopping to look and smell a particularly vibrant red-flowered azalea. 'I hadn't realised there were so many shrubs and trees.'

Near the lake, oak and beech trees that formed a small copse around it were starting to bud up with new leaves, and dotted around the surrounding land were large swathes of daffodils. The undergrowth of the hedge thirty metres away that formed the boundary between the château land and the surrounding fields was dotted with primroses. A wooden bench was tucked under the shelter of a large willow tree planted near the lake and by mutual unspoken consent Pixie and Gwen walked over to it and sat down.

Sitting there, the lake in front of them with the occasional fish movement rippling the surface, the château back in the distance with the glass of the dilapidated orangery twinkling in the sunlight, pigeons high up in the branches of several trees cooing softly, Pixie closed her eyes and let the peace of the surroundings engulf her. Idyllic was the word that summed it up. She remembered sitting on this bench with Frank the day they'd decided to buy the château. They'd sat there in silence for several moments, both happily lost in their own thoughts, delighting in the prospect of living in this gorgeous setting sometime in the future. Not imagining for one moment that all their dreams and plans would never come to fruition.

Pixie stifled a sigh. No good brooding. Life was what it was.

She opened her eyes and glanced at Gwen. 'I'm going to pick some daffs. Fancy a bunch for your bedroom?'

'Please. I'll give you a hand.'

Half an hour later, walking back, both of them carrying a bundle of daffodils, Pixie took a quick look in the barns. One housed a sit-on lawnmower, a stack of logs, a large granite trough and bundles of willow reeds of various lengths all in various stages of drying.

'I wonder who uses the sit-on lawnmower. The grass is certainly well maintained,' she said thoughtfully. The doors on the other, larger barn were closed and padlocked.

'Mmm, interesting. Another puzzle.' She sighed as she turned away. 'I wonder what secrets are locked in there.'

8

Easter Saturday and Pixie drove them into Carhaix for a wander around the large weekly market. The market was the usual mixture of stalls, with local food producers – vegetables, cheese, charcuterie, bread – mixed in with plant sellers, clothing stalls, shoes, hardware, jewellery. The enticing smell of chicken roasting on a large rotisserie with sauté potatoes cooking in the tray underneath wafted over from one of the food vendors on the circumference of the market. Crêpes and galettes were also on offer, including the famous Breton sausage galette. Sweet tooths were catered for with pain au chocolate croissants and cupcakes on sale along with coffee from a mobile catering van.

Pixie and Gwen wandered around for some time simply enjoying the 'Frenchness' of the atmosphere, before returning to a couple of the food and vegetable stalls they'd seen earlier. They both enjoyed sampling some local cheese and charcuterie before buying some of each for lunch. The stallholder laughed at them when they both refused to be tempted by the offer of a slice of the infamous andouille sausage as they bought a roll of stuffed pork, some sausages and a leg of lamb for a traditional Easter Sunday lunch.

The cafes around the marketplace were busy and they decided to stop for a coffee in the village cafe on their way back to the château instead. Which proved to be easier said than done when they got there. A young couple had earlier been married in the mairie and now crowds of people were jostling around in the street, taking photographs and throwing confetti.

Pixie pulled to a halt in front of the local shop and she and Gwen got out and joined the happy crowd. A loud klaxon announced the approach of an old tractor, painted in bright red, white and blue stripes and decorated with flowers and balloons, that was slowly making its way through the village. The trailer behind it had a flowered arch with ribbons blowing gently in the breeze, and a bench placed underneath it on a bed of straw. Pixie and Gwen watched it come to a halt and the driver cut the engine, before jumping down and lowering the back tailboard of the trailer, which converted into two shallow steps.

The driver clapped his hands. 'C'est prêt – allons-y.'

Holding hands, the groom and bride stepped carefully into the trailer and settled themselves on the bench, followed by four tiny bridesmaids, who sat on the straw at their feet. The driver clipped the tailboard back into place before climbing onto the tractor, sounding the klaxon and moving off. Wedding guests started getting into their own cars and a procession was soon following the tractor out of the village, all sounding their horns to accompany the klaxon, which was blaring non-stop.

As the crowd thinned, and the cacophony of noise moved off in to the distance, Pixie saw Fern walking slowly towards them, accompanied by an elderly lady.

'Hi. Don't you just love a wedding?' Fern said. 'Maria is a local farmer's daughter, hence the different bridal transport. I don't think you met Anouk, my first and only mother-in-law, the other evening, did you?' And she quickly introduced them, explaining that Anouk had been her first husband Laurent's mother, who now lived with her and Scott.

'We thought we'd have a coffee here, will you join us?' Gwen asked, gesturing at the village cafe.

'Sounds like a lovely idea, but I'm sorry, I have to get back to the auberge to meet some guests who are due to check in. Another time maybe?' Fern said.

'Why don't you both come up to the château Monday morning,' Pixie suggested impulsively. 'Bring your husband, too.'

'We'd like that. Any chance you'd give us a tour? None of us have ever been inside.'

'Of course. Eleven o'clock all right?'

'Perfect. I'll bring cake,' Fern smiled.

As Fern and Anouk left them, Pixie turned to Gwen.

'Let's forget about coffee here and have it back on our terrace.'

They spent the rest of the day happily pottering around the château and eating both lunch and supper out on the terrace. After supper they sat enjoying a red wine nightcap and looking up at the bright stars appearing in a sky untroubled by light pollution, but the chill in the air reminded them it was still not summer. Before the cooler air drove them indoors, they were treated to a spectacular aeronautical show by a group of bats busy flitting between the trees and the roof of the château.

* * *

The next morning, Pixie was awake early and quickly dressed, pulling jeans and a sweatshirt out of the wardrobe before creeping past Gwen's door, not wanting to disturb her. Downstairs in the kitchen, she made herself a mug of tea and took it out onto the terrace. She loved this time of day and was often up at this hour at home, where the silence was punctuated by the rumble of a distant motorway and the street she lived on coming to life as people began their working day. Here, the nearest neighbour was several fields away and noise from traffic was non-existent. Right now all she could hear was the gentle cooing of pigeons in one of the high pine trees.

Pixie sipped her tea and sighed as she looked out over the parkland. Château Quiltu really was a special place. She and Frank should never have bought it really, it was far too big. A place like this cried out to become a family home, or at the very least a bolthole for people who needed time out from life for whatever reason. Living here, writing and running retreats with Frank would have been such a wonderful thing to have done together. Out of the question now, of course; no way could she do it on her own, but it had been a good dream.

A wave of sadness threatened to engulf her at the thought of how different the rest of her life was going to be now she was alone. Not that she wasn't used to being alone for days at a time. For the last few years, while Frank had travelled more and more in Europe, her own lifestyle had been dictated by the demands of his diary. While he was away, she wrote for long periods every day, freeing up hours for when he was home so they could spend as much time as possible together, particularly at the weekends. But now she was facing a future where there would be no week-ends together, no one to celebrate birthdays and anniversaries with, no one to care whether she was ill or not. She was well and truly on her own and the future looked bleak.

Sitting there, Pixie could sense that all the old despairing feelings that had swamped her so often in the past after every miscarriage were in danger of breaking through the inner wall she'd built around them, keeping them buried. There was no way she wanted to give rein to those desperate feelings that had over-whelmed her every waking thought in those years. Those awful days had taught her a valuable life lesson though. She would get through this. The older and stronger version of herself would survive even without Frank at her side. Besides, the unwritten guarantee that Frank would be a part of her future life had been torn up by the presence of this unknown woman in the cottage.

Just who was she? How long had Frank known her? Was her arrival on the scene linked to him not telling her about the viager agreement finishing? So many questions waited for the woman's return.

Pixie closed her eyes, willing the tears not to fall. Once she'd confronted her, received a few answers and told her to get out, the château would be put on the market and she, Pixie, would return to the UK, pull herself together and get on with the rest of her life.

'Morning. Here, have another cuppa.' Gwen's quiet voice broke into Pixie's thoughts.

Pixie opened her eyes to find her mum standing next to her. 'You're up early.'

'Could say the same about you,' Gwen said as she handed Pixie a mug. 'I don't seem to need as much sleep these days – what's your excuse?'

'I like this time of day. At home, I like to write early in the morning and late at night.'

'You plotting your next book right now then? You were deep in thought.'

'No, bad case of writer's block at the moment. I was thinking about how different life is going to be from now on and...' Pixie sighed. 'Wondering about how our mysterious woman fits into things.'

Gwen took a sip of her tea before cradling the mug in her

hands. 'I admit I'm curious too, but until she returns, best to put it to the back of our minds.'

Pixie gave a resigned nod. 'I know. And I should really be thinking about writing. My deadline is getting closer. Listen,' she said. 'I can hear the church bell tolling for early Easter mass. D'you want to go to a later service?'

'No, although I'd like to have a look around the church sometime,' Gwen answered.

The two of them sat there for several more moments, enjoying the sound of the bells drifting across the fields as they drank their tea. Pixie was the first to make a move.

'Breakfast out here, I think. No, stay there,' she said as Gwen went to stand up. 'I'll get it. Afterwards, we'll have to see if that ancient range works to cook the lamb, otherwise lunch could be a problem.'

* * *

Later that morning, Pixie smeared the leg of lamb with honey and inserted cloves of garlic deep into several small cuts she'd made in the meat.

'D'you want some rosemary to go with that?' Gwen asked, busy peeling potatoes at the kitchen table. 'I saw a bush the other side of the orangery when I had a wander around yesterday. Think there was an abandoned vegetable patch close by.'

'I'll nip out and pick a few sprigs,' Pixie said.

After picking two or three stems of rosemary, she went over to the plot of land that Gwen had thought was an old vegetable patch. Standing there, looking at the leaf-strewn but strangely weed-free ground, Pixie saw green shoots appearing in line and at regular intervals and laughed with delight. Not an abandoned veg plot but an established asparagus bed and the season was just starting.

She shrugged away the thought that someone had clearly been taking care of the plot. If it was 'her', then it didn't matter; if anyone turned up to claim the asparagus, she would apologise to them for helping herself but point out that it was on her land after all.

Back in the kitchen, Pixie placed sprigs of the rosemary on the bottom of the roasting tray with some water and sat the lamb on top. To Pixie's relief, when she switched the ancient cooking range on, it responded with a low hum, not the loud bang she'd half been expecting, and within a minute or two, as she opened the oven door, she could feel some heat.

An hour later, the kitchen was warm, the potatoes were roasting and delicious lamb smells were filling the air.

'Another twenty minutes and lunch will be ready – time for an aperitif and a glass of champagne,' Pixie said.

Gwen had placed a plate of blinis and smoked salmon with a bowl of olives on the table.

Because the weather had clouded over, they sat at the kitchen table and toasted each other with their champagne, 'Happy Easter'.

'I love this kitchen,' Pixie said. 'I imagined turning it into the hub of the château – the place where everyone gathered, not just for food, but company and conversation.' She swallowed a mouthful of her champagne. 'Sad to think really that it's not going to happen. C'est la vie.'

'Maybe the new owner will have a similar vision. The whole place has such a good vibe to it.' Gwen gave Pixie a serious look. 'You'll need to try and make sure the person you sell to is like-minded. Doesn't want to change things radically.'

'Hard to do that from across the Channel, but I'll do my best,'

Pixie agreed. 'The place needs a family really. Right, the lamb should be done, I'll take it out to rest while the roasties finish.'

Pixie glanced at Gwen as the two of them enjoyed their lunch. 'Thanks for coming with me, Mum. At least I'm making some memories of this place, sleeping in the four-poster, cooking and eating, the two of us enjoying time here. If you hadn't come with me, I wouldn't have stayed here alone.' She raised her glass in a toast gesture. 'Thank you.'

Gwen smiled at her. 'Glad to be of service.' She reached for the champagne bottle and topped up her glass. 'Here's to us and the château.'

* * *

After lunch, as they cleared up the kitchen together, Gwen said she was going for a lie-down and to sleep off the effects of the champagne.

'Good idea. I'll just cut the rest of the lamb off the bone and put it in the larder and then I might go up and open my laptop.' The germ of a possible story idea had unexpectedly popped into Pixie's mind earlier and she wanted to write it down before it disappeared.

As she opened the larder door, she noticed the little stack of staple ingredients that Gwen had mentioned earlier. Putting the plate of lamb meat on the marble shelf, she picked up the tins, packets and jars one by one. There was nothing out of the ordinary, day-to-day stuff most housewives would have in their cupboards. But in amongst the olives, pasta, rice, instant coffee granules with their French labels, there was marmite, brown sauce, sugar, rice, custard powder, long-life milk powder, teabags, all with English labels. All ingredients that would have been bought in the UK to bring over to France.

Pixie let out a deep sigh of hurt as the realisation hit her. Food supplies in the larder. Clothes in the wardrobe. Frank must have spent some serious time here in the château. How many times had Frank been here without her? How many times had he been here with his woman? How many times in the past sixteen months had he lied to her? Importantly, why had he taken to coming without her?

Pixie slammed the larder door closed. She had to get a grip and stop asking herself these infernal questions. She was in danger of spoiling this, her one and only stay in the château, and she wanted her memories of the place to be good ones.

Photos, that's what she needed. Tangible memories. Running upstairs, she grabbed both her phone and laptop from the bedside table. Where to begin? Top floor and work her way down, she decided.

Standing in the doorway of what would have been her writing den and library if their dream of moving here had come true, Pixie took a snap, before walking into the room and taking one from another angle, as well as one of the view from the window.

Her bedroom with its four-poster bed was next, and then the other bedrooms and bathrooms. Not wanting to disturb Gwen, she carried on past her room and took one of the long hallway. Downstairs, she photographed the kitchen, the hallway and the two sitting rooms. That should be enough to keep the memories of this Easter alive and Pixie sank into one of the old-fashioned armchairs. Wandering around taking the photos, she'd started to imagine how the château would have been in the past compared to the present day. Could she write a historical story set around life in the château? Doubtful, that genre really wasn't her vogue, she wrote contemporary stories. A modern-day story then? Or even a time-slip one. She opened her laptop. No internet connection here at the château, but she didn't need one to write down her ideas.

Her fingers were soon flying across the keys as she expanded on the original thought and the characters and several scenes for the story came into her mind. The block of the last two months had seemingly disappeared. Before Pixie knew it, over two hours had disappeared and Gwen was standing in the doorway saying the sun had finally come out and asking if she'd like a drink on the terrace.

9

Easter Monday and the sun decided to show its face for Fern, Anouk and Scott's coffee morning visit. Pixie showed the three of them out to the terrace, where Gwen was busy putting cushions on the extra chairs. Scott was carrying the promised cake – a sumptuous coffee and cream gateau, which he placed down on the table with a sigh of relief before straightening up to take in the view.

'Wow – what a backyard you have,' he said. 'Another week or so, those shrubs are going to look amazing. May I come back and photograph them in all their glory?'

'We'll be back in the UK, so I'll miss seeing them, but yes, do. Perhaps you'd send me a copy or two?' Pixie smiled at him.

'Sure thing.'

'Would you like to see around the château before or after coffee?' Pixie asked.

'Before, please.'

'Moi, I stay and talk with Gwen,' Anouk said. 'I think the château it has a grande staircase, non, and my ancient legs don't appreciate too much use these days.'

'Make yourself comfy. We won't be long, the château isn't that big.' And Pixie took Fern and Scott inside. Wandering through, showing off the château and trying to remember the little bits of history that Monsieur Quiltu had told them, Pixie felt a flash of proprietorial pride.

Scott was intrigued by the age of the château. 'Did your Monsieur Quiltu ever mention the possibility of ghosts? A place like this could tell so many stories.'

'Scott, stop it,' Fern said. 'You'll worry Pixie.'

Pixie laughed. 'No, he didn't mention any ghosts, thankfully. And I haven't heard any suspicious noises, like clanking chains or doors unexpectedly banging in the middle of the night. Come on up the stairs to the last floor.'

'What a view,' Scott said as the three of them stood looking out from the windows on the third floor.

Fern turned to Pixie. 'If it's not a rude question, what did you and your husband plan to do with the château? It's a big place for two people.'

'This floor was going to be my office and writing den and we were going to run retreats for... for anyone who wanted to come, basically, in the rest of the house.'

'And now?' Fern probed in a gentle voice.

'Now I shall have to sell it,' Pixie answered, pushing the 'you don't have to, you could keep it' thought away. 'Come on, I'm sure you're ready for coffee and I'm longing for a slice of that cake.'

'That's such a shame. You clearly love it here,' Fern said as they made their way downstairs. 'The place suits you – you look completely at home. Is there no way you can keep it?'

'I don't think so.' Pixie shrugged. 'I just have to accept things don't always work out as you want or expected. Curveballs of life and all that.'

'I certainly know all about those.' Fern smiled as Scott placed his arm around her shoulders and gave her a hug.

Out on the terrace, coffee, cake and conversation flowed for an hour before Fern reluctantly stood up, saying she had to get back to the auberge.

'If, when you've sold the château, you want to visit any time, there will always be a bed for you at the auberge. As a friend, not a guest,' she hastened to add. 'I'd love it if we could keep in touch.'

Pixie felt her eyes brim with tears at her kind words. 'Thank you, I'll definitely keep in touch,' was all she could manage to stutter.

Standing on the front terrace with Gwen, waving goodbye as Scott drove them away, Pixie sighed.

'I think Fern and I could have been good friends if I'd ever come to live here.' She'd forgotten what it was like to have a close girl friend since becoming a full-time writer. When she'd been working as a journalist, there had been one close friend for a time, but only a handful of other women she called friends. Sadly, over the years, life had taken them all in different directions and she'd lost touch with everyone. Of course, these days she met fellow writers when she went to book signings and publisher's events, but making new friends had proved to be difficult. Pixie turned to go back inside. 'Come on, let's clear the coffee things away. It's gone twelve, we need to think about lunch.' She gave a short laugh. 'Honestly, all we seem to do here is eat and drink. It's a good job we don't live here permanently, it would be a full-time battle to keep off the pounds.'

'Why don't we skip lunch? I'm not hungry after that cake and coffee. We could have an early dinner instead.'

'Are you sure?' Pixie glanced at her mother. 'It would give me a couple of hours to get some more writing done.'

'This place inspiring you, is it?'

'More a case of my deadline is getting closer.'

'You go and write then. Don't worry about dinner, I'll see to it.'

Before she settled down in the sitting room with her laptop, Pixie stood for several moments looking out over the gardens. Fern's comments earlier had upset her because over the weekend she had started to feel completely at home here, had even begun to think about a few improvements she would like to make and was cross that with the way things were now it could never be her real home.

And Gwen had been right too when she'd asked the question about being inspired. It hadn't been the pressing deadline alone yesterday afternoon that had made the words flow, it was the whole ambiance of this place that had affected her.

Settling herself in a chair and opening her laptop, Pixie sighed. There was no question about it, she had to sell the place now she was on her own, but did she have to sell in a hurry? It would be wonderful to spend some more time here. Frank had been here more than once, a tiny jealous voice in her head said. Maybe she shouldn't rush to put it on the market, keep it as a second home and come over as often as she could? Delay the inevitability of selling up for what, one or two visits? Or maybe even spend the summer in France?

Pixie tried to push away that thought as it arrived with a sharp intake of breath, but it refused to leave. Spend the summer here – could she? Write her next book in the peaceful surroundings. Was it possible? As a glimmer of hope flooded through her, Pixie decided she'd talk to Gwen about it later, because if Gwen didn't agree, the idea was a non-starter anyway. There was no way she'd abandon her mother to life in the UK whilst she lived and experienced the Breton lifestyle over the summer.

* * *

Left to her own devices, Gwen pottered around, tidying up the kitchen, checking on the food for their evening meal – the last of the lamb, salad and pasta, with the remainder of Fern's gateau for dessert – before making herself a cup of tea and sitting out on the terrace to drink it. And to think about the first and only time she'd visited Brittany before.

Since that early-morning breakfast in Roscoff and the stroll around the harbour with Pixie, forgotten images from over sixty years ago had floated into her mind during the past few days. When Anouk had mentioned places up on the coast worth a visit as they'd chatted that morning, more disjointed memories had flitted into Gwen's mind. Wandering around the ancient town of Morlaix. A picnic near Callac.

She was beginning to regret saying no to Pixie when she'd asked if there was anywhere she'd like to go while they were over here, wishing she'd said *'yes'* instead. But what was the point? Walking around Roscoff itself had been enough to stir her decades-old memory pot with all its regrets and longings.

The childminding job that long-ago summer had come out of the blue and was the result of some serendipitous events. Friends of her parents, the Widdicombes, had left the West Country for London and knew a French family who were looking for help with their children over the summer in France. A job they thought Gwen, who often looked after their two toddlers when they returned to Devon for holidays, would be perfect for.

Once they knew Gwen was interested, they'd arranged everything. She'd found herself caught up in a whirlwind of organisation, including applying for her first ever passport. Finally, when it was all arranged, she took the train to Paddington, where Mrs Widdicombe had met her and taken her home. Sitting in the kitchen drinking tea, Gwen had dared to voice the worrying question. 'What happens if the Dubois family don't like me when they meet me?'

'Unlikely, my dear, so don't worry about that. They know how fond of you I am and that I trust you to look after my two. Anyway, you're on a fortnight's trial and if you are unhappy or things don't work out, they will pay you and buy your ticket home. They're really nice people, so I'm sure you're all going to get along just fine.' And so it had proved.

The next day, Gwen had been shown some of the London sights and in the evening both the Widdicombes had taken her to London Victoria station and waved her goodbye. Gwen, clutching her passport, had boarded the night ferry train from platform two and at 9 p.m. it had departed for Dover and the Calais ferry on the first part of the eleven-hour journey.

From the moment she stepped out of the Gard du Nord concourse, Paris had seduced her. To her twenty-year-old mind, it was the most beautiful city she'd ever seen. Given that she'd only been to London and Bristol at that time, both of which were still recovering from the bomb damage of the war, she realised the comparison was unfair.

The more she explored Paris, with its handsome buildings, the Seine running through the very heart of the city, the numerous palaces, flights of steps and Montmartre – oh, how she loved that place – the sheer romanticism of everything had enchanted her, and she'd never wanted to leave. But in true Parisian tradition the family decamped to their summer house for the month of August, leaving the sweltering city to the tourists.

The prospect of decamping to the countryside of Brittany for the whole of August wasn't something she'd looked forward to, as much as the Dubois family assured her she would enjoy her time there too. A smile played around Gwen's lips as she remembered.

The family had been right. Brittany too, had enchanted her. Besides, she met the love of her life that month in Brittany.

A movement down by the lake caught her gaze and she saw two deer grazing. For several moments she watched, before they trotted away, the white underneath of their tails flashing as they bounced in the direction of the fields beyond the copse. Pixie would adore knowing that there were deer on her land. Such a shame that she was hell-bent on selling the place before she had a real chance to enjoy it.

Gwen sighed. She'd admitted to being dubious all those years ago when Pixie and Frank had told her they were buying this beautiful château in France, but in the last few days she'd come to realise how special the place was, especially to Pixie. The strain that had been etched on her daughter's face in recent weeks had softened, she'd relaxed, and this morning, with Fern, she'd smiled more than she had in a long time. Gwen knew without a doubt, it would do her good to do her grieving over the loss of Frank here. A place they had both loved, but Pixie's only true memory of the two of them together here was from ten years ago. There would be no ghosts of Frank jumping out to hijack memories of holidays or birthdays spent here or point out how different everything now was. She could make new memories for herself in this beautiful place.

Gwen sat there, her tea cold in its cup, deep in thought, trying to figure out how she could subtly nudge Pixie into changing her mind and not be guilty of interfering. Even as she acknowledged to herself that whatever she did, Pixie would regard it as interfering, she was still determined to try. The question was how? Maybe the direct approach would work best, as long as she was ready to backtrack if Pixie got annoyed with her. If nothing else, it might make Pixie have second thoughts, which would be a good thing.

* * *

Some hours later, as Gwen put cutlery and crockery out on the table and wondered about interrupting her daughter, Pixie wandered into the kitchen, stretching her arms above her head. 'Gosh is that the time? Six o'clock. I'm starving now and I bet you are too.'

Gwen nodded and picked up a bottle of wine and two glasses. 'Aperitif on the terrace while we wait for the pasta. I'm guessing you had a good writing session?'

'Yes, I did.' Pixie nodded.

'I saw two deer down by the lake this afternoon. I hope you get to see them before we leave.' Gwen took a sip of her drink before looking at her daughter. 'One more day before we leave and I have to ask, are you still set on selling up because...' she took a deep breath. 'I think you should seriously reconsider about rushing in to it.' She watched Pixie's face, waiting for the inevitable cross reaction. 'Perhaps even forget about selling at all,' she added.

Pixie stared at her for several seconds, the silence between them heavy with foreboding, before Pixie gave a peal of laughter.

'You know what, Mum, I think you're a bit of a witch.' She shook with laughter again at the look on Gwen's face. 'Keeping this place long-term is not an option, but I was intending to talk to you over supper about spending the summer here and waiting until the autumn to put the château on the market.'

'You were?'

'Yes.' It was Pixie's turn to watch her mother now. 'How do you like the thought of spending the next four months here? Because there is no way I'm coming out here and leaving you alone in Devon. Either we both come for summer or I tell Jean-Yves Ropars to put the place on the market before we leave tomorrow.'

'I wasn't thinking about me coming too. Go and sit down, I'll get the pasta,' Gwen said, playing for some thinking time.

She took several minutes draining the pasta, tossing it with some herbs and butter before placing it in a warm bowl. By the time she joined Pixie out on the terrace to eat, she'd come to a decision, but she needed Pixie to answer a couple of questions before she told her yes or no.

'Why the sudden desire to spend the summer here?' Gwen asked.

Pixie didn't answer immediately and Gwen waited for her to finish helping herself to slices of cold lamb and salad and to swallow a few mouthfuls.

'Yesterday and today, for the first time since Frank died, I've been writing and I realised if anyone needed to go on retreat, it's me. And I have the perfect place right here. If nothing else, summer here would be a complete break and rest before returning to the UK in the autumn and getting on with the rest of my life. But I meant it – if you don't come too, I'll forget the whole idea.'

'You're a strong woman and just because you're now a widow,' Gwen paused as Pixie flinched at the word. 'It doesn't mean you can't do those things you dreamed of doing on your own. You could still work towards opening the château as a retreat and living here full-time – if you want to.'

'Right now, Mum, there are two things I want to do. One is to write my next book and the second is to spend the summer here with you. Make some new happy memories. I thought Gus and Sarah might like to come over for a couple of weeks. Bring Charlie, even Annabelle and Harry and Mimi could come, if they wanted to. There's plenty of room. Be a real family summer.'

Gwen nodded thoughtfully. 'That would be good.'

'Please say you'll come. I know I'll be busy writing for a few hours every day, but we can go out and about together, especially when the family are here. We can fit lots of fun in.'

'And the woman living in the cottage? How is that going to affect you?'

'Ah, the mysterious tenant.' Pixie swallowed hard. 'I know I'm going to have to meet her face to face, find out the truth. But as soon as that's happened, I'll tell her she has to find somewhere else. She's nothing to do with me and she's not my responsibility.' Pixie picked up the bottle of wine and poured them both a small top up. 'So are we coming back to spend the summer here or not? We've both got neighbours who will keep an eye on our houses, neither of us have pets to worry about, so there's nothing to stop us, is there?'

'You can be very stubborn,' Gwen said.

Pixie smiled. 'I learnt that on my mother's knees. Come on, just agree we come, you know you want to.'

'Okay, but I have one condition,' Gwen said, twirling the wine around in her glass thoughtfully before looking up at Pixie. 'You're a grown woman who I've always thought had a compassionate nature. I've never seen you being nasty to anyone. I need you to promise me that you will be kind to the woman in the cottage when you meet her. You don't know the circumstances of why she ended up living here, or why Frank didn't tell you about her. Find out her story before you jump to any conclusions. Things aren't always as clear-cut as they may seem. Frank was a good man and he loved you very much, that I know is true.'

Gwen watched the conflicting emotions flit across Pixie's face before she drained her glass of wine. 'I don't know why you're so bothered about a perfect stranger, but I promise I will do my best to, at least, be civil to her, okay?'

And with that Gwen had to be content.

10

After supper that evening, they'd talked about what needed to be organised on both sides of the Channel if they were to spend four months in France. They'd decided to leave behind all the things like bedding and clothes they'd brought with them on this visit, it would mean having to bring less at the end of the month. During this weekend they'd discovered that Monsieur Quiltu, as well as leaving the château furnished, had left an ancient washing machine and vacuum cleaner in the boot-cum-utility room, and there was even a television in one of the sitting rooms, not that they'd switched it on. So it was really a question of bringing over personal stuff – clothes and a few things to make it feel more like home – and organising an internet connection.

The dawn chorus woke Pixie early the next morning and she stayed in bed for some time listening to the birds and watching the sunrise through the tall unshuttered windows. The short holiday had gone in a flash, but, at least, if everything went according to plan, she'd be back in ten days and taking up residence for the summer. A thought that filled her with happiness.

Today, their last full day, would be a busy one. A visit to town, calling in and telling Fern about their summer plans on the way, a quick visit to the notaire to keep him informed of her plans, lunch in one of the restaurants in town to save buying and cooking more food (supper would be a salad baguette from the boulangerie and a glass of wine), and then back to spend their final afternoon and evening at the château.

Gwen was already in the kitchen when Pixie went downstairs half an hour later, coffee on the go and bread in the toaster. 'I've been thinking,' she said, handing Pixie a cup of coffee.

'Please don't tell me you've changed your mind about summer?' Pixie looked at her mother anxiously.

'No, I'm really looking forward to another French adventure.'

'There's a but coming, I can feel it.'

'I'll need to go home for a short visit in June. It's my yearly hospital check-up.'

'Can you bring it forward to next week? Or postpone it until the autumn?'

'Doubt it, you know how busy these hospital departments are.'

'We'll worry about it after we get back tomorrow,' Pixie said, smothering a sigh. 'Let's make the most of our last day here.'

* * *

It was mid-morning when Pixie drove out through the village en route for Carhaix, having stopped off at the auberge to tell Fern their summer plans. Fern couldn't have been happier to hear the news.

'Supper here the first Saturday you're back, yes? I can't tell you how pleased I am you've decided to live in the château, even if it is only for a short time.'

Once in town, Pixie headed for a central car park. 'I've just got time to see Jean-Yves before we have lunch. Do you want to come with me or wait here?'

Gwen shook her head. 'I'm going to find the chocolate shop and buy a couple of presents for the neighbours – bribery in advance for the summer.'

'That's on my way to the notaire's so I'll leave you there. I shouldn't be long, so wait there for me. I could do with buying some in-advance chocolate presents too.'

Jean-Yves was showing a client out as Pixie arrived at his office. 'Madame Sampson, how can I help you today?'

'I wanted to tell you that whilst the château will definitely be going on the market in the autumn, my mother and I have decided to spend the summer here.'

'I am pleased you will at least get to enjoy some time at the château.' Jean-Yves smiled at her. 'Will the tenant in the cottage also be staying?'

Pixie shrugged. 'She hasn't returned, so I haven't met her yet. I'll have that pleasure when we get back at the end of the month. Unless, of course, she appears between now and tomorrow morning when we leave.'

'If you wanted, I could send her an official letter?'

'Maybe after I've met her I'll ask you to do that – put it in writing that she has to leave.'

Jean-Yves nodded and held out his hand. 'Let me know. We'll say au revoir for the moment then. Enjoy your summer 'ere in Brittany.'

Pixie's hand was taken in a firm grip for two or three seconds before Jean-Yves let go and turned back into his office.

'Oh, there is one thing, can you tell me the tenant's name please?'

Jean-Yves stopped, looked back at Pixie. 'Her name is Justine Martin. That is all I can tell you.'

'Thank you.'

Walking back to the chocolate shop to rejoin Gwen, Pixie tossed the name around in her mind, trying to see if it rang any bells. Had she ever met anyone with the surname Martin? Nobody sprang instantly to mind and by the time she reached Gwen, she'd decided it was a pointless exercise.

* * *

After treating themselves to lunch at a smart restaurant in the countryside outside Carhaix, Pixie drove them back to the château and they spent the rest of the day and evening pottering around.

That night, in bed listening to the owls calling through the trees to each other and watching the moon move slowly across the night sky, Pixie realised she couldn't wait to return and spend more time in this special place. Easter here had been good, a portent of what the summer would be like, she hoped. She knew she'd already made a new friend in Fern, and Gwen and Anouk seemed to get on too.

Of course, there was still the disturbing knowledge that Frank hadn't told her the truth about the château being theirs – or about installing this mysterious woman in the cottage. Pixie had this gut-wrenching desire to know everything about this woman, starting with how long she'd known Frank. However hurtful the truth turned out to be, she had to know who she was, why she'd become part of Frank's life, and importantly, what their plans had been before he died.

Pixie wished the woman had returned whilst she and Gwen were still here. She would have insisted on having answers to all her questions, and then told the woman she had to leave before they returned at the end of the month. And that would have been the end of that. Now she had ten days to brood and overthink everything while they were in the UK. But whatever story the woman gave her when she finally turned up, she would soon be on her way.

* * *

Both Pixie and Gwen were subdued the next morning. After breakfast, Pixie went round the château carefully taking her time, checking that everything that should be shut and locked up was. She carried Gwen's suitcase down and went back for her own.

Loading the car, she glanced across at the cottage. Would it be easier to push a note under the door, telling the woman to leave with no explanation given? But then she wouldn't get any answers to her questions. Pixie needed to do it face to face. She needed the woman to know she knew about... about whatever had been going on. Besides, she wanted to see for herself this woman Frank had somehow become involved with. Pixie slammed the boot closed on the car and made her way back to the château.

She pulled the heavy oak front door closed and turned the key whilst Gwen got in the passenger seat of the car and strapped herself in. They both turned for one last lingering look at the château as Pixie started the engine. Together they chorused 'We'll be back' before they both burst into laughter. It was good knowing that she was coming back for the summer. That this visit wasn't the one and only time she'd spend here.

Pixie turned onto the lane for the village. Once in the village, she stopped outside the boulangerie and quickly ran in and bought a couple of ham and cheese baguettes and two coffee eclairs. 'Much nicer than the ones on the ferry,' she said to Gwen, placing them carefully on the dashboard as she got back into the car.

Leaving the village behind and reaching the junction for the main road, Pixie slowed down and came to a halt at the same time as a French registered car approaching the village pulled to a stop on the other side of the road. When the woman driver smiled and gestured she should go first, Pixie raised her hand and smiled in acknowledgement as she looked both ways before pulling out onto the main road and heading for the ferry port.

11

___

As Justine Martin approached the crossroads and slowed down to come to the required stop, a car travelling away from the village also came to a halt directly opposite. Seeing the English car number plates, Justine smiled and gestured to the woman driver to go first. English drivers not used to driving on the 'wrong' side of the road sometimes made mistakes, so she was always super polite and gave way to them. The woman raised her hand in acknowledgement as she drove across to take the road signposted Roscoff. The elderly lady in the passenger seat smiled and waved as well.

While she waited for the road to clear, Justine glanced in the rear-view mirror at her three-and-a-half-year-old son, Ferdie, safely strapped in his car seat and fast asleep for most of the journey. It had been a good Easter holiday at St Malo, even if Ferdie had been spoilt rotten by his grandparents. It had also been the first time for years that she hadn't been lectured or subjected to deep sighs and sorrowful looks from her mother. Thankfully, she seemed to have at last accepted the decision Justine had made as well as the consequences and stopped nagging her about it.

Four years ago, Justine had been inwardly terrified when she'd selfishly made the decision to do something she knew was the right thing for her but not necessarily for anyone else. The action had upset her mother and for months afterwards their relationship had been fraught. Unable to change her mind, her mother had come to accept that it was something Justine needed to do, after repeated warnings about how the consequences could not only be disastrous for her but also painful for the other people involved. 'These things have a habit of taking on a life of their own,' she'd repeated time and time again before making Justine promise not to involve her and her father in the whole sorry business. Justine had promised and gone ahead with her plan.

After the initial heart-pounding meeting to instigate matters, there had been months of toing and froing before things had started to level out, but now almost everyone had come to terms with the consequences of her action. Justine's promise to her mother was still unbroken and her own life had never been better.

She had a beautiful son, a lovely home and she was in the process of turning a basket-making hobby into a thriving business. The only part of her life she'd never envisaged was being a single mother. She'd always wanted children, to have a family within a secure relationship, but that option had been taken out of her hands when she became pregnant. Now she wouldn't part with Ferdie for the world and apart from the lack of a wedding ring on her finger she was in a good place.

Justine hummed softly to herself as she drove through the village. Not long now and she'd be home and could slip back into the routine that had established itself over the past year. Ferdie would be back at the école maternalle every morning next week, which meant she could spend the mornings making sure she had enough baskets in stock for the summer season. She loved having Ferdie at home, though, the place felt empty somehow when he was at school, even though she could lose herself in her work. Goodness only knows how she'd feel when he started at proper school.

She was up to date with her work, but she needed to build up a good supply of stock for the street markets which would start with a vengeance in May as the tourists arrived. As well as her regular weekly stalls at Huelgoat and Châteauneuf-du-Faou, a couple of shops had also asked to stock her baskets and other willow work. There were enough baskets under lock and key in the barn near the cottage to keep her going for several weeks, but she definitely needed to make a lot more baskets before the main summer season. If only basket making wasn't so time-consuming.

Justine glanced in the rear-view mirror as Ferdie woke with a small groan and wriggled in his seat. 'Hi, sleepyhead.'

'Mummy, I'm thirsty.'

'A few more minutes and we'll be home. You can have a drink then.'

Justine drove the remaining short distance down the road towards home. It was so good to be back. Turning onto the château drive, she breathed a sigh of happiness as she saw the château and then her cottage standing to one side. She loved living in this cottage and was still in awe of the fact that she and Ferdie got to call it home.

Stopping outside the cottage, Justine turned off the car engine and pulled up the handbrake. Life was good, summer was on its way and she'd never been happier.

PART II

'It is not in the stars to hold our destiny but in ourselves.'

— *SHAKESPEARE'S SONNETS*.

12

Four days after returning home, Pixie sat at Frank's desk in the study. Well ahead with organising things for spending the summer in France she'd also made a start on sorting through Frank's belongings. She was determined that when she returned here in the autumn, that whatever transpired at the château in the coming months, there wouldn't be the need to face any additional heartbreak of throwing things away. Frank's side of the wardrobe in their bedroom was now empty. She'd divided his good suits, trousers, jeans, shirts and several pairs of leather shoes between the homeless shelter in Totnes and the local charity shop, the rest she'd binned. Sweaters and scarves were in black bags, ready for the next run to the Save the Children shop. That was his clothes sorted. This afternoon, she planned on going through his desk, in particular the papers in the filing cabinet.

Jean-Yves' remark about Frank forging her signature had been niggling away in her subconscious ever since he'd said it. The Frank she knew and loved would never do such a thing, but he hadn't been his normal self for well over a year, who knew what he'd been capable of doing in those months?

Pixie's fingers trembled as she took the official papers out of the folder and found the one she was looking for. The final completion certificate. A sigh of relief escaped her mouth, as her eyes scanned the signatures at the bottom, hers underneath Franks. It certainly looked genuine, if a little untidier than her usual one. The date alongside the signatures corresponded with the date the bank manager had said the château became theirs.

She drummed her fingers on the desk in front of her. *Think, think, Pixie.* She hadn't known it but this would have been the last time she'd had to sign anything château related and she needed to remember when and where she'd signed it to be absolutely certain.

She looked at the date again, searching her memory of that year, of that particular month, and slowly she remembered. Her agent had arranged for a local bookshop to take a large quantity of signed copies of Pixie's latest book for the weeks leading up to Christmas, which had meant a long book-signing session in her office. Her wrist and hand were aching from signing over forty books and there was still at least twenty to do when Frank had interrupted her.

'Pixie darling, I know you're busy, but the notaire wants these signed by us both asap. Could you just pop your signature at the bottom here under mine? Then I can send them back to him today.'

Tired and cross at being interrupted, she remembered irritably signing her signature, not questioning or even looking at what she was signing. No wonder her signature looked a little scrawled. Frank, she now realised with the benefit of hindsight, had chosen a moment when she would be unlikely to ask questions. Well, at least she could now assure Jean-Yves the next time she saw him that she had signed the paper, even if it had been unknowingly.

Pixie sat back in Frank's chair. What had been on his mind that afternoon? He could have told her then it was the final ownership papers for the château, so why hadn't he?

Pixie stretched out her hand and picked up the silver framed photo of the two of them on their wedding day that Frank had kept on his desk forever. Down the years when she'd suggested changing it for a more up to date one of the two of them, he'd refuse. 'Happiest day of my life' he'd say. 'Looking at it always reminds me how lucky I am to have you.'

Pushing back on the chair, Pixie stood up. Installing another woman in the grounds of the château they'd bought together didn't make sense, whichever way she looked at it. She wished Gwen's charitable suggestion that Frank was maybe giving someone a helping hand was behind everything he'd done, but in her mind, that idea didn't hold water. If it was the case, he would have discussed it with her before going ahead, instead he'd acted in secret, keeping everything from her. Hopefully next week when she met the tenant in the cottage at least one of her questions would be answered – even if the answer was unpalatable.

Pixie sighed as she replaced the château folder in the desk drawer before going across the landing and into her own study. There was still a lot to organise before they left in six days. She'd promised Gwen she'd print out the photos of the château she'd taken on her phone and give her copies to show her many friends in the village.

Waiting for the printer to do its stuff, Pixie looked around her office and thought about what she needed to take to France. Notebook, laptop, printer, reference books, desktop computer. She stifled a sigh. The days had long gone when all a writer needed was a pen and paper, but did she need to transfer her whole office to the château?

By the time the printer had finished the photographs, Pixie had decided on her essentials: laptop, her big-screen iMac and the printer. Notebooks she could buy in France and she'd google any research she needed to do.

Pixie flicked through the photos as she picked them out of the collecting tray. There were three of the parkland and one of the lake. Inside the château, there was one of the main sitting room, one of the grand staircase with its suit of armour on the landing and one of the kitchen. She put those seven to one side. There, that should be enough for Gwen to show off with to her friends. The remaining photos were of the other bedrooms and the bathrooms and the empty rooms on the third floor.

Glancing at one of the empty room photos that was out of focus and preparing to throw it away, Pixie froze and stared at it, not believing what she was seeing. In the middle of the out-of-focus fuzz, there was an image of a man with his arms held open in welcome, looking straight at the camera and smiling at her. It couldn't possibly be Frank, could it?

It took several minutes to make her thumping heart and shaking body calm down as she stood there muttering to herself. 'You're being irrational thinking the image is Frank. Besides, there is no image. It's a figment of your imagination. It's just an out-of-focus photo. It's impossible.'

* * *

The evening before they left for France, Gwen walked down to the village hall to say goodbye to her friends for the summer and to enjoy a final session of OldTyme Dancing.

Everyone wished her well, told her they would miss her over

the summer and oohed and ahhed over the photos Pixie had printed out for her.

'Bit posh that. You won't want to come back. Looks lovely though – reckon the club ought to organise a coach outing there – you got enough bedrooms to put us all up!' were just a few of the comments that came her way.

Brenda, a widow and her closest friend in the village, was pleased for her but admitted that, selfishly, she wished Gwen wasn't going for the whole summer. 'I hope you have a lovely time even though I'll miss you. Evenings like this won't be the same without you. Not sure I'll bother to come very often.'

'Brenda, don't talk rot. Of course you'll still come here every week, you'll set otherwise. Got to keep those hips wiggling!' Gwen wiggled her own hips around to emphasise the point and Brenda laughed.

'Make sure you send me the occasional postcard.'

'I promise.'

Gwen's favourite dancing partner, Freddie, came over at that moment and whirled her around on the last foxtrot of the evening.

'Keep an eye on Brenda for me while I'm away, she dances a good waltz, and she needs a bit of cheering up,' she said quietly as the dance finished.

'Will do,' Freddie said. 'Don't worry about her – enjoy your summer. I hear there's a tango class starting up in September, so make sure you're back in time for that.'

As she and Brenda made their way to the door at the end of the evening, Freddie called out.

'Gwen, you make sure you look after yourself with all those Frenchies – we all know what casanovas they are.'

Gwen turned and waved. 'Bit late for that advice – been there, done that, got the T-shirt as the old saying goes.' Chuckling to herself at the thought of watching out for French casanovas, she made her way home.

Once home, she poured herself a small medicinal brandy as a nightcap and carried it upstairs to the bedroom. Her packing was done – two suitcases this time. One was closed, the other open, ready for her toiletries bag and night dress in the morning.

Thoughtfully, she took a sip of her drink. The visit to France at Easter had been for Pixie's sake and this long holiday over there was for her too, but it occurred to Gwen after she'd brightly thrown the 'been there done that' quip back at Freddie that maybe it was time for her to deal with some unfinished business.

Placing her drink on the old-fashioned bedside table with its cupboard underneath, she opened the door and took an old address book and a small drawstring bag off the shelf.

The address book pages fell open to reveal an old black-and-white photo. A swing was hanging from the bough of a tree, a small boy and girl were squashed together on the wooden seat, while standing behind was a taller, older young man holding the swing steady and with a little girl in his arms. The four of them were smiling happily at the camera.

Gwen looked at the photo for several seconds before replacing it between the pages of the address book and purposefully crossing to the open suitcase and placing the book in an empty elasticated pocket on the inside of the case. Picking up the drawstring bag, she eased it open and carefully took out the object inside and held it in the palm of her hand.

Memories of long ago began to crowd into her mind as she stared at the small enamel lighthouse brooch. This small inexpensive piece of jewellery had meant the world to her over sixty years ago, even now her heart quickened as she looked at it, wondering if she should do what she longed to. It was far too late to change anything, but maybe the truth was still out there, if she was brave enough to try and find it.

Gently she put the brooch back in its bag and pulled the drawstrings tight. She'd take it to France and wear it while she was there. Perhaps it would act as a sort of good-luck talisman – not that she believed in things like that – and give her the courage to take the step she'd tried to take years ago and failed.

She slipped the bag into the elasticated pocket of the suitcase, alongside the address book. Maybe this summer she would talk to Pixie about the best summer of her life. She'd also do her damnedest to try to find out the truth about what had happened to make that long-ago summer come to such an abrupt end. Her twenty-year-old self deserved to know the truth even after all these years.

13

Justine took Ferdie to the école maternalle school before driving back into the village to meet her friend Carole for a quick chat in the cafe. Pushing open the cafe door, she smiled as she saw Carole already sitting at one of the tables, nursing a large hot chocolate.

Buying herself a hot chocolate at the bar, Justine carried her drink over to Carole and pulled a chair out. They'd slipped into a routine of meeting up here one morning a week during term time after they'd taken their children to their respective schools. Lola, Carole's daughter, had recently moved up to the école elementary on the outskirts of the village, which meant there was no meeting up at the school gate in the mornings.

'How's things? Heard from your good "landlord" recently?' Carole wriggled her eyebrows suggestively.

Justine smothered a sigh. She wished Carole would stop being so leery about her landlord. Almost from the moment the two of them had become friends and she'd told Carole she lived in the château's cottage, she'd made innuendoes about her 'good landlord'.

'He brings you flowers and chocolates, he gives Ferdie presents. You mark my words, he's not doing that out of the kindness of his heart. One day he's going to expect you to say thank you.'

'Stop it. Honestly it isn't like that. And no, I haven't heard recently,' Justine said, briefly wondering what Carole's reaction would be if she told her the car she drove was a Christmas present from him. She might long to be able to talk about the situation but she'd made a promise and until things could be out in the open for everyone to know, it was better to hug the truth to herself. In an effort to change the subject, she said, 'Ever since we got back from Mum's, Ferdie has been going on and on about getting a dog like my mother's. He's driving me mad, perpetually whining why can't we?'

'The farmer near us will be looking for a home for some pups soon.'

'Not helpful, please don't mention it to Ferdie. I haven't got time for training a puppy.'

'It's good for kids to have pets. Besides, you're quite isolated where you are, be good to have a dog.'

Justine shook her head. 'Maybe. But life is busy enough right now without adding a puppy into the mix. Perhaps in the summer when Ferdie is off school, but then I'm going to be busy doing the markets and earning some money.'

Carole glanced at her. 'You still bringing Ferdie to mine after school on Friday?'

'Yes please, if it's okay?'

'Of course.'

A few minutes later, Justine finished her hot chocolate and stood up. 'Better get going. I've a couple of orders to finish by the end of the week.'

* * *

Driving home, Justine mentally organised her working day. Now Ferdie was back at school four mornings a week, she could settle down into her own working routine again. The two orders that needed finishing were the priority and then she could begin a new basket and make a start on some woven place mats.

She parked behind the cottage and, grabbing her bag and keys, made straight for the barns. She unlocked the padlock on the door of the small barn and slid it open. Different types of baskets were piled alongside each other or hanging by their handles from long display poles Justine had hammered into the wall. On an ancient kitchen table, there were piles of woven bowls of all sizes, wastepaper baskets and square holders. Along the shelves at the side were all her ready-to-use materials: willow, wicker, raffia, alongside the tools she used.

Justine opened her favourite music channel on her phone before sitting down on the three-legged stool and pulling a low working table towards her. Within minutes, she was absorbed in her work, finishing off the first of the commissioned baskets and oblivious to any outside sounds. Two hours later, she'd finished the two baskets and had made a start on a set of six raffia place mats when her rumbling stomach reminded her it was lunchtime.

She stood up and stretched her arms above her head. A good morning's work. With luck, after lunch she'd finish at least three of the place mats before leaving to collect Ferdie.

Not bothering to close the barn door behind her, Justine went to walk around the side of the barn onto the path that led to the cottage, glancing across to the château driveway as she did so, and stopped in surprise. There was a car parked there. Not Frank's car, unless he had changed it, but the car did look vaguely familiar, with its English plates.

She stepped back and stayed out of sight, watching for a few moments as two women went back and forth to the car, before she remembered why the car seemed familiar. It was the English car she'd given way to at the village crossroads when she was coming home after Easter. She recognised too, the elderly lady who had been a passenger.

Justine shivered as a cold band of fear caught her in its grip. Who were these women? What were they doing here? She took several deep breaths, trying to calm herself, and wiped her sweaty hands down her jeans. Only one way to find out.

Pushing her shoulders back, she began walking towards the car, as a deep-rooted fear inside her that something momentous was about to happen, began to fill her body. Whatever it was, she hoped she was strong enough to deal with it.

14

Pixie stopped the car in front of the château with a happy sigh. 'We're back. Summer officially begins today,' she said, glancing at Gwen.

'The shutters are open on the cottage. Your tenant has returned,' Gwen said, looking across the drive.

Pixie felt her spirits drop as she too looked across at the cottage. Happy as she was to be back at the château, she was aware the time of reckoning was drawing closer and she was dreading the confrontation she knew she had to have with the mysterious tenant in the cottage. 'Never mind that for the moment. Let's start getting the car unpacked and sort ourselves out some food, it's lunchtime and I'm starving.'

As Gwen sorted the food stuff in the kitchen, Pixie flung open all the shutters on the ground floor before going back out to the car and starting to carry boxes and suitcases in. Gwen came out to take a bag of jumpers she hadn't been able to squeeze in her case.

'Right that's enough for now,' Pixie said. 'I'll take my computer and office stuff in after lunch.'

They were about to return indoors when they were both startled to see a woman walking towards them from the direction of the barn. Watching the woman as she got closer to them, Pixie was filled with trepidation and a degree of uncertainty. The woman was younger than she'd expected. She waited for her to speak.

'Hello. I'm Justine Martin and I live in the cottage. Are you friends of Frank, come to stay? I expect he told you about me living here.'

Her words fell into a lengthening silence as Pixie stared at her without answering.

Gwen looked at Pixie anxiously before turning to Justine and saying a quiet 'Hello.'

Pixie took a deep breath. Right, she could do this. 'I'm Pixie Sampson, Frank's wife. My mother and I are here for the summer. I don't know your connection to my husband, but no, he never mentioned you to me or the fact that you were living in the cottage.' To her own ears, she sounded like a parrot reciting something she'd been told to say.

'Will he be joining you this summer?' Justine gave her a hesitant smile.

Taken aback by the question, Pixie felt the colour drain from her face and she stared open-mouthed at Justine before managing to stammer, 'No. Of course not.' Shaking, she took the last bag out of the car, slammed the door closed and went into the château.

Gwen gave Justine a sad look. 'The two of you will have to talk later,' she said, before following Pixie in and shutting the oak door.

Pixie had collapsed onto a kitchen chair and was rubbing her tear-filled eyes when Gwen walked in. Pixie looked up at Gwen, stricken. 'She doesn't know that he's dead, does she? How ironic that it seems I'm the one who is going to have to tell her. Unless you...?'

Gwen shook her head. 'No, darling, I think that's down to you, sadly.'

* * *

The tears were streaming down Justine's face before she reached the sanctuary of the cottage. A thousand questions were going through her mind. There could only be one answer as to why Frank's wife had gone such a ghostly colour and answered 'No' in a sharp voice when she'd asked if Frank would be joining her. Something awful must have happened to him.

She sat huddled on the settee sobbing, remembering their short time together. From the beginning, he'd promised he'd always be there for her, but now he wouldn't be. She wished that she'd pushed harder for him to tell Pixie about her. Not listened to his protestations that he needed time to pave the way and he hated the thought of hurting her. She wished too, that she'd seen him on a more regular basis, especially after she came here to live. There was no routine to any contact. His visits and his phone calls were always unexpected and sometimes weeks passed without hearing from him – always explained away by travelling for work. Justine was always happy to see him whenever he could fit her into his life, which was why she hadn't been unduly worried over the past few weeks by not hearing from him. She should have sensed something was wrong.

Justine was trying to pull herself together when there was a knock on the door. She debated not opening it but knew she had no real choice.

'May I come in?' Pixie said.

Justine nodded as she glanced at her watch. 'I have to go out soon.'

'What I have to say won't take long,' Pixie said. 'But first I have some sad news to tell you.'

'I think I've guessed – Frank's dead, isn't he?'

Pixie nodded. 'Yes.'

'When? What happened?'

'It happened back in early March. Motorway accident. Joy-riders crashed into his car.' Pixie's voice was quiet but brusque as if she couldn't bear to voice the information.

'I'm so, so sorry for your loss, Mrs Sampson.' Justine tried and failed to stem a fresh batch of tears. 'That's horrible.' She reached for a tissue from the box on the table. Finding it empty, she sniffed and wiped her hands across her face, defiant under Pixie's gaze.

'How well did you know Frank?'

The unexpected question took Justine by surprise and there was a short pause before she answered. 'I hadn't known him long, about four years, I think, but he was very kind to me.'

'I didn't ask you that. I asked, how *well* did you know him,' Pixie pressed, staring at Justine. 'And why are you living here?'

Justine jumped as the loud alarm on her watch buzzed into the uncomfortable silence that followed Pixie's words. 'I'm sorry. I have to collect my son from the école maternalle.'

'I didn't realise you had a child,' Pixie said. 'He lives here with you? How old is he?'

'Of course he lives here – where else would he live? He's nearly four. I have to go or I shall be late and Ferdie will be upset.' And Justine grabbed her car keys from the table, opened the door of the cottage and gestured to Pixie to leave.

'I have another question – your surname, Martin, is that a married name?'

'No, my family name. I'm not married. Please – I have to go.' Justine slammed the cottage door behind her and ran to her car. Thirty seconds later, she was driving away.

Pixie stood on the driveway watching her go and despite everything, found herself hoping that she was okay to drive in her upset state. At least she'd managed to tell the woman the truth about Frank without breaking down herself, but she still had questions she needed answers to. Pixie sighed and walked slowly across to the château. Justine and her child were not her problem, but how could she evict a single mother with a small child?

Her rehearsed speech of, 'I now own the château and the cottage, both of which I intend to sell later this year. So, I am giving you notice to quit and I'd like you to leave immediately,' had died on her lips before she'd even attempted to speak the words. A second, uneasy question slipped unwanted into Pixie's mind. Could the child be Frank's? And if he was – what the hell was she going to do about it? Ignore or acknowledge?

15

Before she reached the village, Justine pulled over and rooted in her bag for a comb. When she pulled down the small mirror in the visor and saw the state of her face, let alone her hair, she groaned and searched hurriedly for some concealer to try and hide the redness around her eyes in case she saw anyone. Sitting there, she took several calming deep breaths before she drove the rest of the way to the school.

Ferdie was waving a picture he'd painted as he came out into the school playground. 'Look, Mummy, it's Gangan's dog. Can we have a dog?

'You've painted him beautifully, we'll pin it on the board in the kitchen when we get home,' Justine said, ignoring his question. She scooped him up and lifted him into the car quickly. Getting a dog had moved even further down a long list of wants at the moment.

She handed Ferdie one of the flapjack biscuits that she always carried in her bag, knowing that he needed something to eat the moment he came out of school, otherwise he became cranky quickly. And today she couldn't cope with cranky.

Not wanting to go home straight away, she took the road that led down to the river, about three kilometres away. There was a small playground with swings and a trampoline and Ferdie loved it there. While he amused himself, she'd use the time to think about the future.

To her relief, the playground was deserted when they arrived and Ferdie ran off to jump around on the trampoline. Sitting on a nearby log bench to watch him, Justine let her thoughts wander back to the scene in the cottage.

Pixie had said she had something to say other than telling her the sad news about Frank but had never got that far. Justine sighed. She didn't need a crystal ball to guess that Pixie intended to give her notice to quit the cottage. When Frank had promised the cottage was hers and Ferdie's to live in for as long as she wanted, she'd taken a lot of convincing that he meant it. She remembered throwing her arms around him in the end and thanking him profusely.

Shame he'd never got around to telling Pixie about their arrangement. All those months when he kept saying he knew how hurt she would be and once he'd sorted a few things out, he'd know when it was the right moment to tell her. Justine smiled wryly to herself. The right moment had never arrived and now it was too late. Pixie Sampson must surely be wondering about who she, Justine, was, and why Frank had let her live in the château cottage. Doubtless there would be a lot of questions next time they came face to face.

Justine let out a deep sigh. She'd promised Frank that she would leave it to him to tell his wife the truth, saying it was his secret to tell, not hers, but she knew if the truth ever became known it wasn't only Pixie Sampson who would be hurt.

What were she and Ferdie going to do now? The first option to come to mind, just leave, disappear out of Pixie's life, she pushed away. If only it were that simple. There was so much to take into consideration. Did she stay here in Finistère or move completely away? Back nearer her parents? Finding somewhere else to live that she could afford wouldn't be easy, finding storage for her basket-making stuff would be another problem. But uprooting Ferdie from both his home and school at the same time would be so hard on him, especially when she'd tried to give him some stability in his young life.

Justine smiled as she saw him bouncing on the trampoline, arms flailing and shouting with glee.

'Mummy, you bounce too!' Ferdie shouted as he saw her watching.

Justine shook her head.

'Pleeeze.'

Oh what the hell, there was no one here to criticise.

Justine kicked off her shoes and joined Ferdie on the trampo-line. For five minutes, she jumped and bounced all her worries out of her head, concentrating on playing with her son, staying in the middle and avoiding the safety net around the edges of the trampoline.

'This is fun, but we have to go home soon,' she said, as Ferdie landed on his bottom next to her as she took a quick breather.

'No no, want to stay,' and Ferdie was up and jumping again.

'Okay, two minutes, but that's it. When I call you, you come. I'm getting off now.'

Justine's legs felt like jelly as she climbed back onto the ground and she wobbled as she walked towards the car. Leaning against it waiting for her legs to stop trembling, she began to worry about what was likely to happen now. If Pixie did plan on telling her to leave, and that surely had to be a high possibility, she'd need a plan.

Would Pixie agree to her staying in the cottage if she offered to pay rent? Frank had always insisted he didn't want her to worry about paying rent, but as her business had started to take off, she'd religiously put some money away every month. Not a lot but enough to give her a cushion, and now her baskets were selling well, paying rent wouldn't be a problem. Offering to pay rent had to be worth a try. If her offer was refused, which was, of course, a distinct possibility, then she'd have to ask for time and think of a plan B.

In the meantime, she and Ferdie would stay out of sight back at the château as much as they could in an effort to put off the next meeting with Pixie for as long as possible. To think that less than twenty-four hours ago she'd thought she had her life mapped out for the summer – and the foreseeable future.

'Come on, Ferdie. Time to go home.' The words, 'while we still have one' remained unspoken.

* * *

When Pixie returned to the château after Justine had driven off, she found Gwen sitting out on the terrace. Lunch things were still on the table, although Gwen had eaten something and poured herself a glass of rosé. Gwen took the bottle out of the wine cooler and poured Pixie a generous measure before pouring herself a smaller one.

'Thanks. I feel in need of this,' Pixie said before taking a gulp.

'How did she react?' Gwen asked.

'She was in a terrible state before I got there. I told her about Frank, but I couldn't tell her I needed her to leave,' Pixie said, sinking down onto a chair before taking another large gulp of her drink, hoping it would calm her down. 'Didn't feel I could hit her with that news straight away, the state she was in.'

'There will be time enough for that,' Gwen said.

'She's got a child. A boy. He's three – nearly four.' Pixie paused. 'She also said she'd known Frank for about four years.'

'Oh.'

'Exactly.'

'Doesn't necessarily follow,' Gwen said, her voice trailing away.

'No, but it would explain his behaviour over the château and letting her live in the cottage.'

'Did you learn anything else?'

Pixie shook her head. 'No. She had to dash off to collect her son – oh, his name is Ferdie – before we got any deeper into the whys and wherefores of the conversation.'

The two of them sat in silence, each deep in their own thoughts for several moments.

'So, while she knows about Frank, we know nothing more about her, apart from the fact she has a child,' Pixie said, before draining her glass and placing it on the table. 'But whatever the truth turns out to be it doesn't change the fact that I'm selling the château in the autumn and she has to leave.' She stood up.

Gwen looked at her. 'Aren't you going to eat anything?'

'I'm not really hungry. I'll clear the table and then we need to start settling in. Tomorrow we'll need to do a supermarket shop for the weekend. It's Labour Day on Saturday, May the first, so the shops will be closed, with only the boulangerie open for a short time in the morning.'

'Does Fern know we're back?'

Pixie nodded. 'Yes, We're off out on Saturday evening for supper at the auberge. But now unpacking calls.'

Once in her bedroom, Pixie opened the first of her cases and started to place things in drawers and on shelves. Opening the carved doors of the large Breton armoire, she winced as she saw Frank's new clothes still hanging there. She'd forgotten to pack them up ready to be donated somewhere. They'd just have to stay there for now and she pushed them to the far end of the rail.

The first suitcase emptied, she zipped it up, pushed it under the bed out of the way and reached for the second one. The urn with Frank's ashes had been an impulsive last-minute addition to this case and was one of the first two things she saw as she undid the buckles and straps on the old-fashioned case. She'd had some absurd notion that she couldn't leave him behind, that they had to spend the summer at the château together. She picked up the silver framed photo of Frank that was the first thing she saw every morning when she woke up and placed it on the bedside table. Returning to the case, she held the urn carefully while looking around for inspiration as to where to put it, him, while she decided where to scatter them. She certainly didn't want them in full view, forcing her to look at them every day. A photo was one thing, a happy reminder, ashes were another thing altogether.

'If you weren't already dead, Frank Sampson, I could cheerfully murder you right this minute. Why didn't you tell me what was going on – surely after all our years together I deserved that? Right, you're going in the armoire for now. Out of sight, out of mind, until I decide what to do with you.'

And she marched back over to the armoire. Kneeling down, she placed the urn in the far corner on the floor underneath Frank's clothes, before standing up and slamming the door shut.

16

The next two days were busy ones for Pixie and Gwen. A visit to the small hypermarket in Carhaix took care of several hours on their first full day. They stocked up not only on food and wine, Pixie also bought candles, cushions and a couple of throws which, together with the things she'd brought from England, she hoped would turn the château into a home from home for the summer.

Pixie smiled as she saw a large display of the flowers known as 'the friendship flower' in France, muguets, in the gardening and plant section of the hypermarket.

'I'd forgotten about the tradition of giving these lily of the valley flowers on May Day,' she said, placing half a dozen pots on top of the shopping in the loaded trolley. 'We can take a couple to Fern and Scott tomorrow and toast King Charles IX for starting the annual gesture way back when.'

Back at the château, Gwen took charge of putting the food away in the kitchen, while Pixie carried the rest of the shopping in, placing most of it in the sitting room where the television was. It was a lovely room, although the dark oak panelling and the polished wooden parquet floor, combined with the dark leather furniture, did give it a somewhat sombre feeling. By the time Pixie had placed her cream throws over the settees, candles on the mantlepiece and a cream rug on the floor in front of the wood burner, the ambience of the room had become more welcoming.

As a final touch, she put three pots of muguets together in a large ornamental china bowl she found in a cupboard and placed it on the low carved wooden table in front of one of the settees. The perfume they gave off was wonderful and she bent and sniffed it appreciatively.

From time to time, as she passed one of the tall windows, she glanced across at the cottage. Justine's car was parked to one side, but there was no sign of her or her son. Part of Pixie wanted to go over and have the conversation she'd not managed the day before faced with Justine's obvious distress over Frank. Justine needed to be told that the château was going up for sale at the end of summer, giving her no alternative but to start looking for somewhere else in the next few weeks. If she gave her enough time to find somewhere else, Pixie couldn't be accused of evicting the two of them in a fit of spite, which, for some reason, made her feel better.

There was also that other conversation she wanted to have with Justine, starting with the question that she'd failed to answer yesterday – 'How well did you know my husband?' Which would lead on to the next, inevitable one, 'Is he Ferdie's father?' If the answer to that second all-important question was what she'd started to suspect, Pixie had *that* question to ask herself – what was she going to do about it? Acknowledge or deny? Accept or reject?

The thought of having that conversation, though, filled her with dread. Her life had changed so much in the last few months and something deep inside told her once she lifted the lid on this particular Pandora's box, life would be in free fall once again. And right this moment Pixie wasn't sure whether she could cope with whatever Justine had to tell her. Perhaps it would be better to take Jean-Yves up on his offer to write a formal letter asking her to vacate the cottage as soon as possible. In the meantime, she intended to avoid the cottage and its occupants as much as possible.

The next day, Saturday 1 May, Pixie spent some time deciding where to put her desktop computer and printer. She'd really have liked to set things up in the room on the third floor, but there wasn't a desk up there or even a table she could use. In the end, she decided on the second sitting room at the front of the château where there was a large extending table, which would comfortably hold both computer and printer and leave space for files and printouts, as well as any reference books she might buy, together with the scraps of paper she always seemed to generate when she was writing.

While in England, she'd emailed an internet provider and organised the setting up of an account and had been promised that it would be up and working by next week. Fingers crossed that would happen.

As they prepared to leave on Saturday evening to drive to the auberge for supper, they could hear childish laughter coming through the open windows of the cottage.

'Someone sounds happy,' Gwen said.

Pixie gave a non-committal 'Mmm' as she placed a pretty gift bag with wine, chocolate and three pots of muguets on the back seat of the car. She looked at Gwen as she got in the car.

'Not seen that brooch for a long time. I remember you wearing it a lot when I was a child.'

Gwen smiled as she touched the lighthouse brooch pinned to her silk scarf. 'I couldn't come back to Brittany without it.'

Pixie glanced at her questioningly, but Gwen smiled at her serenely and didn't say anything else, so Pixie turned back to concentrate on her driving.

The door to the auberge was open when Pixie and Gwen arrived and by the time she'd parked and picked up the gift bag, Fern had appeared to welcome and usher them inside.

'Happy Labour Day,' Pixie said, holding out the bag. 'Hope you've haven't been working too hard for this evening though.'

'Thank you. You didn't need to bring anything.'

'Wouldn't dream of arriving empty-handed,' Pixie answered.

Scott, waiting for them in the kitchen with Anouk, handed glasses of champagne around.

'To new friends and summer in Brittany,' he said, raising his glass in a toast.

'I'd hoped we'd eat out on the terrace, but there's a bit of a nip in the air, so it's supper around the kitchen table tonight – not so formal as the dining room,' Fern said. 'I invited Belinda and Alain from the campsite for the evening too, but Belinda rang earlier to apologise. Campers due to check in late this afternoon broke down on the way and aren't expecting to arrive much before ten o'clock, so they have to stay on site until then.'

'I love your kitchen,' Pixie said as they all sat down at the table. 'I would have liked to do something similar up at the château but...' she shrugged. 'We'll use it this summer and leave whoever buys it to update it.'

'Perhaps summer here will change your mind about selling,' Anouk said.

Pixie shook her head. 'Perhaps, but I don't expect it to.' She glanced at Fern who was busy placing their Coquille Saint Jacques starters on the table. 'Did you know there's a tenant in the château's cottage?'

'Yes.'

'Have you met her? Do you know anything about her?

Fern shook her head. 'I've met her briefly but I don't know a lot about her. She's French and she and her son have been living there for over a year, I think. She makes beautiful baskets.

'I thought she was English,' Pixie said, surprised. 'She has no trace of a French accent. Jean-Yves, the notaire, says I need to make sure they leave during the summer, otherwise it could be a problem selling the château in the winter.'

Anouk nodded. 'That would be the winter truce that prevents evictions for the five months of winter. Can be a real problem for landlords.'

'Jean-Yves is a very well-respected notaire,' Fern said. 'He'll know the best way to deal with it.'

'Have you lots of plans for the summer?' Scott asked.

'A few, but I've got to work while I'm here, I've got edits and a deadline to meet for my next book,' Pixie said. 'But I'll make sure Mum and I have plenty of fun too.'

'You're a writer?'

Pixie nodded. 'For my sins, yes. Monday morning, after this holiday weekend, my routine will be back in force.'

'What d'you write?' Fern asked.

Pixie smothered a sigh. This was the bit she disliked. She never hid the fact that she was a writer, but people's reaction when they knew what she wrote and heard who she was could make or break a friendship. She could only hope the three people around this table would continue to see her as Pixie. Maybe she could get away without telling them her pen name.

Gwen joined in the conversation and put paid to that thought.

'She writes under a pen name. Didn't think people would take her seriously as Pixie,' Gwen said before proceeding to tell them who she was. 'She's very popular,' she added. 'Several bestsellers.'

Pixie registered Fern's surprise as she jumped up and left the kitchen, running into the dining room and returning seconds later with a copy of Pixie's latest book. 'I've got them all. I love your books.'

Pixie smiled. 'That's a relief. Could have been embarrassing if you hated them. But please, keep it to yourself. Here in France, I'm more than happy to be known as just Pixie for the summer. Can I help?' she added as Fern stood up to fetch the main course.

'No thanks. Scott will get the salad out of the fridge while I get the lasagna out of the oven.'

'She has me well trained,' Scott said as he stood up.

* * *

Driving back to the château a couple of hours later after an evening filled with good food and lots of laughter, Pixie felt happier than she had done for months.

'That was a fun evening,' Gwen said. 'We'll have to return the favour – maybe when the family are over next month?'

'Good idea,' Pixie said, coming to a stop outside the château. 'Here we are, home.' As the words left her mouth, she realised that it did indeed feel like coming home.

17

Monday morning, Pixie was awake at five thirty and pulled on jeans and a sweatshirt before creeping past Gwen's room and going downstairs. The kitchen with its terracotta tiles was cold and Pixie shivered as she pushed a coffee pod into the machine and waited for it to do its stuff. If ever a kitchen cried out for an Aga, this one did. There was even a large inglenook for it. Pixie pushed the thought away and picked up her drink.

In the sitting room, she placed her mug of coffee on the table and pulled a rug in front of her chair before sitting down and switching on the computer. Her editor had emailed the edits for the manuscript she'd finished and sent to the publisher that awful day back in March, so it was more than time to knuckle down and do them. The germ of the idea she'd jotted down involving the château and worked on when they were here at Easter would have to wait.

She took a sip of coffee while she waited for the machine to boot up, thinking about the suggestions and alterations her editor wanted. A few minutes later, her mug was empty and she started to work on what would hopefully be the final draft, losing herself in the story.

The slamming of a car door a jolted her out of her concentration sometime later. A quick glance at her watch – eight fifteen. Probably Justine leaving to take Ferdie to school. She could ignore it, nothing to do with her. Men's voices and a banging on the front door told her she was wrong and, in a daze, she went through to the hallway and opened the front door.

A large white builder's pick-up truck was parked on the drive and in front of her stood two men, one middle-aged, the other in his twenties – father and son judging by the colour of their hair. The younger one's still a vibrant red, the elder's flecked with grey.

'Bonjour,' she ventured.

'Bonjour, Madame Sampson, *aujourd'hui nous sommes ici pour commencer. C'est bon, non*?' The elder man waved a roll of paper at her. '*J'ai les plans.*'

'Commence? Plans?'

'Your writing room and library.'

Pixie stared at him. 'I'm afraid there has been some mistake.'

'Last year 'e wanted me to start, but I am too busy. I promise 'im the first week in May, and voila! I, Jerome Blanchet, keep my promise. Monsieur Sampson 'e is 'ere? He will tell you.' He smiled at Pixie.

'No. He's not here. He's dead.'

The smile vanished, to be replaced by a look of horror as Jerome visibly shrank at her words. 'Non.'

Pixie, feeling guilty for the abrupt way she'd broken the news, nodded, before taking a deep breath. 'Come in and show me the plans.'

Leading the way up to the third floor, Pixie heard a muttered conversation going on between the two men who were clearly nonplussed by the news about Frank and what they should do.

'Ah, the wood for the shelves, it is 'ere already,' Jerome said, looking to the far end of the room.

The plans when the two men unfurled them and held them up for Pixie's inspection were perfect. Frank had clearly given the space a lot of thought. He'd really wanted the room to be a perfect retreat for her.

She bit her lip as the out-of-focus photo with its fuzzy image of him in this room holding out his arms to welcome her slipped into her mind and she took a deep breath.

'How long would it take to do?' Pixie asked. 'And would there be much noise?'

'I 'ave reserved May for this job and the noise would be kept to a minimum. We close the door too, no dust downstairs.' Jerome looked at her anxiously.

Pixie laughed. Dust was the least of her worries. Noise, on the other hand, while she was trying to write was far from ideal. But she was two floors down and afterwards she'd have her ideal writing room for the rest of summer and the converted space would surely appeal to any prospective buyers of the château.

'And you came today ready to start?'

Both men nodded.

'I'll leave you to it then.'

Jerome held out his hand and shook it vigorously when Pixie took it. 'Merci madame. We begin.'

Pixie was laughing as she went back downstairs.

Gwen was in the kitchen making coffee and raised her eyebrows at her.

'We have the builders in for the next month,' Pixie said. 'Frank had apparently arranged for the conversion to be done on the top floor. I didn't like to disappoint them. I'll just nip up to the boulangerie for some croissants for our breakfast and for their elevenses. I guess French builders, like English ones, will need feeding during the day.'

* * *

Driving back, a bag of still-warm croissants on the dashboard, Pixie passed Justine and Ferdie going into the village. She held her hand up in acknowledgement, a slight smile fixed on her face, but determinedly didn't look directly at Justine or the child sitting in the back.

Back at the château, sitting out on the terrace enjoying breakfast, Pixie sighed contentedly. The first morning of her writing routine might have been disturbed but she'd got a good two hours in and the day was still young.

'Gus sent me a WhatsApp message just now,' Gwen said. 'He and Sarah would definitely like to come over sometime in June for a fortnight, Charlie too. Annabel and her family will most likely come for a few days while they are here. That's okay, isn't it? I told him it was.'

'Yes, of course. Oh, this summer is going to be such fun.' Charlie, footloose and still playing the field at thirty, was fun to have around, while Annabelle, married to Harry, was now the mother of Mimi, an adorable five-year-old little girl. Fleetingly, Pixie wished Frank was still alive to enjoy spending time here with them. He would have adored playing host to them all. She finished her coffee. 'I'm going to get another hour or two in. Will you sort out the builders for elevenses if I haven't surfaced by then? Call them down rather than carry stuff up. See you in a bit.'

* * *

Once Pixie had disappeared into the sitting room, closing the door behind her, Gwen cleared up the breakfast things before going upstairs. She could hear the murmur of men's voices and footsteps pacing around and couldn't resist carrying on up the next flight of stairs to see for herself what was happening.

Jerome happily showed her the plans and explained. 'Monsieur Frank, he 'ad wanted it to be a surprise for 'is wife.'

After she'd told them to come down to the kitchen at eleven o'clock for coffee, she left them to it and went to her room, hoping Pixie's decision to let the work go ahead was a good omen for the future.

Gwen had a shower and pulled on a pair of blue cotton capri trousers and a stripy Breton top, pinning the lighthouse brooch on the left-hand side with a happy smile. She ran a comb through her hair before picking up her phone, the old address book and a notebook and going downstairs. Time to try out the internet connection and to form a plan of campaign for when she could start to do some sleuthing.

Jerome and his son had been down for their morning break and Gwen had cleared the mugs and plates away and was ready to go back out on the terrace when she heard a vehicle coming up the drive and parking at the side of the château. The scruffily dressed man that greeted her when she went outside was in his sixties, she guessed, and his weather-ravaged face indicated an outdoor life.

'Bonjour,' she said cautiously.

'Bonjour. Je suis Marcel – le jardinier. Today I cut the grass, okay? Then I see to the asperge.'

Nonplussed, Gwen smiled and he strolled away in the direction of the barn, reappearing a moment or two later and giving her a cheery wave as he turned the sit-on mower in the direction of the parkland. Sitting on the terrace watching as Marcel expertly drove the mower up and down the grass, she wondered if Pixie was aware she had a gardener. It certainly explained why the grounds were so tidy.

An hour or so later, when Marcel parked the mower back in the shed and made his way to the old vegetable garden and the asparagus bed, she waited a few moments and then followed him. He was cutting asparagus and placing it in a neat pile and glanced up at her.

'You 'ave the asperge for lunch today,' he said.

'Merci. Have you worked here at the château for a long time?'

'Oui. I work for Monsieur and Madame Quiltu for many years. My father, he began the garden business and when I left school I joined 'im. Now sadly, he 'as gone and I work alone.' He folded the pocket knife he was using to cut the asparagus before straightening up and looking at her. 'I 'ope you are 'appy for me to continue. Monsieur Sampson he assured me that he didn't 'ave the time to garden. In summer, I come for the day once a week.'

'You need to speak to my daughter, but I'm sure she will want you to continue.'

'Bien. Now I weed,' and he picked up a hoe lying on the ground and began to carefully turn and air the ground around the asparagus plants.

'Would you like a cup of tea?' Gwen asked

Marcel shook his head. 'Merci, mais non.'

'I'll leave you to it then,' Gwen said, turning to go.

'The asperge,' Marcel said, pointing to the pile on the ground. 'You forget.' He glanced at her. 'Peut-être you like me to plant some lettuce and tomato plants here? There is still time.'

'That sounds like a good idea, thank you,' Gwen said, picking up the cut asparagus and making for the kitchen. She promised herself the next time she saw Marcel she'd ask him a bit about the history of the château, maybe even quiz him a little about Justine. Knowing how village grapevines worked, there was always the chance he'd heard something that could help explain her presence at the château and in Frank's life.

18

During the first week with the builders there, things settled down into a routine. Pixie got up with the sun and wrote for a few hours, relishing the peace and quiet. Gwen rose early on the second day, ready to walk to the village for the breakfast croissants, only to find that Pixie had already driven in and collected a dozen croissants and two baguettes.

'I've ordered two dozen for tomorrow to freeze so we'll always have some handy.'

'I was looking forward to the daily walk,' Gwen grumbled. 'I need the exercise. I'm used to being out and about in the village at home every day and going dancing once a week.'

'I know but the walk to the village and back on your own is a step too far for you,' Pixie said gently. 'Don't want you overdoing it.'

'Don't you start mollycoddling me, my girl. Walking is one of the best exercises. I'm certainly not going to sit around on my jacksy all summer.'

'I don't expect you to. I just don't want you going for long walks on your own, that's all. Once these edits are out of the way, we'll go for walks together, okay?'

'I give you fair warning, I'm not going to sit around waiting for you. I also intend to get stuck into some gardening. Marcel was saying we should grow some salad stuff alongside the asparagus. And the flowerbeds and urns could do with some tender loving care.'

Pixie, knowing that she too, could do with more exercise after hours of sitting in front of the computer, promised to help Gwen in the garden, so long as Gwen didn't overdo things.

As Gwen prepared lunch every day, Pixie organised their evening meals, which, like all their meals, were usually eaten out on the terrace.

Weekends though, were different. No builders. No early-morning writing for Pixie – that's not to say she didn't do any work, she read through, edited and made notes over Saturday and Sunday so that when Monday arrived, she could carry on with the next section.

Saturday mornings, they joined the crowds in Carhaix market before a quick visit to a supermarket for the things they couldn't find in the market. Saturday lunch was always the plat du jour in whichever cafe took their fancy.

Pixie had kept to her decision to avoid Justine and had yet to meet Ferdie, although Gwen told her he was a sweet little boy.

'When did you meet him?' Pixie demanded.

'Justine came over one afternoon when you were writing to return the key Frank had given her to keep an eye on the place and to let the builders in. She seemed relieved when I told her you were busy. I hung the key on the board in the kitchen,' Gwen said. 'I offered her a coffee, but she wouldn't stay. Ferdie was allowed to accept a chocolate biscuit though, so we must remember to get some more in the village tomorrow morning.'

'Did you learn anything?' Pixie couldn't stop herself from asking.

'If you mean did I quiz her with questions for the few moments she was here? No, I didn't.'

Pixie hesitated. 'Does... Ferdie look like Frank?'

'Only in that he has blue eyes and fair hair – but then so does Justine.' Gwen shrugged. 'You're going to have to talk to her soon.'

'I know. Sorry, excuse me, I just want to write something down I need to add to the edits before I forget it,' Pixie muttered, desperate to be alone, and she left Gwen weeding one of the large flower urns by the front door.

Instead of going back to the computer in the sitting room, Pixie ran upstairs to her bedroom and closed the door, before flinging herself down on the bed to stare unseeingly up at the ceiling. Above her head, she could hear Jerome and his son packing their tools away for the day and, within minutes, she heard their footsteps as they descended the stairs before walking past her door to reach the main staircase.

Turning her head, she saw the out-of-focus photo she'd propped against the framed one of Frank on the bedside table. Every time she looked at it, the image of Frank somehow became sharper, willing her to believe in the impossible – that Frank had been in the room that day.

She knew that he would be disappointed in the way she was behaving towards Justine and Ferdie. He'd always been first in line to offer help to people in need. He'd empty his pockets of his last penny to give to beggars outside supermarkets, as well as handing them a bag of food. Was Justine merely someone 'in need' like Gwen had suggested? Someone Frank was giving a helping hand to?

Pixie leant across and reached out for the photo, looking directly at the image, smothering a deep sigh. 'I loved you so much, Frank. I thought we were soulmates and I trusted you with my life. Why didn't you tell me about the château? Or about Justine? I never ever thought you'd keep such momentous events secret from me.' Tears dropped onto the photo and she wiped it down on the bed cover before replacing it on the bedside table.

Whatever had been on his mind over the last year or so, deep down she knew that they had a strong marriage, that Frank still loved her. She closed her eyes and swallowed hard, trying to rid her mouth of an unexpected sour taste. Gwen was right. She needed to talk to Justine who was the only person who could tell her what had been going on.

Something banged above her head. Had the builders left the door open, a window unlatched?

There it was again.

Pixie took a couple of steadying breaths, forcing herself to get up and go and check everything was all right upstairs. Opening the door which the builders had closed behind them, Pixie stood on the threshold, surveying the room.

Studwork, ready for the tongue and groove planking to be attached, now lined three walls – the long back wall with its old-fashioned tiled fireplace, one of the side walls and the spaces on the front wall between the two dormer windows. The other side wall, the interior of the round tower, was freshly painted a pale yellow and shelves of varying lengths and depths had been fixed inside the curve.

Pixie moved across to the shelves and gently rubbed her hand along the smooth surface of one. She smiled. It really was going to be the room of her dreams. Frank had always been so good at knowing what she'd like.

She moved around the room, looking to see if something had fallen down. The builders had left their tools in a neat pile by the far window, could one of them have fallen out of place? No, they were so neatly arranged. All the windows were closed and latched. Nothing anywhere to indicate what had made the noise. If it had been louder she'd have suspected one of the many pigeons who inhabited the trees in the parkland had banged against the window, but it hadn't been that kind of noise.

Turning, she looked at the fireplace and saw that one of the decorative tiles had fallen off and was lying in the grate. Could that have been what she'd heard? Doubtful. It had been more of a door-banging type noise. Thankfully, the tile hadn't broken. Jerome would be able to fix it back in place, she was sure. She bent down to pick it up and place it on the mantlepiece where it would be safer. Something small and gold in the corner of the grate caught her eye. A signet ring. Pixie picked it up and gave an involuntary gasp as she held it in her hand. How on earth had it got into the grate? It was the ring she'd bought Frank for his fiftieth birthday; the one he'd said he'd lost. His initials were engraved on the front of the square of gold; the date and the words 'I love you', followed by her initials engraved in tiny letters, were on the inner side of the chunky ring.

Fingering the ring, she remembered how a week before the accident he'd been upset when he'd admitted to her that he couldn't find it and had no idea where it had gone. She'd planned on buying him a replica for his birthday this year. She sighed. She missed him so much. Whatever had been on his mind over the last year or so, deep down she knew that they had been the soulmates she believed them to be. If she were honest with herself too, she knew that he would expect her to do the right thing by Justine and Ferdie, for whatever reason they had come into his life.

Pixie took a deep breath. She needed to go and see Justine, warn her about the château being put up for sale soon. Avoiding her because she was afraid of learning a bitter truth and not wanting them in her life was cowardly. She'd go across to the cottage right now and speak to Justine.

Thoughtfully, Pixie stared at the ring she was holding for several seconds before she slipped it on to the middle finger of her right hand. As she did so she was conscious of a gentle breeze, like a happy sigh, blowing through the room.

19

Justine was in the small barn working on a basket while Ferdie played with a set of farm animals and building bricks on a play mat set down in the corner, when a shadow fell across the doorway.

'I thought we should have a second start,' Pixie said quietly. 'I wasn't exactly friendly before.' When Justine didn't answer, she took a deep breath. 'I wondered what was locked up in this barn. Did you make all these baskets?'

'Yes.'

'And this is Ferdie?'

'Yes. Ferdie, say hello to Mrs Sampson.'

'Hello, Mrs Sampson,' Ferdie said, concentrating on his play and not looking up.

'Ferdie, you should look at people when you speak to them,' Justine said quietly.

'Hello, Ferdie, it's nice to meet you,' Pixie said and received a brief smile before he turned his attention back to his game.

Justine waited for Pixie to speak, but Pixie was looking at

Ferdie and appeared to be miles away. In the end, Justine broke the silence.

'Is this a social visit or did you want something?'

'Oh, I'm sorry, I was miles away. First, I want to thank you for returning the key.'

'No point in me having it now that you're living here.'

'Quite. There is something I need to tell you though.'

'Let me guess – you're giving me notice to quit the cottage.'

Pixie gave a brief nod, her smile not quite reaching her eyes.

'I thought that was what you wanted to say the other evening.' Justine hesitated. 'Would you consider letting me stay as a paying tenant when you return to England at the end of the summer?'

'It's not that simple. I'm selling the château after summer, so that's not possible.'

Justine felt her heart drop at Pixie's words. 'How much notice are you actually giving me then? A week? A month? Summer? It's going to take time to find somewhere to live and to work.' Justine gestured at the baskets.

'I realise that. I also realise that Frank wouldn't want me to put you out on the street, so how about you plan to leave here by the end of September when we'll be leaving to return to the UK. If you start looking now, you may even find something sooner than you expect.'

'I miss Frank,' a small voice said from the corner. 'I wish he wasn't dead. He promised we could live here forever.'

Justine smothered a gulp of guilt as she jumped up and ran across to Ferdie, pulling him into her arms and holding him tight. As he buried his tearful face into her shoulder, she bent and kissed the top of his head. She'd thought he was so engrossed playing farmers that he wouldn't pay any attention to the conversation going on over his head. She should have known better.

Pixie's quiet voice broke through her despair. 'I'm sorry. We all miss Frank, but nothing, it seems, lasts forever.'

Justine looked up to ask her to leave, but Pixie was already walking away.

'Fancy a cup of hot chocolate?' Justine said, looking back down at Ferdie.

'With marshmallows?' Ferdie asked, looking up at her with a hopeful smile.

'Just this once.'

'Yes.'

Back in the cottage, she sat Ferdie down to watch his favourite Thomas the Tank Engine video while she went to the kitchen and mechanically began the process of making them both a hot chocolate. Stirring the hot milk and watching the squares of chocolate melt as she dropped them into the saucepan and swirled them around, she wondered why she'd been so naive as to expect the idyll she'd been living in for the past fourteen months to continue.

The life she'd built up for herself with Frank's help was over. She was back to square one. Only this time the move would be upsetting not only for herself but also for Ferdie. He was settled at school and he loved living in the cottage. Changing home and school at the same time would be difficult for him – finding a new home in the same area would have to be her main goal.

Equally important, though, was earning enough money at the summer markets to give her a deposit and a couple of months' rent in hand. She'd managed to save some money in the last year but not enough to last more than a few months. And so long as it didn't rain on market days during the summer she knew her baskets would sell well, but rain kept the tourists away. She could sell the car Frank had given her, buy something smaller and cheaper to run and use the balance for living if she got desperate.

And she always had the option of returning to live with her parents, who she knew would welcome her back.

Giving the hot chocolate a final stir, she poured the drink into two mugs before putting the saucepan in the sink to soak. Of course there was always the last-ditch option of telling Pixie the truth. Break the promise she'd made.

Justine pulled a face. There was no way she could do that. No, the best thing would be to stay out of Pixie Sampson's way as much as possible while she was living here. Shouldn't be too difficult. Three or four morning markets a week as summer progressed meant she would be out most days and Ferdie would be at school. Summer holidays might be more of a problem, Ferdie did like spending time playing outside the cottage, riding his trike up and down the drive. No point in worrying about the holidays at the moment, they were weeks away. She'd worry about the holidays when July arrived.

Reaching for the packet of marshmallows, she popped two on top of each mug before pulling her shoulders back determinedly and picking up the mugs. A promise was a promise, she'd have to be desperate to break it. And she hadn't reached that stage yet.

* * *

Gwen was out on the terrace reading when a visibly upset Pixie flopped down on a chair next to her. 'Well, that went well – not.'

Gwen gave her a concerned glance.

'I've finally told Justine she has to vacate the cottage because the château is going on the market soon.'

'Is she okay about that? How long did you give her?'

'Until September. She was expecting it apparently, but that didn't make it any easier, especially when Ferdie started to cry and said that he missed Frank.' Pixie slumped back in her chair.

'Frank had promised him he could live here forever. Honestly, Mum, I feel like I'm the villain in all this. What am I supposed to do? If I tell her she can stay and then nobody wants to buy the place with a sitting tenant, I'll be stuck with a millstone of a property around my neck for who knows how long.'

'It's a difficult one,' Gwen said. Before she could say more, Pixie spoke again.

'Besides, I still don't know the truth about her and Frank. I'd sort of hoped Justine would blurt the truth out about why she was here. Surely she must realise I need to know how she ended up living here rent-free at Frank's insistence?'

'Sounds like you'll have the chance to get to know them better over summer – if you want to that is,' Gwen added hurriedly as Pixie stared hard at her.

'Not sure it wouldn't make the situation even more difficult to deal with if I became friends with her. Come what may, the château is going on the market and the cottage needs to be empty when that happens. No. Best if I keep my distance, I think.' Pixie placed her hands on the arms of her chair to push herself up.

'Is that Frank's ring you're wearing?' Gwen asked, surprised.

Pixie nodded. 'Would you believe, I found it upstairs after the builders had left this evening.'

Not having told Gwen about the out-of-focus photo with the image of Frank, she didn't feel the need to explain about the noise and the weird breeze she'd felt rustling through the upstairs.

'He told me he'd lost it but didn't know where. Obviously realised it was over here and couldn't tell me. How it ended up in the grate in the attic room is anybody's guess.' She stood up. 'I'll go and start dinner.'

While she scrubbed a couple of jacket potatoes and put them in the oven to bake before preparing a salad, Pixie thought about Ferdie. He looked such a sweet little boy, the kind of child she had always imagined she and Frank would have together. She had to admit to feeling a little warmer towards Justine too. She clearly adored Ferdie, but there was an air of apprehension hanging over her. Or was that just when she was around Pixie? She must know that Pixie had several questions she wanted answered – questions that would reveal her vulnerability, no doubt.

The most important question out of all of them though, was one she dreaded hearing the answer to. That question was the one she'd desperately wanted to ask the moment she'd learnt of Ferdie's existence. Was he Frank's son? Part of her was beginning to long for that to be true, although another part wasn't sure how she'd cope if that did turn out to be the case.

20

Gwen was making a start on clearing the various urns and pots that were dotted around the terrace and garden one afternoon so they could be replanted after a planned visit to a garden centre at the weekend, when Marcel made an unexpected appearance.

'What are you doing here? Not your normal day?' Gwen asked, smiling at him.

'I 'ave brought you lettuce, tomatoes, peppers. I thought it enough to begin, oui?' Marcel held out the small wooden pallet box filled with plants.

'Merci,' Gwen said as she followed him past the dilapidated orangery to the kitchen garden.

'I stay and 'elp,' Marcel said, placing the pallet box down. 'The tomatoes will go there, at the back, the peppers there and the lettuce near the front,' he said, pointing out the patch of ground he'd cleared ready for planting.

For the next hour Gwen dutifully followed behind Marcel, pushing the plants firmly into the ground and then watering them with the hose.

'This hose makes life so much easier than a watering can,' she said.

'My papa 'e had the Quiltus pipe the water 'ere and instal the 'ose when the kitchen garden and the orangery were in constant use,' Marcel said. 'J'ai adoré l'orangerie when I was growing up. With its citrons, orange and grapefruit trees, always the smell it was wonderful in the spring with the blossoms. And the pêches, mm.' He glanced in the direction of the orangery. 'A shame it falls into disrepair so bad. Peut-être Madame Sampson, she restore it?'

Gwen shook her head sadly. 'Not in her plans at the moment, but never say never.' She carefully watered the last of the lettuces before glancing up at Marcel. 'Did Monsieur Sampson ever say to you he'd like to restore it?'

Marcel nodded. 'I only saw 'im the once, after he moved Justine and her son into the cottage, before that we talk on the telephone, but he talked about 'ow he wanted to restore it.'

'I love the baskets Justine makes. So clever. And little Ferdie is so sweet.'

'She keeps 'erself to 'erself that one,' Marcel said. 'Works 'ard. Not an easy job doing the markets.' He bent down and picked up the empty pallet box. 'Bien. I 'ave finished here. I see you next week – unless I see you at the Fest-Noz tomorrow night?'

'A Fest-Noz involves dancing, right?' Gwen said, her face lighting up at the thought, even if it would be just Breton dancing. 'When and where?'

'Begins at six o'clock at the village school and is always good fun. A bientôt.'

'A bientôt,' Gwen echoed, inwardly vowing to mention the Fest-Noz to Pixie over supper.

After Marcel had left, she washed her hands and went up to her room for her iPad before coming back down and sitting at the kitchen table. Time to check on some addresses, starting with the Paris one. She hadn't got very far when she'd tried before.

Taking a deep breath, she carefully typed in the name A. Dubois and, opening her old address book, copied the Paris address into the search bar. Not recognised. She typed the house number and street name alone. Nothing came up. The Dubois family appeared to no longer own the Paris house. Next she tried the Roscoff address. This time, the name 'Puglisi, Anton' came up.

Gwen closed her iPad and the address book. That was that then. The Dubois family had clearly sold on both houses. She was a silly old woman expecting to find him still living in one or other of the family houses over sixty years later. Things didn't work like that these days. People moved about. It was probably for the best – what would they have found to say to each other in all honesty. No, it had just been the foolish dream of an old lady.

She patted the lighthouse brooch that she wore every day now. She had her memories. They would have to be enough.

* * *

That evening, as the two of them ate their chicken salad sitting out on the terrace as usual, Gwen said casually, 'You remember it's a fête day again tomorrow? The last one of the month.'

'Another one? That must be at least one a week all through May,' Pixie said. 'The French certainly love their fête day holidays.'

'Marcel was saying earlier that there's a Fest-Noz at the school tomorrow evening. It's in aid of the school funds. I thought it would be fun to go.'

'Do you want to go? I'm not sure Breton dancing is my scene,' Pixie said.

'The fact that I bought the subject up should tell you that, yes, I would like to go,' Gwen answered crossly. 'You don't have to get up and dance if you don't want to, although I shall. I rang Anouk earlier and she said the three of them are going, so it would give you a chance to catch up with Fern. She was asking how you were you. You also promised that we would have fun this summer. Hasn't been much evidence of that so far.' That might be a bit of a below-the-belt remark, but Gwen didn't apologise for it.

'Okay, we'll go to the Fest-Noz tomorrow,' Pixie agreed, before finishing her salad and reaching for her wine glass.

Gwen sighed. She was beginning to suspect that Pixie was still locked into grieving for Frank and, as well as keeping her distance from Justine and Ferdie, was using writing as an excuse not to socialise at all, even with Fern and Scott. Although Saturdays and Sundays, when Pixie didn't shut herself away writing, and they went out and about were always good fun.

In truth, she was quite happy herself spending time at the château doing the gardening, preparing meals, chatting to the builders, walking into the village to have coffee with Anouk. She was as busy here as she had been at home, apart from the OldTyme Dancing Club, but the dancing tomorrow was sure to be good.

Pixie and Gwen decided to walk to the village in the early evening as parking was sure to be difficult. 'I can always come back and fetch the car if you're too tired after all the dancing you plan on doing,' Pixie said as they set off, smiling at the look Gwen gave her. 'Meant to tell you earlier, Jerome said this evening as he left they'll be finished this week. It will be good to have the room finished, but I shall miss having them around.'

'I'll definitely miss having my elevenses with them,' Gwen replied.

The sun was still shining as they walked along enjoying the wayside flowers, ragged robins, cow parsley and a patch of tall bluebell-shaped flowers that neither of them knew the name of. Up above their heads, the elderflower trees were in full blossom and blackbirds sang as small birds darted from side to side.

Nearing the village, they heard the distinctive sound of Breton music filling the air. Pixie could pick out the sounds of bagpipes, accordion, guitar and possibly a violin, she thought. Once in the village, they saw a stage had been set up in the school playground and four musicians were playing a lively piece of music. In front of them, a large circle of people holding hands were dancing a traditional gavotte dance.

'That looks fun,' Gwen said, starting to clap in time to the music.

They stood watching for several minutes before making their way over to Fern and Scott whom they'd spotted sitting with Anouk on some temporary benches at the side of the playground.

Scott instantly went to get them a drink at the makeshift bar and returned with a tray containing not only small glasses of chouchen but also crêpes, galettes-saucisses and slices of Far Breton.

'A veritable feast,' Pixie said. 'Thank you. May I pay you for Gwen and myself.'

Scott shook his head. 'My treat. Besides, the food looks delicious, but I can't vouch for the drink. All they told me was it's a traditional drink from Brittany, it's a sort of mead and it's 14 per cent alcohol.'

Anouk looked at Gwen and winked. 'And traditionally it makes your head spin.'

Pixie took a tentative sip. 'It's, um, different. Quite sweet.'

'Wouldn't want too many,' Fern said.

'Well, before my head starts spinning, I'm going to dance.' Gwen looked at them. 'Who's joining me? Pixie?'

'Maybe later.'

'I have to warn you I'm still a beginner at this Breton dancing, but I'm game.' And Scott held out his hand to Gwen. 'Let's go.'

Pixie sipped her drink slowly and nibbled a piece of the sweet egg custard-like flan, Far Breton, figuring it would go better with that than one of the hot sausage galettes.

'How's things?' Fern asked.

'Good. The weeks have just flown by. I'm sorry I haven't been in touch – how about coffee one morning next week? I can show you my new library and writing room then. Oh.' Pixie stopped speaking as she saw Ferdie walking towards them holding his mum's hand.

'I'd forgotten my tenant and her son would, of course, be here,' Pixie said in a quiet aside to Fern.

Justine gave a general 'Hello' to everyone as she drew level with them.

'Justine, Ferdie. Hello. Are you having fun, Ferdie?' Pixie asked, looking at the little boy rather than Justine.

Ferdie nodded solemnly. 'We're going home soon. Mummy says we can't stay late. Your cake looks nice. I like cake.' Ferdie looked at her hopefully.

Pixie risked a glance at Justine. 'Is he allowed some?'

'Yes, but, Ferdie, it's really, really rude to ask for cake,' Justine said.

'I didn't ask. I just said I like cake,' Ferdie pouted.

Pixie held out a piece with a serviette. 'Here you are, Ferdie. Enjoy it.' She gave the little boy a tentative smile and was rewarded with a big grin.

'Before you start eating, say thank you and goodbye,' Justine said, clearly desperate to move on and not wanting to make conversation with Pixie.

'Thank you, Mrs Sampson. Bye.'

Justine caught hold of his hand again and led him away, but not before Pixie heard him ask, 'Mummy, why is Mrs Sampson wearing Frank's ring?'

Pixie took a deep breath as she realised both Fern and Anouk were looking at her, clearly sensing the awkwardness of the meeting. She rubbed her forehead and closed her eyes. 'Frank had made a private arrangement with Justine regarding the cottage. It came as a complete surprise to me when I arrived and I still have no idea why it came about. Only Justine knows that and she hasn't yet volunteered the information.' Pixie paused. 'I guess Scott would describe it as Justine invoking the fifth amendment in case she incriminates herself. I know she is hiding something, but I will find out the truth somehow.'

21

Two days later at five o'clock, Jerome interrupted Pixie in the sitting room, asking her to go upstairs to check she was happy with everything and that there was nothing else she wanted done in the room.

'You like?' he asked.

Looking around, Pixie nodded. 'Yes. I love it. It's perfect.' The tongue and groove panelling had been painted the same soft yellow as the tower wall and the floor had been relaid with some light oak panels, creating a luminous and airy space. 'You've transformed it. Merci beaucoup. Shall I pay you now or will you send your invoice?'

'There is little to pay – just the electrician's bill, which I will send you. Monsieur paid me in advance.'

After Jerome had left, Pixie went back up and stood in the middle of the room, imagining how she'd furnish it if life had turned out the way she and Frank had planned. Her desk would go in the space between the two dormer windows, a French daybed loaded with cushions placed alongside the side wall opposite the shelves, which would be filled with books, a radio

and speakers on the top shelf, candles and photographs inter-
spersed between the books on the other shelves. In the fireplace
on the back wall, there would always be a large vase of fresh
flowers and two white pillar candles standing either side. On the
floor, two or three cream deep-pile woollen rugs scattered
throughout the room.

'Oh Frank, I do wish you could be here and see this, share it
with me. Thank you for arranging it.'

Close to tears, Pixie closed her eyes in an effort to keep them
at bay and sighed. Standing there, she felt a sudden gentle warm
breeze, like the one she'd experienced before, drifting around the
room and ruffling her hair. She didn't dare open her eyes in case
she broke the spellbinding moment because that was what it felt
like – a spell.

'I thought I'd come and see the transformation,' Gwen's voice
broke into her reverie.

The breeze gave one last gentle puff before dying away and
Pixie opened her eyes, feeling a strange sense of contentment
flowing through her body as she turned to smile as Gwen came
into the room. 'It's exactly as I wanted.'

'I love the paintwork and those shelves,' Gwen said. 'I can see
you writing well up here.'

'Not going to happen. I won't be using it.'

'Why on earth not? We're here for another three months,
nothing to stop you using it, if you want to.'

'There's no point.' Pixie shrugged. 'I'm settled at the dining
table downstairs now, and that's far too heavy to even think about
moving it up here, even temporarily. And buying stuff to furnish
the room would be a waste.'

'The point is would it make you happy working up here,
which has to be worth something? More memories of the place
for a start. Your decision.' Gwen shrugged and decided to change

the subject. 'There's a vide-grenier this Sunday at that campsite near the village, Camping dans La Forêt, if you fancy going? Could be fun. One never knows what one might find at these things.' Gwen looked at her hopefully. 'Shall we go?'

'We'll go, but remember we are only here for the summer, no point in buying anything for the château.' Pixie gave her a warning glance. 'Agreed?'

Gwen nodded. 'Of course. Come on, it's time you were organising supper. I fancy an aperitif tonight, by the way.'

'It's pizza and salad tonight, so not too much organising to do.'

Pixie followed Gwen downstairs, trying to analyse her feelings and pushing the sense of disappointment she felt knowing that she wouldn't be using her new office-cum-library. Gwen was right, she should use it, but it simply wasn't practical to furnish a room that she would only use for a few months before selling up.

* * *

Sitting on the terrace half an hour later with a couple of drinks and garlic bread nibbles, watching Justine playing ball with Ferdie in the distance down by the lake, Pixie felt her heart contract and she looked away. This is what the château needed: a family.

'Annabelle, Harry and Mimi are still definitely coming while Gus is here, aren't they?' she said, turning to Gwen.

'Yes. Why?'

'This place is perfect for kids to run around and have adventures in. Be a shame for Mimi to miss out this summer.' Pixie stood up. 'The oven should be hot enough for the pizza now. No, don't get up, you stay there. Do you want another G & T or a glass of red with the pizza?'

'Glass of red please.'

Once she'd put the pizza in the oven, set the timer and thrown a quick salad together, Pixie collected wine glasses, cutlery and plates and took them outside to find that Gwen had wandered off to join the ball game down by the lake. Watching from the terrace, it looked like a classic game of 'pig in the middle', with Ferdie shrieking with laughter as he jumped, trying to catch the ball as Justine and Gwen threw it to each other, just out of his reach.

For a few seconds, Pixie contemplated joining them before deciding it would make Justine uncomfortable. She hadn't seen her to speak to since that brief meeting the night of the Fez Noz. Keeping her distance was proving to be easy, but deep down Pixie was realising it was pointless. In reality, the only way she was going to learn the truth about what had been going on during the last year of Frank's life was by becoming Justine's friend, not her enemy. She was the only person who could tell her the truth now.

Every time Pixie saw Ferdie she couldn't help but look for similarities between him and Frank. She'd already convinced herself that his eyes were the same smokey blue, as for his smile – pure Frank. It was a puzzle really why Justine hadn't told her the truth in the hope it would stop the eviction. The château, though, was going on the market whatever happened.

Maybe it was time for her to talk woman to woman with Justine, tell her that she'd guessed Ferdie was Frank's son and that she'd like to get to know him, both of them, better over the summer. Frank, she knew, would want her to make the effort.

Pixie pushed her shoulders back, determining on a plan. She'd stop avoiding Justine, get to know her instead, and then, when they were friends, ask her for the truth about Ferdie.

Seeing Gwen walking up from the lake hand in hand with Ferdie, and chatting away to Justine, she decided now was as good a time as any to put her plan into action.

'Anyone for pizza?' she called.

She saw Justine give a shake of her head as Ferdie yelled, 'Me' and grab him by the hand before he could run up.

Pixie turned in disappointment and went into the kitchen as the timer buzzed. Clearly it was going to take time and patience to get Justine to trust her.

Gwen was sitting on the terrace pouring wine into the glasses when she took the pizza out.

'Justine said thanks for the offer, but she'd already got supper waiting for them in the cottage.'

'I'm sure she has. The pizza's not big enough for four really so probably a good thing,' Pixie said. 'I've been thinking about what you said earlier about using the new room, making the best of things for the summer we're here.'

'And?' Gwen's voice was hopeful.

'Furnishing my new writing room isn't really a practical idea, but I'm going to buy a barbecue and one of those pizza ovens in the garden centre. They can stay as part of the fixtures and fittings when I sell. With the family coming soon, I think they'll be well used. Good idea?' Pixie looked at Gwen, a bright smile on her face hiding her inner thoughts. As much as she wanted to use the writing room, she was starting to realise it was going to be a big enough wrench leaving the château at the end of summer without adding a perfect writing room into the frame.

22

Trying to get a fractious Ferdie to eat his sausages after hearing the magic word 'pizza' being offered by Pixie was difficult and Justine was fast losing patience with him. It didn't help that she felt bad about saying no and she definitely didn't need him crying and calling her a meanie. Her immediate reaction to Pixie's unexpected invitation had been a definite, No. The last thing she wanted to do was to eat with Pixie and her mother. As much as she liked the older woman, Pixie made her feel uncomfortable and guilty, but she hadn't stopped to give any thought to Ferdie's love of pizza. Why had Pixie issued the sudden invitation to them anyway – was she developing a conscience about turning them out of the cottage?

'Come on, Ferdie, eat your sausages. They're your favourite.'

'Not. Pizza favourite.'

'If you eat your sausages, we'll have pizza at the weekend.' Justine knew she was resorting to bribery. 'If not, well, I don't know when we'll have pizza again. And there is also the fact, of course, that if you don't eat them, you will go to bed with a rumbling tummy, because there is nothing else to eat.'

Justine's mobile rang at that moment and she picked it up, glancing at caller ID as she did so. Her mother. Tempted as she was not to answer right away, she knew she had no choice. Her mother would ring every five minutes until she answered.

'Salut, Maman,' Justine said, automatically slipping into French. 'How's things with you and Dad?' She wandered away from the table, leaving Ferdie to eat, or not eat, while she talked to Brigitte. She didn't want him whining to 'Gangan' about not being allowed to eat pizza with Mrs Sampson.

'All good. Your favourite uncle is here with us at the moment. He sends his love.'

'Give him mine,' Justine said. Her uncle and godfather was a special man and she was sorry she didn't get to see him as often as she, and he, would have liked. 'We'll have to have a catch-up soon.'

'He's on the move again. Talking of coming back to Brittany, so if you're still in the château when that happens, you'll be able to. Now, why don't you come up here and see us soon? If not soon, how about planning a visit for for Ferdie's birthday?'

Justine bit her lip. She'd left herself wide open there. She laughed. 'I expect Ferdie will want his best friend, Lola, to come to tea. Besides, it's not long since I came back from you.'

'What's that got to do with anything? You know you're welcome any time. For a holiday – or longer. I still think it would be better for you to come back 'ere and live. You being so far away is ridiculous.'

Justine smothered a sigh. Living near her parents would make life easier on so many counts but harder in other ways. Her mum, with the best intentions in the world, wouldn't be able to stop making suggestions and interfering. 'Well, I can't come at the moment. I'm busy making baskets and getting ready for the morning markets.'

Her mother gave an exasperated 'Tch,' before saying, 'What's happening with the château now that Frank is no longer with us?'

'No idea,' Justine lied. She hadn't told Brigitte about Pixie and Gwen being at the château for the summer and didn't intend to now. Or the fact that she had to move out of the cottage. She knew how her mother would react. Better to tell her afterwards when she'd found somewhere else to live – or needed to move back home like her mum wanted. 'I expect I'll hear something soon. Either from his wife or the notaire.'

There was silence at the other end of the phone.

'Anyway, Mum, we're just having tea, so I'll love you and leave you. Love to Dad. Talk soon.' And Justine ended the call before Ferdie could demand to 'talk to Gangan'.

Talking to her mum had brought back the disappointing reception she'd got from the four letting agencies she'd been in touch with. Without exception they all told her that there was no chance of finding anywhere before summer was over. Every available property was being rented out as a holiday let. The advice had been to come back in September when there would be winter lets available from October. Justine needed to be moved and settled by September, ready for Ferdie's new term, besides which a winter let was no good. She didn't want to have to move again in the spring. The alternative was to find a private rental. Perhaps Carole would know of something or somebody who could help. Next time they met up she'd ask her.

* * *

The visitors' car park at Camping dans La Forêt was busy on Sunday when Pixie and Gwen arrived at midday. Walking through the campsite, following vide-grenier signs pinned to trees and fixed to posts, Gwen commented on how inviting it all looked.

'I've never fancied camping in a tent, but these chalets look really cosy. Well-spaced too. I wouldn't mind staying in one of those.'

The path they were following finished at the entertainment area – a large concreted space where all the stalls and tables had been set up.

'There must be at least seventy or eighty stalls,' Pixie said in surprise. 'Where to start?

'We're sure to find some bargains here,' Gwen said. 'You might even find a desk for your writing room.'

'Mum! There's no point in buying anything. We're just look-ing.' Pixie wasn't sure that Gwen was even listening as she walked off towards a table with an eclectic mixture of stuff, from jewellery, kitchen paraphernalia, DVDs and ornaments to baby clothes.

For the next hour, the two of them wandered from table to table, Pixie sticking resolutely to her no buying policy and sighing every time Gwen picked something up.

The second-hand book table with its selection of English paperbacks was a magnet though, for both of them. Even Pixie couldn't resist buying a couple.

'Time for a coffee,' Pixie said, looking across at the takeaway window of the cafe. To her surprise, Fern was working behind the counter.

'I managed the place for a season or two when Belinda and Alain first took it over,' she explained. 'But once Scott and I were married I didn't have the time to do both the auberge and this. I still help out from time to time and I make some of the cakes for them – try the Breton apple cake, that's one of mine.'

Pixie and Gwen took their coffees and cake and sat at one of the outside tables to enjoy them while indulging in a spot of people-watching. Pixie's phone rang just as they were thinking of re-joining the crowds and checking out some more tables.

'Hi, Gus. Everything okay? Annabelle's changed her plans? You're all coming at the same time? No, not a problem. What about Charlie – is he still coming? That's fine. Yes, Mum's fine too. See you all next week then.' She pressed the end call symbol. 'Annabelle's coming earlier than planned. Harry apparently can't make it, so she's going to follow Gus and Sarah as she's not happy about driving all the way on her own.'

'And Charlie?'

'Typically Charlie, no definite date. Expect him when we see him.' Pixie stood up. 'I love my nephew dearly, but he is impossible to tie down. Come on, I saw a plant stall earlier. We might find some plants suitable for the urns and pots since we keep missing the opening times at the garden centre.'

Pixie was congratulating herself on buying nothing more than a basketload of plants, geraniums and cosmos mainly, at the plant stall when she saw the pair of Lloyd Loom chairs.

'They'd be perfect in the new room,' she said. 'What a pity.'

'Go on, be a devil,' Gwen said. 'You know you want to. I'll ask how much they are.'

As Pixie went to protest, a voice behind her said, 'Bonjour, Madame Sampson. I hope you are well?'

Pixie whirled round and came face to face with Jean-Yves.

'Bonjour,' she echoed as she registered he was holding the hand of a little girl clutching a big pink teddy.

'My granddaughter, Jade. My daughter is at work today, so I've been commandeered for childminding. And like any French papa, I can never refuse the little one.'

Gwen returned. 'The price is – oh, sorry.' She looked from Jean-Yves to Pixie.

'Mum, this is my notaire; Jean-Yves Ropars, my mother, Gwen. And this is his granddaughter, Jade.'

'Enchanté, madame,' Jean-Yves said, shaking Gwen's hand. 'You are buying something from here?'

'The wicker chairs,' Gwen replied. 'I think they're a good price, but the man can't deliver and I don't think they will fit in the car. Shame. I was going to buy them as a present for Pixie's new room.'

'They will fit in my car. I am happy to deliver,' Jean-Yves offered.

'Perfect, thank you,' Gwen said, turning back to the vendor before Pixie could voice her objection.

'I am so sorry about my mother. You really don't have to do this.'

'I am glad to help. It is not a problem,' Jean-Yves said, smiling at her.

'The chairs are yours,' Gwen said, returning to their side. 'Now, how do we get them back to the château?' And she smiled at Jean-Yves.

'I would suggest I collect them later today. Once the vide-grenier closes, I will be able to drive down through the campsite and pick them up. Is that all right for you?' he asked, turning to Pixie.

She nodded. 'I hate putting you to so much trouble.'

'Pixie, it's no trouble, I'm happy to help.'

'Thank you.'

'I'll tell the vendor the plan and I'll see you later then,' and Jean-Yves turned away.

'Thank you for the chairs, but I am so cross with you for

involving Jean-Yves,' Pixie said to Gwen when he was out of earshot.

'He didn't appear to mind in the slightest,' an unrepentant Gwen replied. 'Anyway, he offered.'

'You manipulated him shamelessly,' Pixie said before laughing at the wide-eyed innocent look Gwen gave her.

* * *

Once back at the château, Pixie decided to skip lunch as she was still full after the large slice of apple cake she'd eaten earlier and went straight into the sitting room to do a few hours' writing, telling Gwen she'd like to finish the edits completely and send them to her editor before the family arrived.

It was gone seven o'clock when an immaculate dark green 4x4 pulled up outside and Jean-Yves got out. Pixie smiled as she went to greet him.

'Somebody's been busy in the garden. It's all looking a lot better than it did,' Jean-Yves said as he opened the back door of the car and lifted one of the chairs out, placing it on the ground before reaching in for the next one.

'That's down to Marcel and my mum, she loves gardening and I've been busy writing.' Pixie picked up the chair and moved it out the way as Jean-Yves stood the second one on the ground before slamming the door closed.

'Right, where do you want them?' he asked.

'Oh, don't worry about that. We'll leave them in the hall for now and I'll carry them upstairs later.'

Jean-Yves gave her a look and an exaggerated sigh. 'The new room is on the top floor, isn't it?' And he picked up one of the chairs and was off. 'I'll come back for the other one.'

'No, I can manage one, it's not heavy.' Pixie picked up the remaining one. Not heavy but definitely awkward to carry and she'd barely reached the first landing before Jean-Yves came back down the second flight of stairs and relieved her of the chair, carrying it effortlessly up the final flight.

'Jerome has done you a good job here,' Jean-Yves said as they stood together in the room. 'The room looks good. D'you want the chairs put in any particular place?'

'Maybe by the far window and the shelves. It's not as if there is going to be any more furniture up here.'

'Not even a desk or a table?'

Pixie shook her head. 'There isn't a suitable one in the château. I'm quite happy using the dining table downstairs, although I might bring my laptop up here occasionally now I've got a chair. Especially when the family arrive in a few days.'

'Family?'

'My brother and his wife, with their adult children and a granddaughter, are coming for a few weeks. Now, may I offer you a coffee or a glass of wine?'

'Coffee would be good, thank you.'

Gwen was sitting out on the terrace when they got downstairs and Pixie left Jean-Yves chatting to her while she organised coffee. Gwen had the coffee primed ready to go, plus a plate of sweet biscuits, together with a plate of savoury cheese and olive crackers placed on the kitchen table. Pixie smiled to herself, Gwen had clearly taken to Jean-Yves.

When she carried out the tray with everything on it, the two of them had wandered off to look at the dilapidated orangery. Pixie placed the tray on the table and went to join them.

'So sad to see it like this. I remember when it was a sight to behold with oranges, lemons and grapefruits in large boxed containers – like those at Versailles. There was even a peach tree espaliered along the back wall. Marcel and his father always made sure it was well protected in winter.'

'Did you know Monsieur and Madame Quiltu well?' Pixie asked.

'My parents did. The Quiltus socialised a lot before they got old and ill. There were some great parties here. I think your husband, he had plans to renovate the orangery?'

Pixie nodded. 'It was going to be his retirement project. I'm afraid it will be down to the next owner to save it now. Coffee's on the table, it will be getting cold.'

As they returned to the terrace, Justine drove in with Ferdie and parked by the cottage. Getting out of the car and unlocking the cottage door, she waved in acknowledgement before hurrying Ferdie inside.

'Have you told Mademoiselle Martin that she has to vacate the cottage?' Jean-Yves asked.

'Yes. I've given her until September to find somewhere else.'

'That's a generous amount of notice.'

Pixie shrugged. 'It's not actually a problem her living there, we rarely see her, and the little boy is a sweetie.' The fact that she was still hoping to learn the truth about Ferdie's parentage before they left was immaterial.

'So you are still intending to sell the château?'

'Yes. One summer in France and then it will be back to England and reality.'

Jean-Yves gave her a philosophical shrug. 'C'est la vie, I guess.'

He took his leave of them ten minutes later, saying he had some paperwork to catch up on before work in the morning. Pixie walked to his car with him.

'Thank you once again for playing delivery man.'

'My pleasure – any time I can help, you only have to ask. Au revoir for now.'

The intense look he gave her left Pixie in no doubt that he was serious about helping her, but she was left with the strangest feeling that behind his words there was something more he wanted to say. Something important he wasn't telling her.

23

Pixie was busy for the next few days, getting ready for the imminent arrival of the family. She was determined that this summer should be one to be remembered, full of fun, laughter and memories – happy ones to carry with her once she'd sold the château and returned to England.

She spent a couple of hours online researching pizza ovens and gas barbecues before heading into town to put her newly acquired knowledge to the test and ended up ordering a combined barbecue and pizza oven, that she fell in love with to be delivered the next day. Telling herself it was a practical solution and would look wonderful on the terrace, she managed not to baulk at the price as she handed over her card. A new fridge-freezer from the electrical shop on the industrial estate was next on the list. When Gwen gave her a quizzical look on seeing the list of proposed purchases, Pixie shrugged. 'Fixtures and Fittings.'

One afternoon, when she was finishing making up the last bed ready for the family, she heard the throaty roar of a motorbike coming up the drive. Gwen was downstairs so she'd leave her to deal with whoever it was, she decided, before she heard a man's voice and a deep laugh. She knew exactly who that was and ran downstairs to be immediately picked up and swung around in a bearlike hug.

'Charlie, my favourite nephew! How lovely.'

'I'm your only nephew,' Charlie protested.

'There is that. Your dad said to expect you anytime, but I didn't think you'd arrive this early. I warn you now, you're going to be put to work. I have a long list of things to do before everyone arrives.'

'And there I was thinking about leisurely lunches in the French countryside and fine dining of an evening under the stars,' Charlie said as he released her.

'Oh, you'll get those and more,' Gwen said. 'Right now though, coffee and cake do you?'

'You bet, Grandma. Then I need a tour of this place. It looks amazing.'

Sitting out on the terrace, Pixie and Gwen listened as Charlie filled them in on his current news, the major piece of which was he'd been made redundant from the estate agency where he'd worked for five years.

'So at thirty I'm jobless, footloose and fancy-free.' He hesitated. 'I haven't told Dad yet, but I've also given up the London flat.' He glanced at Pixie. 'Hoping I can stay around here for a bit longer than the planned holiday?'

'We're here until September and you're welcome to stay but the place is going on the market then.'

'What about the plans you and Uncle Frank had to live here?' Charlie asked.

'Things change, as you've discovered. Any idea what you're going to do in the future?' Pixie said, turning the conversation back to him. 'Find another agency to work for?'

'I was thinking of something completely different, like doing a cookery course. I don't want to be a chef in some poncy restaurant, but I quite fancy a pub restaurant serving good food.'

'You've always liked cooking,' Gwen acknowledged. 'And I've taught you everything I know, so you're off to a good start.'

Pixie and Charlie looked at each other and laughed. Gwen's disasters in the kitchen had been well documented down the years, although, to be fair, she had improved.

'We'll happily be your guinea pigs while you're here,' Pixie said. 'Consider yourself in charge of the kitchen from now. What are you like with barbecues?'

'I'm a man – I'm a brilliant cook with barbecues.'

'How about building them? Follow me,' and Pixie stood up and led Charlie over to a large package standing on a pallet. 'Pizza oven-cum-barbecue. Do you reckon you can build it? I got rather carried away in the shop, didn't really think about setting it up.'

'Sure,' Charlie answered confidently. 'On one condition – I get to be the first to cook on it.'

'It's a deal.'

As they turned to go back to Gwen, Charlie noticed the two figures down by the lake. 'Who's that?'

'My tenant in the cottage. Justine and Ferdie, her little boy. Frank had agreed they could live there. You'll meet up with them in due course. In fact, once the pizza oven is up and working, I'll invite them both for supper.' No need to tell Charlie that Frank had installed Justine in the cottage – or how bad she still felt about upsetting Ferdie the other evening.

'Is there anywhere I can put my bike? Looks like it might rain tonight and I don't have a cover for it,' Charlie said, looking up at the sky.

Pixie pointed out the two barns. 'Justine works in the smaller one and keeps it locked, but there's plenty of space in the other one.'

'Thanks. I'll get the panniers with my stuff in off and push it over there. And then I'll come in and get organised.'

'Organised?'

'You told me I was in charge of the kitchen, so I've got an evening meal to cook tonight.'

'Charlie, you really are my favourite nephew.' And Pixie linked her arm through his. 'As you're cooking, I think I might just go and finish my editing, after I've given you the guided tour and shown you your bedroom, of course.'

Charlie was as good as his word. Not only did he cook dinner that evening, but afterwards he opened the booklet that was taped to the pizza oven package and spent the rest of the evening trying to get to grips with the instructions. 'Jeez, why do they make everything so complicated,' Pixie heard him mutter at one point.

The next morning, Pixie was up early as usual to get a writing session in before the day overtook her and was amused to find Charlie already in the kitchen making himself coffee.

'Thought I'd make an early start. That barbecue is going to take some figuring out.' And he disappeared with his drink out onto the terrace.

Pixie took her own coffee and went into the sitting room and switched on her desktop computer. She'd finished the edits last evening, now she wanted to do a last run-through before sending them off to her editor. An hour later, they were gone and she sat back with a satisfied sigh. Now, not only was she was free to enjoy the family holiday, she could also start to concentrate on all those notes and ideas she'd jotted down on her laptop before abandoning them to get the edits done.

Giving in to a sudden impulse, she picked up her laptop and

climbed the two flights of stairs to the new room. She placed her laptop on the seat of one of the chairs before dragging the two chairs closer together.

Picking up her laptop, she sat in one of the chairs before pulling the other close enough in front of her to place her shoe-less feet on the cushion. Perfect. Sitting like this she didn't need a table.

Pixie opened the laptop, pressed the power button and waited for the machine to boot up. A deep breath of pure contentment escaped from her lips as she looked around. Frank organising the conversion without her knowledge had been such a surprise, but sitting up here now she had a strong, comforting sense of his presence. Without a doubt, there was a special atmosphere to the room, both calming and inspirational.

Two hours later, she pressed save and closed the laptop. She'd fleshed out her original germ of an idea and the story was beginning to shape up nicely. Her main character had started to come alive in her mind which was always a thrill. But now it was time to see what the rest of the world was up to.

There was no sign of Gwen as Pixie went downstairs, in fact the château was unusually quiet. Charlie was out on the terrace and the pizza oven-cum-barbecue was beginning to take shape. The bottom section was in place and fixed to the ground and the second section – the firepit and the barbecue – was ready to be attached.

'Looking good,' she said.

'Not as difficult as I feared in the end,' Charlie replied. 'Grandma's gone to the village to meet Anouk for coffee. Said if she's not back for lunch, don't worry. She'll ring if she needs a lift home.'

'Okay. Reckon we'll be able to fire this up tomorrow evening?'

Charlie nodded.

'In that case I'll just pop across to the cottage and have a word with Justine.'

'She's working in the barn,' Charlie indicated with his head. 'I saw her going across earlier.'

'Thanks.'

In the barn, Justine was putting the finishing touches to a shopping basket and looked up in surprise when Pixie appeared.

'Hi.'

Pixie registered the wary note in Justine's voice. 'I wanted to apologise for the pizza debacle the other evening. My fault entirely. I should have checked with you first. I guess you've seen my nephew building a state-of-the-art pizza oven out there? I'm planning on firing it up tomorrow evening if you'd like to bring Ferdie to join us? About six o'clock so he's not too late for bed.' She braced herself for a curt refusal of the invitation as Justine looked at her without speaking for several seconds.

'Thank you. He'd like that.'

At Justine's words, Pixie realised she'd been holding her breath. 'Good. See you then.'

Pixie turned and walked away before Justine could see how emotional the acceptance had made her feel. Tomorrow evening she was determined to try and get to know both Ferdie and Justine better.

24

The next day, Pixie was busy putting finishing touches to all the guest rooms and making sure the château was looking its best, ready for everyone's arrival the following day. Beds were all made, water and glasses on the bedside tables, some bedside reading in Gus and Sarah's room and Annabel's, towels, soap and shampoo in the bathrooms, lots of soft toys on Mimi's bed. Tomorrow morning she'd cut some roses from the garden and put them in vases on the dressing tables.

After lunch, she and Charlie drove to the largest supermarket in Carhaix, where she told him to buy whatever ingredients he needed or wanted to cook with.

'I warn you, I love French supermarkets. You'll regret letting me loose in here,' he said.

Pixie laughed. 'Just this once, go mad. We've got a brand new fridge-freezer to fill and you've got eight mouths to feed every day for the next couple of weeks. Need to remember, though, children tend to prefer plain food.'

By the time they'd bought bottles of wine and champagne

and were stood in line for the checkout, they'd filled two trollies to the brim.

Pixie whispered to Charlie. 'I'm glad we're not behind us. This is going to take ages.'

Pixie unloaded the car back at the château, while Charlie disappeared to fire up the pizza oven, leaving Gwen to help Pixie put everything away. The larder shelves were all but groaning with the weight of food placed on them and the drawers of the new fridge-freezer were stuffed full. Gwen had already organised plates, serviettes, cutlery and glasses out on the terrace table.

Once he was happy with the pizza oven fire, Charlie started preparing the pizzas. 'Three big ones should do it for tonight' he said, rolling out the dough he'd bought from the supermarket bakery. 'Next time, I will make my own dough.'

Once the dough was rolled, Charlie began to grate cheese, drained the mozzarella and some olives before slicing some pepperoni and tomatoes. He smeared tomato paste over the three rounds of dough and started to layer everything on top.

'Time for a pizza party,' he said and Pixie and Gwen helped him carry them outside.

Justine and Ferdie were on their way over from the cottage and, as soon as he saw them, Ferdie ran ahead.

'I love pizza,' he said to Charlie. 'I can eat loads.'

'I'd better get cooking then,' and Charlie pushed the first large pizza into the oven.

'Ferdie, would you like a glass of lemonade?' Gwen asked.

'Please.'

'Justine, glass of wine? What about you, Charlie – beer or wine?'

'Wine please, Grandma,' Charlie said.

'You're too big to have a grandma,' Ferdie said. 'You've got to be little to have one. I've got one, she's called Brigitte, but I call her Gangan, not grandma.'

Everyone laughed and Charlie stooped down to talk to Ferdie. 'If you're lucky, you never get too big to have a grandma. They boss you about however old you get, but they always love you.'

Ferdie nodded seriously. 'It's like having two bossy mummies.'

'And this bossy mummy is saying that's enough, drink your lemonade.' Justine gave him a look that brooked no argument.

Ferdie glanced at Charlie, a look on his face that clearly said, 'see what I mean?' before taking a sip or two of his drink.

'I've just realised – I haven't introduced you two,' Pixie said. 'How rude of me. Charlie this is Justine. Justine, meet my nephew Charlie – he's staying with us for a while. I think Ferdie has made a splendid job of introducing himself.' And Pixie smiled at Justine.

'I think he's almost four going on fourteen sometimes with the things he comes out with,' Justine replied, shaking her head.

'When is his birthday?' Charlie asked.

'The twentieth of July, would you believe? Right at the beginning of the summer holidays. That is some pizza oven. I've never seen one quite so big or complicated before.'

'It's a bit OTT really and I definitely didn't think about how I would get it put together before buying it,' Pixie confessed. 'If Charlie hadn't arrived when he did,' she shook her head. 'Let's just hope it cooks a good pizza. We'll try out the barbecue another time.'

Ten minutes later when they'd all had a slice of the first pizza and the next two were cooking, the unspoken verdict was that the oven did indeed cook a good pizza. As Charlie cut up the second pizza and gave Ferdie another slice, Pixie looked at Justine and took a deep breath. If she wanted to talk to Justine tonight in private, now would be a good time.

'Would you like to see what the builders have done to the top floor?' she asked.

'Yes, I'd like that. It's such a great space,' Justine's voice faltered a little.

'Come on then, while Ferdie is occupied.' Pixie stood up. 'I'm taking Justine up to see the new room. Back in a tick.' She saw a concerned look flash across Gwen's face and gave her a brief smile, trying to convey everything was good.

As they walked up the main staircase side by side, Pixie glanced at Justine. 'We didn't get off to the best of starts, did we? I owe you another apology for that. I reacted badly to your presence here. It was such a huge shock, to be honest, and coupled with the fact that Frank had neglected to tell me about finally owning the château...' her voice trailed away.

'I can understand that,' Justine said. 'I kept urging Frank to talk to you sooner rather than later, but he kept saying he couldn't find the right moment. He finally decided he'd tell you everything when he brought you here after the work had been done for your new writing room and he could show it to you.' She bit her lip. 'Which proved to be too late in all respects. Like I said, sooner would have been much better.'

They walked along the corridor of the first floor in silence. As they passed open bedroom doors and before they started to climb the final flight of stairs, Justine said. 'The bedrooms look very welcoming.'

'Thank you.'

Opening the door of her writing room, Pixie stepped aside to let Justine enter first. A few seconds passed before Justine spoke.

'What a wonderful room. Just how Frank described to me how he wanted it for you.'

'Frank discussed the conversion with you?' Pixie asked, wondering why he would have done that.

'Yes. He was so excited about organising it when he met Jerome. Spent ages up here with him explaining what he wanted.'

Pixie twisted Frank's ring around on her finger. 'I found his ring up here in the fireplace. He told me he'd lost it but said he didn't know where.'

'He was so upset when he lost that ring,' Justine shook her head before giving a deep sigh. 'I'm sure it would have been easier all round if only he'd been honest from the start. I'd sort of hoped that that was what would happen when I moved into the cottage.'

Pixie held her breath, waiting for her to continue. Was Justine referring to the fact that Frank hadn't told her about the viager scheme finishing, or something else? Was she about to confide in her? Finally tell her the truth about her relationship with Frank?

But all Justine added was, 'I do miss him. Ferdie does too. Talking of Ferdie, I'd better get back down to him before he wonders where I've got to.'

Pixie resisted the urge to say Charlie and Gwen would be entertaining him, just tell me what you were to Frank, but she wasn't brave enough right then to push for the truth. Their fragile friendship needed to be stronger before she took that risk because once she knew the truth it couldn't help but change things. And whether that would be for better or worse, she had no way of knowing.

As they reached the ground floor, Justine turned to Pixie. 'It's such a shame you are selling and I'm not saying that selfishly wishing you weren't, but I think Frank would have liked you to stay, expected even, come what may. You and the château suit each other.'

Justine walked away as Pixie stared after her. Justine was the second person to tell her she suited the place. Well, whatever they might mean by that, staying wasn't an option. Frank's double life made that an impossible choice.

Two hours later, back at the cottage, Ferdie was tucked up in bed, fast asleep, and Justine was sitting on the settee with a glass of wine and a slice of cold pizza, courtesy of Charlie, on the table in front of her. Once she'd admitted to liking pizza cold, he'd insisted on her taking a large slice because she was leaving the party early.

Sitting there drinking her wine, Justine thought about the evening. Ferdie had been well behaved and she sensed the three adults liked him. Ferdie himself had been captivated by Charlie and had followed him around devotedly. Gwen had been her usual friendly self and obviously happy to have her grandson staying. Pixie had definitely thawed towards her, although there was still a certain reservation about her. Justine sensed that the Pixie she'd been with tonight, gentle, nice and happy, was the true one, not the abrasive one she'd apologised for being earlier. Frank had been right wanting to protect and not hurt her, but the full truth, if it ever became known, would still be a painful cross to bear.

At one point, Justine had sat there, smiling to herself as she listened to the banter between the three of them. Banter that had its roots in a family history that showed how close they all were. Banter that Frank, as Pixie's husband, would have been familiar enough to join in with, whereas she was an outsider.

For the most part it had been a good evening, except for the briefest of moments when a memory of another evening spent sitting on the terrace showed up in her mind. Not long after she'd moved into the cottage, Frank had arrived for an overnight visit and they'd sat together under the starry night sky, with Ferdie asleep in his stroller alongside them. It was one of several evenings when she tried and failed to persuade Frank to tell Pixie about them.

'The timing's all wrong,' something he was to say on several occasions in the future, not knowing that the right time was never going to arrive for him.

Perhaps now, given the circumstances, it was a good thing that at the end of the summer she and Pixie would go their separate ways – she with the secret still intact and Pixie in blissful ignorance.

25

The next day, Pixie and Gwen made sure everything in the château was as it should be, while Charlie, having cleaned the pizza oven and swept the terrace, took over the kitchen and began prepping food for both lunch and dinner. By the time Sarah phoned to warn them of their imminent arrival, 'Just approaching the village,' everything was ready.

Pixie, waiting outside the front door looking for non-existent weeds in the two urns with their tumbling petunias, found herself hoping that during the next couple of weeks everyone would make some wonderful memories of their time here. Family memories that would become more and more precious down the years to her as this summer in the château became a distant memory.

She watched as Gus's car swept into the drive, followed by Annabelle's. Pixie smiled as car doors opened and everyone got out.

'Welcome to Château Quiltu, everyone. It is so good to have you all here.'

The next few moments passed in a flurry of hugs and kisses

between Pixie, her brother, sister-in-law, Sarah, and Annabelle, her niece, as well as Mimi, her great-niece.

'Come on in, everyone, and I'll show you to your bedrooms and then Mum and Charlie have got lunch ready out on the terrace.'

'Charlie here already?' Gus said. 'That's a surprise.'

'Arrived a couple of days ago and saved my skin with a new pizza oven-cum-barbecue.'

'Can I go find Charlie?' Mimi demanded.

'He and Great-Grandma are round the front. Mimi, there is a lake in the garden and there is only one rule for this holiday, but it is a strict one. You are not to go anywhere near the lake without a grown-up. Anywhere else but not the lake. Understood?'

Mimi nodded, 'Yes, Auntie Pixie,' before dashing off to find Charlie.

'This is lovely, sis,' Gus said as she led the way indoors. 'Makes me want to move to France immediately.'

Sarah and Annabelle both loved their bedrooms and Annabelle gazed longingly at the large claw-legged old-fashioned bath in her bathroom. 'I might have to bribe one of you to keep an eye on Mimi later. A long soak in that bath is calling to me.'

Back out on the terrace, Gus went straight over to Gwen and gave her a hug and a kiss. 'How are you liking France then, Ma?'

'I'm loving it. Brittany has always been one of my favourite places. You're looking tired.'

'Didn't sleep on the ferry, that's all,' Gus shrugged off Gwen's remark.

'Here you go, Dad. Good to see you.' Charlie handed both Gus and Gwen a glass of champagne before going over to Sarah and giving her a tight hug. 'Champagne for you, Mum? Annabelle?'

Once everyone had a glass of bubbly, Pixie raised her glass.

'Here's to a wonderful holiday. Santé.'

Charlie had placed a few nibbles on the table – crisps, olives and peanuts – and once those had gone, he began to bring lunch out. Cold meats, cheeses, baguettes, a big green salad, tomato and mozzarella salad. 'Tonight I'll fire up the barbecue,' he promised Mimi as he poured her a glass of lemonade. 'And we'll have beef burgers.'

Pixie made a large cafetière of coffee after lunch and they sat around chatting and discussing plans for the holiday. The general consensus appeared to favour a few day trips further afield, Quimper and Concarneau were mentioned, as well as local market visits, but staying in and mooching about at the château came out on top as the favourite for the adults. Mimi kept shouting, 'Beach. Beach. I want to go to the beach.' Until Annabelle promised she would take her 'one day next week, if you're good.'

They were all still sitting on the terrace when Justine and Ferdie arrived home. Gus raised his eyebrows and looked at Pixie as Justine gave a wave of acknowledgement in their direction, which Charlie returned before getting up and walking over to her.

'Justine had an arrangement with Frank. She and her son, Ferdie, have lived in the cottage for over a year.'

'Pays rent, does she?' Gus asked.

Pixie sighed. Her brother always did cut straight to the chase. She put it down to him being an accountant. 'No. I think she kept an eye on the place – unofficial caretaker type thing.' She knew she would have to tell Gus her suspicions eventually, but right now she didn't want to spoil the happy atmosphere.

Gus nodded thoughtfully. 'That would make sense, it is a bit in the middle of nowhere here. But, still, he should have charged some rent. Typical of Frank though. He always was one to help the underdog.'

Five minutes later, Charlie returned with Ferdie holding his hand. 'Mimi, meet Ferdie. Him and me are going for a walk down by the lake – wanna come with us?'

'Yes,' and Mimi was up and running.

Watching Charlie lope down through the parkland with Mimi and Ferdie, Pixie realised keeping the little girl happy for this holiday was going to require more than the occasional day at the beach.

* * *

The days settled down into a relaxed holiday routine for everyone except Charlie and Pixie. Charlie took his kitchen duties very seriously and while lunch was generally something with salad, dinner was another matter. Even Gus professed to be impressed with his son's cooking abilities. On the evenings when the main course constituted of barbecued meat or fish, Charlie went to town on the accompanying dishes and desserts. He also spent a lot of time with Mimi, especially while Ferdie was at school. Setting up camps with old blankets in the parkland, finding a tyre and strong rope and creating a swing from the tall oak tree at the side of the small barn. All things Mimi shared happily with Ferdie every afternoon when he returned from school. Within forty-eight hours, the two children had become firm friends and played happily together. When Pixie unearthed an ancient croquet set hidden on a shelf in the utility room, it was Charlie who cleaned it, set it up ready for all of them to play and taught them the basic rules of the game.

Pixie, although not as involved with the cooking of the meals, or as busy as Charlie, kept on top of all the washing up, with Gwen's help. Never had a dishwasher been missed so much and she was sorely tempted to go and buy one. Sarah and Annabelle helped too, of course, but Pixie didn't think it fair to ask them to do too much. It was meant to be a holiday and Annabelle, in particular, looked as if she could do with a rest.

The days they went out on trips, Gwen went with them. Once down to Quimper, another to the west coast and one to Lac de Guerlédan, which gave Pixie and Charlie a much-needed breather.

Mid-afternoon usually found Ferdie racing across to see Charlie and play with Mimi. At first, Justine tried to keep him back at the cottage, not wanting him to intrude or to be a nuisance. Both Pixie and Charlie reassured her that he wasn't intruding or getting in the way and everyone was grateful that Mimi had a playmate. With the children spending so much time together, it was inevitable that Justine became more involved with the family as the days went by. Pixie became used to seeing her around the place.

Justine always took Ferdie home when Annabelle said it was bedtime for Mimi, so that the adults could enjoy the rest of the evening child-free. Several times it was suggested that once Ferdie was asleep she could slip back and join them, but she always refused, despite the cottage being so close.

Pixie was happy with the opportunity of seeing a lot more of Ferdie and getting to know him better. Every time she saw him, she studied him surreptitiously, trying to find any likeness to Frank she could. Pixie welcomed Sarah's unexpected suggestion that perhaps Mimi and Ferdie could have a sleepover one night so that Justine could spend the evening with them. But for some reason or other Justine always said no.

Two days before the end of the holiday, the six of them were sitting around on the terrace after dinner, relaxed and remi-niscing about previous family holidays as the end of the current one approached, when Pixie had a sudden thought.

'Jean-Yves was telling me that years ago this place hosted a lot of parties. Why don't we follow in their footsteps? We could have one for your last night here? I don't know many people, but I could invite the few I do know. Nothing too complicated – maybe a champagne and pizza party? Barbecue food is a bit messy, isn't it? Pizzas are easy enough aren't they, Charlie? Not too much work for you? What d'you all think? A family party to remember from our summer at the château.'

'A champagne and pizza party sounds fun,' Charlie said. 'But I insist on making some desserts as well.'

'That's settled then. I'm going to organise a party for your last evening.'

26

Justine was in the cottage Thursday evening writing up her accounts after a couple of busy market days in Châteauneuf-du-Faou yesterday and Huelgoat today. Ferdie was in bed exhausted. After school, she'd taken him and Mimi down to the lake for a picnic and some pretend fishing with bamboo rods and chunks of bread. The two of them had squealed with delight when they'd seen a frog jump from lily pad to lily pad. Completely made up for the fact they didn't catch any fish. Not that Justine had expected them to. She was pretty sure frogs and newts were the only inhabitants of the lake. Ferdie was going to miss Mimi so much when they left this weekend.

If Justine were honest, she would miss her too. Not only Mimi but the whole family. They'd welcomed and included Ferdie and her so naturally into much of their holiday, she felt comfortable in their presence. Even Pixie had seemed relaxed and friendlier towards her.

A gentle tap on the door startled her. Charlie was standing there when she partly opened it holding two containers and with a bottle of wine tucked under his arm.

'I'm guessing you haven't eaten yet? Fancy joining me for a home-cooked takeaway?' He looked at her, a hopeful smile on his face.

'Yes please.' Justine smiled as she opened the door fully and let Charlie in.

While Charlie sorted the food onto plates and opened the wine, Justine cleared the table of her books, straightened the throw on the settee and plumped the cushions, fetched cutlery and glasses and flicked the switch on the orange salt lights on the mantlepiece.

'Did you not eat with the family tonight?' she asked as Charlie placed two plates of risotto on the table before pouring them both a glass of wine.

'No. I wanted to have supper with you, so I left Pixie in charge of serving up. Cheers,' and he handed her a glass.

'Cheers,' Justine said.

'Eat your risotto while it's hot,' Charlie instructed. 'No dessert until you've finished it.'

For several moments they both ate without speaking, although Justine did make several appreciative noises, before saying, 'This is delicious.'

'I do have a couple of ulterior motives though for feeding you tonight,' Charlie said.

Justine looked at him and waited.

'First, Pixie is organising a party for the last night of the holiday and you and Ferdie are invited – on one condition.' Charlie looked at her. 'Ferdie has a sleepover with Mimi so that you can't disappear like Cinderella halfway through the evening.'

'I'm not sure,' Justine started before Charlie interrupted her.

'Why won't you let him sleep in the château? He does want to.'

'It's hard to explain. Since the day he was born, there hasn't been a night when I haven't been there for him if he called out in the middle of a bad dream or something. If he woke up in a strange place and I wasn't there, he wouldn't know what to do, who to go to. And the château is so big.' Justine knew her fears were unfounded, and she was being irrational. Ferdie slept very deeply and rarely woke up, but the thought of him wanting her and not finding her scared her.

'Okay. How about this. When he and Mimi are tired, we put them both to bed in the château. Knowing my niece, she'll jabber away and keep them both awake. You or Annabelle can pop up to check on them, but you'll at least be able to join the party on the terrace. When you're ready to come home, I'll pick a sleeping Ferdie up and carry him over and place him in his own bed. Sound a good plan?'

Justine gave in and nodded. 'Have to warn you, Ferdie is no light weight.'

Charlie stretched his arms out and flexed his muscles, which, Justine had to admit to herself, were seriously impressive. 'Not a problem. Right, that's sorted. You're coming to the party. More wine?'

'A little. You mentioned a couple of ulterior motives earlier?'

'I did,' Charlie sighed. 'I have a feeling my dad is building up to have a serious talk about the future with me, and I'd rather he didn't yet. So coming here tonight is also serving a purpose as an avoidance tactic.' He took a drink of wine. 'Because I don't have any answers to give him, which will only make him crosser and crosser. It's not that I don't have plans, I just have to work out how to put them in place. So I'm staying out of his way as much as possible.'

'What do you do?' Justine asked.

'Don't hate me, but I'm a qualified estate agent. Rather, I was until I was made redundant a few weeks ago. Now I fancy a complete change of direction – something I know Dad will not agree with. I want to cook.'

'Why is that a problem? Gus has been eating your food since he arrived, he knows how good it is.'

'But his son cooking for a living will not be a good career move in his eyes. You see, I don't have aspirations to be a three-star Michelin chef, I want to cook good food in an ordinary place, maybe even teach people how to do it themselves.' Charlie shrugged. 'I know once I've worked out a business plan and Dad can see I've thought it through, he'll be supportive. Mum's on my side already, so between us we'll talk him round.'

'I think Pixie will help too, won't she?'

Charlie nodded. 'I'm hoping she'll be part of my support group. Anyway, enough about me. I want to know about you. You're a bit of a mysterious woman. You're French, but you don't have a French surname, you speak English like a native, nobody knows why Frank gave you the cottage to live in and you make baskets for a living. Very nice baskets too, I must add.'

'Did you say something about dessert? We've both finished our main course,' Justine said, playing for time. She had no intention of lying to Charlie, but she couldn't tell him the whole truther either.

'Dessert, yes,' and Charlie collected the plates and went over to the kitchen, returning to the table a minute later with a miniature strawberry pavlova each.

'Mmm,' Justine said, picking up the spoon and small fork Charlie had placed on each plate, breaking into the meringue and taking a bite. 'There's nothing mysterious about me,' she said, looking at Charlie, knowing he was waiting for her answer. 'But I daresay people have made up their own stories. My mother is French, my father is English and I actually speak Spanish as well. As for the cottage, I met Frank when I was in desperate need of somewhere to live and he simply offered me this place. End of story.' Justine scooped another mouthful of strawberries and meringue before giving Charlie a look that she hoped would tell him that particular subject was now closed. 'As for the basket making, it was a hobby that I've managed to turn into a business.'

'How do you cope with Ferdie and doing the markets?'

'Most of the regular markets are mornings only, so I drop Ferdie at school and head off. Depending where it is, I can be a bit late setting up, but...' Justine shrugged. 'And then I'm back at the school gate at midday to meet Ferdie. If I have a problem, I have a good friend, Carole, who will meet Ferdie for me. School holidays can be a bit of a problem, but usually things sort themselves out.'

'If you need any help this summer, don't forget I'm here and happy to be roped in as childminder.'

'Thanks.' Justine smiled at him. 'I'll remember.'

Charlie left not long after and Justine closed the cottage door behind him thoughtfully. She wasn't sure how she felt about Charlie planning on staying around for the summer. He and Ferdie got on so well and it was good for Ferdie to have a man in his life as a role model. Charlie was a nice man, too. One of the nicest she'd met for years. She liked Charlie and she sensed that he liked her as well – tonight's unexpected supper had shown her that – and under different circumstances maybe they could have become more than the friends they were already becoming. But if the secret that stood between herself and Pixie ever became general knowledge to Pixie and Charlie's family, knowing the truth would surely change the friendship between herself and Charlie forever.

From now on, she'd be careful to keep Charlie at arm's-length.

She remembered him flexing his arm muscles earlier and pushed the thought he was seriously fit away. Being more than friends with Charlie was a complication in her life she didn't need.

27

The day of the party, Pixie and Gus spent several hours together sorting out decorative lights for the evening. Gus climbed up and down the stepladder, threading strings of silver fairy lights through the camellia trees nearest the château and around several of the shrubs. Another string was wound around the trunk of the big chestnut tree near the top of the drive. Yet another long string of golden lights was fixed to the château wall the terrace ran along. At the front entrance, Pixie wound a string of lights around each of the granite urns, while Gus fixed a string of twinkling white lights around the door portal.

Charlie spent the afternoon in the kitchen, making dough and preparing the pizzas. In the fridge, chocolate brandy mousses and creamy lemon syllabubs stood alongside a bowl of raspberries for the individual meringue nests that were in an airtight tin in the larder.

Pixie had telephoned Fern the day before, inviting her, Scott and Anouk. 'And perhaps you'd like to bring your friends, Belinda and Alain? It would be nice to finally meet them.' She paused before continuing. 'I was wondering about inviting Jean-Yves and his wife. Do you think he would like to come?'

'Why wouldn't he? But he doesn't have a wife. She died a few years ago.'

'Thanks for telling me. I would have hated to upset him.'

After putting the phone down from Fern, Pixie telephoned Jean-Yves.

'I realise it's short notice, but it would be lovely if you were free,' she'd said. 'My way of thanking you for the other day. There will be thirteen of us and two little ones if you can come, so not a big party.'

'I'd love to come, thank you for the invitation.'

'If you'd like to bring anyone, Jade, your daughter, please do. See you tomorrow about eight o'clock.'

Once Charlie was happy with the food side of things, he created a playlist on Pixie's laptop of French music and sultry jazz. This was playing in the early evening as Charlie fired up the pizza oven and Sarah, Gwen and Pixie ferried things to the table. By seven thirty, everything was in place and Annabelle and Mimi promised to keep an eye on things with Gus while the others went and smartened up.

By five to eight, the lights at the entrance were switched on in a welcoming gesture, even though it was still quite light, and everyone was out on the terrace, Charlie had placed the first of many pizzas in the oven and Gus was opening a bottle of champagne.

Justine and Ferdie walked across from the cottage, Justine carrying one of her small baskets with a bottle of champagne inside. Ferdie was carrying a bag and excitedly told everyone, 'My jim-jams are in here. I'm sleeping with Mimi tonight, but then Charlie is going to carry me home.'

'Let's take them upstairs, Ferdie, and show you Mimi's room, then you can both come down and have a slice of pizza,' Annabelle said.

Justine turned to Pixie and handed her the basket. 'This is for you. The bottle has been in the fridge all day, so it's cold if you want to use it tonight.'

'Thank you. We didn't expect you to bring anything. I love the basket,' Pixie said. 'I'll put the bottle in the fridge. Why don't you join Sarah and Gwen. Gus, glass of champers needed for Justine.'

Closing the fridge door, Pixie heard a car parking in the drive and went through the hallway to greet whoever it was. She spotted Jean-Yves and an elegant young woman.

'Bonjour, Pixie. This is my daughter, Marien, mother of Jade.'

'Lovely to meet you, Marien. Come on through, both of you, and meet my family.'

Fern, Scott and Anouk arrived soon afterwards, together with Belinda and Alain, and the party was underway.

The fairy lights everywhere came into their own as daylight faded away and Mimi and Ferdie were taken upstairs to bed an hour or so later. Justine tucked Ferdie in and kissed him goodnight. 'Be a good boy and go to sleep. I'm just downstairs. And, remember, Charlie is going to come and carry you to the cottage when I go home.'

'Mimi and I can talk for a bit, though, can't we?' Ferdie asked.

'Not too long.'

Justine and Annabelle left the bedroom door open and the landing light on.

'He'll be fine,' Annabelle said. 'Right, a second glass of champagne has my name on it, not to mention another slice of pizza.'

Justine smiled. She felt tired and dispirited tonight for some reason now she was here and wished she was back in her own cottage, far away from these people with their smiley faces and bonhomie. She hadn't expected to see Jean-Yves, the notaire, here and had said 'Hello' apprehensively, grateful when he'd returned her greeting politely.

Back down on the terrace, Charlie was just cutting slices of yet another pizza and placing it on plates. He handed her one. 'You look a bit sad tonight, what's up?'

'Bit tired, that's all.' No way was she going to admit to Charlie how worried and overwhelmed she suddenly felt about the future, finding somewhere to live, keeping the secret. The secret that was at the root of her problem. He'd think she was mad if she told him what she'd promised never to tell four years ago. He wouldn't understand why she'd allowed herself to be persuaded to wait until the time was right to tell the truth. 'You make a good pizza,' she said, hoping to change the conversation. 'Love all the fairy lights Pixie has put up.'

'Makes it look a lot like Christmas to me.' Charlie smiled. 'Do you like Christmas?'

'Not so much these days, although last Christmas was good because Frank…' she stopped, realising that she was about to say how special Frank had made it for her and Ferdie. She wasn't used to champagne and Gus had topped up her original glass a couple of times, which must have loosened her tongue.

'Frank what?' Charlie asked.

'Because Frank had let me move in to the cottage and Ferdie and I decorated before I drove up to my parents for the holiday. Will it be all right if I go and get myself a glass of water in the kitchen?'

'Stay here. I've got to fetch the desserts, I'll bring you some back.'

'Thanks.'

Justine wandered over to sit with Gwen and Anouk in time to hear Gwen say, 'So it's a date then. When I return, you and I will brave the luncheon club together. Check out the talent,' Gwen gave a mischievous laugh. 'See if any are worth getting to know.'

'Where are you off to?' Justine asked.

'The UK, tomorrow with Gus. Just for forty-eight hours, then I'll be back,' Gwen answered. 'Can I bring anything back for you or Ferdie? English delicacies you can't find over here?'

'I can't think of anything, but thank you.'

By the time Charlie returned with water and a tray of desserts, Justine was feeling calmer and, after a large glass of water, resolved not to drink any more champagne for the rest of the evening.

Charlie sat with her for a bit before returning to the check on the pizza oven. Once the food was finished and the pizza oven was cooling down, Charlie came over with a plate and held it out to her.

'A cold final slice of your favourite four cheese pizza?'

'How can I refuse?' And Justine took a slice. 'Still avoiding your dad?' she whispered.

'No, I wanted to spend some time with you,' Charlie said. 'And ask you something.'

Justine smiled and bit into her pizza slice, conscious that Gwen and Anouk were sitting close enough to hear the conversation.

'Would you let me take Ferdie and you to the coast one weekend?'

'Ferdie would love that, but you don't have a car. We could go in mine if you like,' Justine said, wondering where her resolve not to get close to Charlie had gone.

'Pixie will probably lend me hers. Next Sunday then?' When Justine nodded, Charlie said, 'It's a date then.'

'A date? You go, girl,' Gwen said, looking at Justine.

Justine laughed. 'See what you've done. Now everyone will be thinking you've asked me out, when really it's a treat for Ferdie.'

Charlie shrugged philosophically. 'They can think what they like. I know it's because I want to spend time with you both.'

It was eleven o'clock when Justine said she was ready to go home and asked Charlie to carry Ferdie over to the cottage for her. Together they crept into the bedroom, where Mimi was sleeping peacefully on her side with a thumb in her mouth, while Ferdie was spreadeagled across the bed clutching one of the soft toys.

Charlie bent over the sleeping boy, whispering reassurance, as he gently scooped him up and carefully began to carry him downstairs, out of the château and back to the cottage. Justine had left the lights on and quickly opened the door and showed Charlie upstairs to Ferdie's bedroom, where Charlie gently laid the boy on his bed, still clutching the toy.

'Night night, Charlie,' Ferdie muttered sleepily.

'Night, Ferdie.'

'Too late for a coffee?' Charlie asked when they were back downstairs, standing in the sitting room looking at each other.

'Much too late. Thank you for carrying Ferdie across,' Justine said, opening the front door. 'See you in the morning.' No way was she encouraging Charlie to stay any longer. The champagne had already weakened her resolve not to get too close to him. She wasn't going to risk letting her guard down any further and she closed the door.

As Charlie wandered back, deep in thought, to join everyone, Gus fell into step beside him.

'You arrived here early, Pixie tells me you're staying for the summer – is there something you'd like to tell me?'

Charlie took a deep breath and decided to come clean with

his father. 'I was "let go" as they say, from the agency a few weeks ago.'

'It happens. You've been there long enough to receive a reasonable cheque. So, what next? Any plans?'

'Nothing concrete, but I definitely want a new direction.' Charlie hesitated. 'I'm thinking of catering, as in cooking for a living,' he added, making sure his dad understood.

'Well, you are a good cook, you've proved that this week – reckon you're Michelin star material?'

Charlie laughed. 'I knew that's how you would react! Dad, I don't want to do that kind of cooking. I want to cook food like I've done this week. Maybe open a small restaurant or bistro. I just have to figure out the where and the why fors. That's why I'm taking summer off. To make proper plans.'

Gus nodded thoughtfully. 'Right. When you've decided, let me know if I can help in any way.'

'Thanks Dad, appreciate that.' And with that the two of them arrived back on the terrace.

* * *

Shortly after Justine had left, Jean-Yves made his way across to Pixie. 'Marien has made a new friend I think with your niece,' and he glanced across to where Annabelle and Marien were busy chatting away. 'It is a pity the holiday finishes tomorrow. I think also the two little ones would have played together well.'

Pixie was about to say, 'Yes, next time I must get them together', but then remembered there wouldn't be a next time and smiled sadly. Next year Mimi would be taken on holiday somewhere else.

'I would be very happy, Pixie, if you would have dinner with me one evening next week?' Jean-Yves' voice pulled her back to the present.

Surprised at the invitation, Pixie looked at him before smiling. 'Thank you, I would like that very much.'

'I will ring you. Now, I must collect Marien and get her home.'

Fern, Scott and Anouk left at the same time, together with Belinda and Alain, and the family set about clearing up the party debris. Gus and Annabelle went round turning off all the outside lights, while Sarah and Gwen tackled some of the washing up, but at Pixie's insistence stacked the rest in the kitchen to be dealt with in the morning. 'You've all got a long day tomorrow, you need to get some sleep.'

It was nearly midnight before she and Charlie checked the pizza oven fire was well and truly out and made their own way upstairs.

Before she went to bed, Pixie climbed the stairs to her writing room. The moon was shining in through one of the dormers and Pixie stood for a moment in silence, just breathing in the atmosphere. Up here she felt she could sense Frank's presence more than anywhere else in the château.

'I missed you tonight, Frank. I so wish you could have been here. I wish too, I could have thanked you in person for this lovely room.'

As the moon went behind a cloud and the room darkened, Pixie sighed and went downstairs to her bed, where she soon fell into a deep dream-filled sleep.

She and Frank were lying wrapped in each other's arms in the four-poster and Frank was telling her how much he loved her. 'And this party tonight will be the first of many so long as you stay here and don't sell the château. All your dreams will come true here and the château will be a home to the family we always wanted. Promise me you'll still live here and won't sell our dream home.' Pixie reached out and touched his face. 'I promise I won't sell the château.' Frank gave a happy smile and pulled her back into his arms.

Pixie woke with a start, reaching out for Frank, convinced that he really was in bed with her, only to find herself clutching a pillow close to her chest and the bed empty. She hugged the pillow tighter. The dream had felt so real and to hear herself promise Frank that she wouldn't sell the château made her close her eyes in despair. In truth, so much of her longed to keep the place, to live here forever, but the reality was that keeping it was also a dream. Wasn't it?

28

The mood at the château the next morning was a downbeat one, with everyone feeling sad that the holiday was over and it was time to leave. The knowledge too, that this holiday had been a one-off hung in the air, nobody shouting 'we'll be back'. Instead plans were made over a late breakfast of croissants out on the terrace to meet up later in the year when summer was over and Pixie was back in England. Gwen, unable to cancel her routine yearly check-up at the hospital, was going back with them, returning to France as a foot passenger on the Pont Aven in two days.

'Time to go,' Gus said, finishing his tea and standing up.

Slowly everyone made their way through the château and out to the drive. Gwen was travelling with Gus, and Sarah with Annabelle and Mimi.

As they started to get into the cars, Justine came over, with Ferdie running ahead of her clutching one of Justine's smaller hand-made raffia baskets. The basket was filled with a colouring book, crayons, a tiny Breton doll and a packet of sweets. Shyly Ferdie held it out to Mimi, already strapped into her car seat, before returning to hold Justine's hand and wave goodbye. 'Bye bye, Mimi.'

Pixie hugged everyone and wished them a safe journey. 'Mum, I'll be at Roscoff to meet you in two days' time.'

Both cars gave a toot as they turned out of the drive and disappeared from view.

Pixie sighed. 'It was fun, wasn't it, having the family here?' she said, glancing at Charlie and then at Justine. 'I guess it's going to take us a day or two to get used to the quiet again.'

Charlie glanced at Ferdie. 'Wanna give me a hand cleaning the bike?'

Ferdie nodded vigorously.

'Sorry, I should have asked you first,' Charlie looked at Justine. 'Is that okay with you? I'm not planning on starting it or anything.'

'It's fine so long as he's not in the way.'

'My mate, Ferdie, in the way? Never.' Charlie ruffled Ferdie's hair affectionately and the two of them walked off to the barn, with Ferdie chatting away excitedly.

Pixie watched them go with an indulgent look on her face. 'It's wonderful to see Charlie with Ferdie – they really get on, don't they?' Pixie turned to Justine with a smile. 'Join me for a coffee before I start stripping beds?'

'Thanks. Would you like some help with the beds afterwards?'

Pixie shook her head. 'It'll keep me busy and take my mind off how empty the château is now that everyone has gone.'

Sitting out on the terrace with fresh cups of coffee, Pixie wondered if it would be a good moment to try and get Justine to open up and tell her the truth about the relationship she'd had with Frank. What the hell, she needed to know the truth and the only person who could tell her that was Justine. She'd give a gentle probe and see what happened.

'Ferdie is a lovely little boy, a real credit to you. The kind of son I always dreamt of having but sadly never did,' she added softly, not looking at Justine.

'Frank told me how desperate you were to have a child. All the tests and fertility treatment you endured,' Justine said.

Pixie caught her breath. Why would he discuss such an intimate matter with the younger woman if he hadn't cared deeply about Justine?

'It wasn't easy on Frank either, he longed for a family too.' Pixie paused for a moment, remembering how hard those years had been. 'But in the end we both had to accept that it wasn't meant to be. I think, to be honest, when we reached the decision to stop trying and to accept things, Frank was relieved. I must have been hell to live with at times. Over the years, we got through it together. The shared pain made us closer than many married couples, I think. At least I thought it did, but now I'm not so sure.'

'I'm really sorry. I think you would have made a great mum.' Justine fiddled with her cup on its saucer. 'I know you don't understand why Frank said Ferdie and I could live in the cottage without telling you. All I can say is he had his reasons and would have told you eventually.'

Pixie looked at Justine and waved her words away with an impatient gesture. 'But he's not here now and you are. I want you to tell me the truth.'

Justine bit her lip. 'I'm sorry, I can't. I made a promise.' She stood up. 'Thank you for the coffee, but I think I should go now.'

'What would you say if I told you I'd guessed the truth,' Pixie demanded. 'I can't say I'm not hurt about him having an affair and having a child with you, but...' She stopped in shock as Justine let a burst of hysterical laughter escape.

'You think I had an affair with Frank? You want the truth?

Okay, here's the truth. Yes, I did love Frank but there was no affair. I loved him like a daughter,' Justine paused. 'Because that's who I am. Frank's daughter. Which makes Ferdie his grandson. And that's why he let us live in the cottage.'

Justine turned and ran away with tears streaming down her face.

A stunned Pixie sat, unable to move, as the realisation hit her that Frank had a child. A child he'd deliberately kept secret from her. She had been wrong in her initial assumption about Justine, but the truth she'd just learnt raised even more questions than answers. The knowledge that Frank had got what she had been unable to give him, a daughter and a grandchild, hurt so much as to be unbearable.

Pixie sat there, the tears flowing unchecked down her cheeks until her blouse was soaked and she was forced to go indoors and change.

PART III

'Love all, trust a few, do wrong to none.'

— *ALL'S WELL THAT ENDS WELL. SHAKESPEARE*

29

Knowing that Ferdie was with Charlie, who would look after him and bring him home if she didn't go looking for him, Justine shut herself in the cottage. How could she have been so stupid as to blurt out the truth like that to Pixie of all people? Frank had been so determined she wasn't to be hurt by the revelation that he had a daughter that he'd made her promise to leave it to him to tell Pixie. Only he hadn't and now the father she'd barely got to know was dead, leaving her and her mother to deal with the fallout.

Justine gave a deep sigh. Her mother, Brigitte, was going to be absolutely furious with her. Four years ago, she had been angry enough with Justine for daring to go against her wishes and look up her biological father. Arguing that it wasn't just about Justine and her wants – other people were in danger of being hurt if she went ahead with her plan to contact him. 'Frank, he not know of your existence when you were born, why does he need to know now? In fact, I doubt that he will want to know.'

'Because I want to learn about my roots,' a stubborn Justine had answered. 'You've never hidden the fact that you were a

single mother and Dad adopted me when you two married. Why
shouldn't I want to know more?'

When she'd insisted on going ahead with contacting Frank,
Brigitte had tried another tack. 'William has been a wonderful
father to you – how d'you think he's going to feel?'

'I've asked him. He knows he will always be my dad and he
understands why I have to meet Frank. Why don't you
understand?'

Brigitte hadn't answered.

To Justine's question, 'Why didn't you tell Frank about me?'
Brigitte had merely shaken her head and shrugged, 'I had my
reasons.'

But when Frank, who, after the initial shock, had most definitely wanted to know about her, had asked the same question
when they all met up for the first time at his request, Brigitte had
looked at him and said quietly, 'You and Pixie were so much in
love, I didn't want a baby with another woman who you no love,
to be responsible for breaking up your marriage.'

Both Brigitte and Frank had made Justine promise that she
would keep her mother's identity a secret from Pixie if she should
meet her before Frank had told her everything. Justine had
promised readily, not expecting to have to keep the secret for so
long. At the time, Frank had already been promising for nearly
three years to tell Pixie about her and she'd assumed that now he
owned the château he'd tell Pixie about her and the château at
the same time. Justine could feel herself tearing up again, if only
that elusive 'right moment' for Frank to admit the truth had
arrived. And yet he'd let her move into the cottage, so he must
have been preparing the ground during that time for telling Pixie,
only to go and die so cruelly and unexpectedly.

Now that Pixie knew who she was, Justine had no doubt that
she would demand to know her mother's identity. And the

answer to that, Frank had told her, would upset Pixie almost as much as learning that he had a secret daughter. Apparently Brigitte and Pixie had been good friends at one time.

With Frank dead and Pixie knowing her true identity, would Brigitte step up and do what Frank should have done and confess to her erstwhile friend that she'd had an affair with her husband years ago? Somehow Justine couldn't see her mother braving the wrath of a wronged wife.

Justine poured herself a glass of water and took a couple of sips.

The cottage door opened and Ferdie called out. 'Mummy, are you here?'

'Yes, I'm here,' Justine said as Ferdie ran in, followed by Charlie. A Charlie who stood in the doorway looking at her, taking in her red eyes and tear-blotched face before moving across and taking her in his arms and looking at her seriously.

'Are you okay?'

Justine nodded. 'I think Pixie might be in need of some company right now though.'

'Have you two had words?'

Justine shook her head. 'Not words exactly. I unintentionally blurted out something I don't think she really wanted to hear. She certainly wasn't expecting it.'

'Ah.' A worried look of understanding crossed Charlie's face. 'I'd better go then, if you're sure you're okay. I'll see you later.'

Justine nodded again, unable to speak, as Charlie turned away and she held out her arms to Ferdie. 'Mummy would love a hug right now.'

Ferdie ran straight into her arms, and she pressed him to her.

* * *

After she'd watched a distressed Justine run away to the cottage, and allowed her own tears to run unchecked down her face, soaking her blouse, Pixie dragged herself into the château. She splashed her face with cold water, changed her top for a cotton sweater and made her way upstairs to her writing room before sinking down on one of the chairs.

Question after question leapt into her mind. How long had Frank kept the knowledge of Justine's existence away from her? Had he ever intended to tell her he had a secret daughter? Who was her mother? Did she know her? Had Frank really led a secret life away from her for years that she'd been in the dark about? Did she want to know the details?

Pixie shuddered. It was all too much to take in. And the fact that Frank had a grandson was a bittersweet addition to the conundrum.

'There you are,' Charlie said, running up the stairs and bursting into the room. 'Been looking everywhere for you. Justine said you might need some company. Why are you both so upset?'

'Because everything has changed. Ferdie isn't Frank's son like I was foolish enough to be beginning to believe, he's his grandson. Which makes Justine his—'

'Daughter,' Charlie said, sitting down on the spare chair. 'I have to admit, I did wonder. There's a certain resemblance, especially when she smiles.'

Pixie looked at him. 'You saw that? Why didn't I? I jumped straight to the conclusion that she and Frank...' her voice wavered. 'I was constantly watching Ferdie, convincing myself that he looked like Frank.'

'He does. But he looks like Justine too.' Charlie hesitated. 'Is Justine being Frank's daughter so bad?'

Pixie closed her eyes and nodded. 'Yes, it truly is.'

'Why?'

'Because it means that at a time in our lives when I was going through hell trying to have a baby, he found consolation somewhere else and was unfaithful to me.'

Charlie was silent.

'Maybe he was unfaithful to me with more than one woman? Maybe it was with a work colleague? A friend of mine?' Pixie wrung her hands together, her fingers catching on Frank's ring and she twisted it round and round. 'I don't know what to do now,' she said. 'I don't think I can face Justine today, but I am going to have to soon. There are things I need to know. Starting with who her mother is and how long the affair with Frank went on.' She groaned in despair. 'I wish Mum was here.'

'She'll be back the day after tomorrow,' Charlie answered. 'Do you want me to pick her up?'

'Thanks for the offer, but I'll go. At least in the car we can talk without fear of being interrupted.'

30

Gwen pushed her small case onto the bottom shelf in the locker room on the 'Pont Aven' ferry, relieved she didn't have to drag it around with her for the next six or seven hours. She made her way out onto the deck, resolving that as soon as the boat was underway and the Devonshire Cornish coastline began to fade into the distance she'd make for the cafe and find some coffee and a croissant. First, though, she was determined to spend some time in the fresh air and enjoy watching all the activity on the water as the boat left port, making for the open Channel.

The summer weather was perfect for the journey, with the sea as calm as it ever was, something for which Gwen was grateful for. She watched as people took photos of the frigate passing them on its way into the Devonport Docks, as the ferry reached open water and picked up speed. Standing there looking out to sea, Gwen became lost in her thoughts.

The last forty-eight hours had passed in a blur. Gus and Sarah had stayed with her for the two nights, but Annabelle and Mimi had carried on up the motorway to home, anxious to see Harry. Yesterday, Sarah had driven her to the hospital for her appointment, which, thankfully, had given her the all-clear for another year. This morning the three of them had got up early for Gus and Sarah to drive her to the ferry port for the early sailing and now they too, would be on their way home to Carmarthen. Gwen had the strangest feeling, as if she too, was now on her way home. How could that be? Her home was in Devon, not France, but stepping on board the boat, she'd felt such a wave of incomprehensible relief – a sense of looking forward to returning to the château, to going home.

Would there have been any developments with finding out who Justine and Ferdie were exactly? She knew and understood how much Pixie was hurting over the fact that Frank had kept two such major secrets from her in the last few years. Gwen still found it impossible to believe he'd set out to hurt her deliberately, even if it had been a calculated decision on his part to lie by omission. She was convinced he must have had good reasons for acting the way he did. And the sooner the truth was out in the open, the better. Once Pixie knew the truth, she could deal with it.

Since they'd been at the château, Gwen had seen Pixie slowly come back to life after the shock of Frank's death. If only she could somehow persuade her to at least think about a future in France, Gwen suspected the healing process would be further helped. Over the last few weeks, Gwen had come to the conclusion that it would be the biggest mistake of Pixie's life to sell the château at the end of summer. Mistakes could rarely be rectified, however much one regretted making them. Something she could give a masterclass in if she was ever asked, starting with her own very first mistake: never returning to Brittany until this year.

A group of children came past, the eldest a girl holding a toddler boy firmly by the hand, and a little girl of maybe five, who was concentrating on hopping first on one foot and then on the other and then twirling around. 'Jessie, just stop it, walk properly. We need to find Mum and Dad. We can have some breakfast then.'

Gwen smiled before following them back inside. Wandering around the boat in search of coffee, she bought a magazine in the shop and decided she'd come back and find something for Ferdie later. Such a sweet little boy, a credit to Justine. Gwen sighed. She was a lovely young woman and from the way Charlie was around her she guessed that he thought the same too.

She spent the next few hours reading her magazine, looking out of the window at the endless waves and making small talk with various people who, from time to time, sat down opposite her. Before lunch, she ventured into the gift shop and found a boxed toy tractor and trailer for Ferdie. From the cafe, she bought a salad and cheese baguette and a bottle of water and ate her lunch out on deck, waiting for the first glimpse of the French coast bathed in sunlight in the distance.

* * *

Gwen knew something had happened the moment she walked through from passport control into the arrivals hall and saw Pixie standing there waiting for her. It took all the willpower she possessed not to start asking questions straight away. She simply returned Pixie's greeting hug and kiss and didn't argue when Pixie insisted on taking her case. Pixie would tell her everything once they were in the car on their way home. Gwen just prayed that whatever had happened to cause her daughter to look so tired and tense hadn't been any sort of life-or-death emergency.

They were in the stream of traffic leaving the ferry-port before Pixie spoke.

'Mum, I'm sorry, I should have asked – your hospital appointment? It went all right?'

'Consultant said all was fine and he'd see me in a year,' Gwen said. 'So, come on, Pixie, put me out of my misery – you don't look as if you've had a wink of sleep since I've been away. What's happened?'

'The morning you left Justine and I had a major fallout. I accused her of having an affair with Frank. She was furious, so furious that she yelled the truth at me. She's his daughter. Ferdie is Frank's grandson.' Pixie's voice trembled and died away.

'Ah.'

'Charlie wasn't remotely surprised and you don't sound it either.'

'To be truthful, I'm not. So now instead of being furious with Frank for installing his mistress and love child in the cottage, you can relax and get to know his daughter and grandson,' Gwen said, trying to inject a note of optimism into her voice.

'It might have happened a decade or two ago, but I can't accept their presence just like that. I have so many questions. Frank was still unfaithful to me. I need to know how long the affair went on for, but most of all I need to know the name of the woman and whether I knew her.'

'Have you asked Justine?'

'No. I haven't seen her. I think we're both practising avoidance techniques.'

'Well, as you're the one who wants answers, I think you're going to have to be the one to contrive a meeting.'

Pixie concentrated on her driving for a few moments. 'The thing is, Mum, whilst I have this need to know, I am also so scared. What if it was a friend? Or even some woman he just picked up?'

'I hope for Justine's sake it was a friend, or, at the very least, a name you recognise,' Gwen said quietly. 'But what you have to remember – none of it was Justine's fault. You can't hold her responsible for being born. She has, after all, given Frank, and you, a grandson.'

Pixie sighed. 'You're right. Tomorrow while Ferdie is at school, I will talk to Justine. But first, tonight, I need to talk to you and Charlie about a dream I had recently – and what I do about it.'

Gwen looked at her as a little flame of hope sprang up. Was Pixie going to change her mind and keep the château as a second home after all?

* * *

Back at the château, Pixie went straight upstairs and, sitting in her favourite chair by the window overlooking the driveway, opened her laptop. There was no way she could concentrate on writing at the moment, but she had some serious thinking and researching to do before she put her idea to Gwen and Charlie at suppertime.

By the time Charlie shouted up the stairs that supper was ready, Pixie was ready to talk about her idea.

Charlie had prepared a simple supper of sauté potatoes with a Spanish omelette and salad, followed by stewed apple topped with fromage frais. He poured a glass of wine at each place setting before returning to the kitchen to fetch the omelette, neatly cut into three portions. 'Right, help yourself to everything,' he said, then glanced at Pixie. 'There is something I need to tell you.'

Pixie gave him a worried look. 'Nothing wrong is there? You're not on the move again, are you?'

'No. I'm planning on taking Justine and Ferdie out for the afternoon this Sunday.'

'And you can't fit them both on the bike, so you would like to borrow my car?'

Charlie smiled. 'I was hoping you might offer, but we can go in Justine's. Knowing how upset you've been, learning about Justine and Ferdie, I hope you don't feel that I'm consorting with the enemy.' He glanced at Pixie anxiously before adding quietly, 'I like Justine a lot.'

'I'm still getting my head around who they both are. If I'd met Justine under different circumstances, I'm sure we would have liked each other from the beginning. Knowing the truth has changed things, no doubt about it,' Pixie said. 'In fact, I wanted to talk to you both about that this evening. Hear your opinions on something.' She picked up her wine glass and took a sip. 'You're welcome to take my car for the outing if you would like to.'

'Thanks.' Charlie looked at her curiously, waiting for her to continue.

'Let's eat first, serious talk can keep for afterwards,' Pixie said.

They were all reaching for their dessert when Pixie started to speak again. 'Since we came to the château at Easter, I've had some funny experiences here. This for instance.' She reached into her pocket and placed the out-of-focus photo on the table, which Charlie picked up. 'Do you see what I see in there?'

'I can see the outline of a man holding his arms out – is that what you see?'

Pixie nodded. 'To me that is Frank. There's more strange things. Several times, when I've been in my writing room, there's been a warm breeze ruffling my hair, nothing else in the room is disturbed. And then, after the party, I dreamt Frank was in bed with me. We were cuddled together like we used to and he was asking me not to sell the château because it could become the family home we'd always wanted. In the dream, I promised him I wouldn't sell. And then I woke up.' Pixie took a self-conscious sip of her wine. 'I know it all sounds a bit airy-fairy but...' she shrugged. 'Scott asked if there was a château ghost because the building is so old. I'm pretty sure there isn't, but I'm totally convinced that Frank's spirit is here. Either that, or I'm going mad.'

'No, I don't think you're going mad,' Gwen said quietly. 'Some things just can't be explained away logically. The question now though is; are you going to keep the promise you made in your dream and not sell the château? And if so, what does that mean for you in the future?'

Pixie hesitated, not sure how her next words would be received. 'Firstly, it means that I will have no reason to evict Justine and Ferdie. They will be able to remain in the cottage like Frank planned. Secondly, and this depends on how you two react to my tentative ideas.' She turned to Charlie. 'You've told me you want to cook for a living. How about becoming my partner and running this place as a retreat with me? We could run courses for writers, artists, photographers and would-be cooks? And, of course, you'd be in charge of all meals.'

'My tentative answer is a very firm, yes please,' Charlie said without hesitation.

'What about you, Mum? How do you feel about moving here permanently and being a part of Château Quiltu Retreat?'

'Pixie darling, I'm way too old to be of any use helping you run the place, I'd just be in the way.'

'Nonsense. You'd be our front-of-house person – you're so good with making people feel at home.' Pixie looked at her anxiously. 'If you don't want to move here permanently, I'll have to think again because I'm not leaving you in Devon on your own, okay?'

'Sounds to me like you're trying to bully your own mother into agreeing,' Gwen muttered.

Pixie smiled at her. 'Maybe I am, but it's with the best intentions in the world.' At that moment, the sound of Pixie's mobile ringing in the kitchen was heard and she jumped up to answer it. 'Talk amongst yourselves for two minutes.'

Picking up the phone from the kitchen table, the caller ID showed her it was Jean-Yves.

'Hi. How are you?'

'Wondering whether I could buy you that supper I promised you one night this week? Maybe tomorrow?'

'That would be lovely, thank you.'

'I'll pick you up at seven o'clock then. A bientôt.'

'A bientôt,' Pixie echoed as she returned to the terrace. 'That was Jean-Yves. I'm having supper with him tomorrow evening.'

31

After taking Ferdie to school the next day, Justine returned to the cottage intending to make herself a cup of coffee and some toast. She'd slept badly again for most of the night, only falling asleep at five thirty and then sleeping through the alarm. It had been a real struggle to get Ferdie to eat his breakfast and get him to school on time. Making something for herself hadn't been an option. Coffee was definitely needed now though before she went across to the barn to start on an order of five baskets for a new shop customer in Rosteren.

Justine leant against the work surface after cutting and flattening two pieces of stale baguette and forcing them into the narrow slots of the toaster and then pressing the button on the coffee machine.

Waiting for the two machines to do their stuff, Justine tried to marshal her thoughts into some sort of order. She had no doubt that Pixie would be over at some point demanding to know who her mother was, not that she could or would say.

Justine smothered a sigh. She hadn't phoned her mother yet to tell her that Frank's wife was living in the château for the summer. That piece of information alone would be enough to set her mother off, add in the news that Justine had actually told Pixie who she was, well, that would have a similar effect to lighting a Catherine wheel on Bastille Night. The sparks would fly everywhere. She'd leave off telling Brigitte until she saw her again, it would be easier that way.

A gentle tap on the cottage door and Justine caught her breath, before squaring her shoulders and going to open the door.

'May I come in?'

Silently Justine held the door open and Pixie walked in.

'Is something burning?'

Justine let the door go and ran back to the kitchen. 'Merde! My toast. I've never understood why French toasters are so ridiculously narrow they can't manage a teacake let alone a piece of baguette.' She unplugged the toaster and threw a tea towel over it, picked it up and carried it outside. 'I'll leave the door open for a bit. I'm about to have a coffee, would you like one?'

'Please.'

Justine poured two mugs of coffee and held one out to Pixie. 'Sorry, I don't have any milk. Ferdie had the last of it for his breakfast.'

'It doesn't matter. I quite like it black.' Pixie took a deep breath. 'I'm sorry about the other day, accusing you of... you know, but I do have questions I need the answers to.'

'I don't mind answering your questions,' Justine said. 'But there is one question that I won't answer and I think it's probably the one you desperately want to know.'

'Your mother's name?'

'That's the one and I'm afraid I was sworn to secrecy and made to promise I wouldn't tell you.'

'Frank's death has changed things, surely?'

'My mother is still alive and she insisted on me making the promise as much as Frank.'

'Okay. I'll leave that one for the moment. Where did you grow up?'

'Mostly here in Brittany, St Malo. My mum married William when I was about one and he adopted me. I had a great childhood and I adore William.'

'Did your mother tell Frank she was pregnant?'

'No.'

'All the time you were growing up there was no contact between you and Frank or your mother and Frank?'

Justine shook her head. 'Never.'

'So when did you feel the need to contact him and why?'

'About four years ago. As for why,' Justine shrugged. 'I wanted to meet him, see if I'd inherited any characteristics of his and ask if he had any regrets. Then when I became pregnant with Ferdie, I also wanted to know his medical history in case there were any nasties lurking in it for the future. You know, diabetes or heart problems. Mum was totally against me making contact from the beginning. Tried to forbid me from doing it. She said other people were involved and could get hurt.' Justine gave Pixie a defiant look. 'I'm sorry about that, but I'd do it again. I loved having Frank in my life. I think he was happy to have me in his too, despite all the complications.'

Pixie nodded thoughtfully. 'I'm sure he was.' She hesitated. 'And you. How did you end up a single mum? It must be hard.'

Justine, registering a softer tone in Pixie's voice, nodded. 'I'd been in a relationship for about eighteen months and I thought Patrice and I were good together. I was wrong. The moment I told him I was pregnant he virtually ran out of the door.'

'Did Frank see Ferdie many times? Did they bond?'

'After we came to live here, a few times. He and Ferdie got on really well.' Justine hesitated. 'He saw him as well when he came to St Malo.'

Pixie stiffened. 'He met up with your mum again?'

'The two of them talked. Frank was cross that he hadn't known about me, told Mum that he would have helped, especially in the early days when she was alone. He thanked William for looking after me – and then the two of them went off to the local bar. They got on well.'

'Why did he offer you the cottage?'

'I was renting a grotty flat outside St Malo and was looking for somewhere to live and to run my business from. Mum and William had suggested I moved back in with them, but I didn't think it fair. Frank thought the cottage would be ideal. He was right, it has been perfect and both Ferdie and I love it here.' Justine sighed. 'I know you want me to leave and I will as soon as I can find somewhere.'

'We'll have to talk more about that later, but for now, please stay. I'd like a chance to get to know you both better. I think Frank would want that too.' Pixie smiled at Justine.

'I know he would. He was longing for the day, for the time to be right, when he could bring you here and we could meet. He was convinced we would like each other.'

'I wish he had done that in the very beginning,' Pixie said. 'Keeping you and Ferdie a secret for so long after you came into his life was cruel all round. I do find it hard to forgive him for that alone.'

32

Later that evening, Pixie was on the terrace talking to Gwen and Charlie, secretly hoping that she'd see Justine and Ferdie before Jean-Yves arrived to take her for the promised supper date. Charlie had fired up the pizza oven earlier and two pizzas were ready to go. She wondered how Jean-Yves would react if she suggested they stayed here for supper. No, she couldn't do that, it would be beyond rude.

'Do you know where you're going this evening?' Gwen asked.

Pixie shook her head. 'No idea.' She glanced across towards the cottage, but there was no sign of Justine or Ferdie. 'I was hoping to say goodnight to Ferdie before I left.'

'You're looking nice tonight,' Gwen said. 'Don't see you in a dress very often.'

'I wasn't sure what to wear, to be honest. Hopefully this and my pashmina will be smart enough for somewhere posh and not too OTT for anywhere else.'

'Jean-Yves is just coming up the drive,' Charlie said, carrying a bottle of wine and some glasses out to the table. 'Off you go and have a good evening.'

Pixie went through the château and out of the main entrance as Jean-Yves brought the 4x4 to a stop. She quickly opened the passenger door and got in. To her relief, Jean-Yves didn't appear to be dressed overly smartly – cream chinos and a pale blue shirt, a cashmere sweater waiting on the back seat.

'I thought we'd go for a stroll by the Lac Guerlédan before supper at my favourite restaurant in Saint-Aignan.'

'Sounds good. I haven't been there for years. Lots of boats as I remember.'

'I used to keep a boat there years ago. Do you sail?' Jean-Yves asked.

'I did back in the day. Gus was keen as a teenager and I went along with him for lessons, most of which I've probably forgotten by now. It was fun, but somehow it was one of those hobbies that vanished out of my life after university and real life began.'

'It happens. Maybe one day I can tempt you out on the water again?'

'Maybe,' Pixie said non-committally.

The village was bustling with both locals and tourists when they arrived and as they strolled along looking at the boats and enjoying the atmosphere, Jean-Yves was greeted several times by both men and women. Most times he simply said 'Bonjour' as they walked past, but one woman was more persistent and stopped them, kissed Jean-Yves on both cheeks and insisted on being introduced to Pixie.

'Martine, this is Madame Pixie Sampson, an English client of mine.'

Pixie, feeling the keen scrutiny of Martine and suspecting she was maybe being weighed up as a rival for Jean-Yves' affections, which was just silly really, smiled politely as she shook the offered hand with a ring on every slender finger.

'Désolé, Martine, but we have a dinner reservation. A bientôt.' And Jean-Yves cupped his hand on Pixie's elbow and led her away. 'My sister-in-law. I think the English expression that explains it best is – on behalf of the family, she likes to keep tabs on me.'

Pixie laughed. She'd been surprised when Jean-Yves had introduced her as an English client, she'd thought tonight was about being friends, but now she understood. He was protecting himself from a nosy family member.

'Are you still close to your wife's family then?'

'I've known them all my life. Deidre and I grew up together, lived in the same village, went to the same schools, colleges, different universities, but we were a couple from the beginning. Childhood sweethearts.' He was silent for a moment. 'It never occurred to either of us our relationship would ever end, certainly not in the way it did.'

'What happened?' Pixie said quietly.

'Deidre had an allergic reaction to a hornet sting, officially called an anaphylaxis, which requires immediate medical atten-tion. Quite simply, it took too long to get her that treatment, we were out walking in the Parc d'Armorique, miles from anywhere. It was a dreadful time.' Jean-Yves shook his head. 'Even six years later I find it difficult to accept how quickly it happened.'

'I'm so sorry,' Pixie said. 'It must have been so hard for you and Marien.'

Jean-Yves nodded. 'But as people kept telling me, time heals while life goes on. It's true, of course, but it was the last thing I needed to hear and for months I wanted to punch everyone who said it. I didn't, of course,' he said, smiling at Pixie. 'I joined a gym and broke their punchbags instead. Right enough. Let's go eat and cheer ourselves up,' and Jean-Yves took her across to the waterside restaurant where he'd booked a table. Here he was greeted by name again and they were taken out to a table on the terrace.

'What a great location for a restaurant,' Pixie said. The terrace was above the water and jutted out over the lake so diners had a panoramic view over the wide expanse of the lake.

Once they'd ordered their food and drinks – a non-alcoholic beer for Jean-Yves and a glass of wine for Pixie – Jean-Yves said. 'How's life been at Château Quiltu this week? Interesting I hope.'

Pixie smiled. 'Interesting doesn't even begin to cover it. I've made a decision and I've also discovered something.'

Jean-Yves looked at her. 'Tell me the decision first?'

'I've decided not to sell the château. Charlie is coming in with me as a partner and we're going to run it partly as a retreat, but we'll also offer courses in various things – writing, painting, photography and cooking. It's going to take some setting up, so it will be next year before Château Quiltu Retreats opens for business, but that's the new plan.'

'I'm so pleased you've taken this decision. If I can help in anyway – especially with planning and French bureaucracy – you know you only have to ask.' And Jean-Yves gave Pixie such a beaming smile at the news that she laughed.

'Thank you. I'm glad you're pleased.'

'And now the discovery you have made? A secret door leading to a cellar maybe? Treasure at the château.'

Pixie laughed. 'No nothing like that.' Before she could say more, the waiter appeared at their table with bowls of steaming mussels. For several moments they both concentrated on their food.

'So what is this discovery of yours?' Jean-Yves asked.

'Justine Wilson is Frank's daughter and Ferdie is his grand-son.' Pixie glanced at Jean-Yves. 'Did you know that?'

'Not officially, no. But I did suspect that was the connection. Frank told me that they were both very dear to him, particularly the little boy, but it was a complicated situation and he needed time to sort things.'

'Complicated doesn't begin to explain it. I do wish though, that Frank had been able to confide in me about his unknown daughter the moment she contacted him – which was four years ago. I can't help feeling that I let him down in some way, that he was so worried about my reaction to the news that he didn't know how to tell me.' Pixie shrugged. 'I'll never know the answer to that, so best I try and put it out of my mind.'

'I think perhaps he was trying to protect you, trying to find a way to tell you without blowing your world apart. How did you react when you discovered the truth?' Jean-Yves asked gently.

'Honestly? Pretty badly, so I guess he was right to be worried. I'd goaded Justine about having an affair with Frank and she flipped.' Pixie bit her lip, remembering the scene. 'I apologised and asked her to tell me who her mother was. Apparently that is a question too far as she's promised not to say.' Pixie sighed. 'Knowing only half the story is incredibly frustrating.'

'Tell me, which came first: your decision not to sell or the knowledge that Frank had a daughter and grandson?'

'Deciding not to sell.'

'That's good.'

'Why?'

'Because you didn't take the decision under pressure from anyone. You made it of your own free will.'

'And that's good?' Pixie looked at him and waited for an explanation.

'Yes, in two ways. First, you're moving forward with your life, but also because under French inheritance laws Justine, as Frank's daughter, has a claim on the château. It's complicated but, put simply, she would have to agree to you selling it and the majority of the sale money would be hers.'

Pixie slumped back in her chair. 'Even though I am the sole owner of the château now?'

Jean-Yves nodded. 'You don't have any children and she is Frank's heir.'

Pixie picked up and drank the wine in her glass. 'May I have another glass of wine please?'

'Of course. Would you like the name of a gym and a good punchbag as well?' Jean-Yves asked, a definite twinkle in his eye.

Out on the terrace, Gwen watched as Justine and Ferdie made their way over to the château five minutes after Pixie had left with Jean-Yves. Was that deliberate? Gwen wondered. She'd guessed that Justine had intentionally kept her distance. Ferdie, of course, had no such inhibitions and ran happily up to her when she held out her arms.

'Hello, Gwen. We're having pizza with you tonight.'

'I know, Charlie has made them especially for you. You know I went to England recently? Well, I brought you something back.'

'For my birthday? It's soon and Lola is coming for tea.' Ferdie's little face was lit up with excitement. 'I wish Mimi could come too, but she lives far far away.'

'No, it's not a birthday present. I bought it just because I thought you'd like it.' Gwen reached under her chair and picked up the toy tractor and trailer package from where she'd hidden it.

'Thank you. Can I open it now and play with it?'

Gwen nodded.

'I'm going to show Mummy and Charlie first.' And Ferdie sped off towards the pizza oven where Justine was standing talking to Charlie.

Watching him, a long-ago memory of another little boy playing in a Brittany garden up on the coast not seventy kilometres away slipped into Gwen's mind. That special summer in the late 1950s when she'd looked after three small French children aged eight, five and three. A little boy called Thomas was the five-year-old, sandwiched between two sisters who alternated between spoiling him and being cross with him for not doing what they wanted when they bossed him around. Thomas had positively lived for the weekends when his big brother arrived and the two of them did things without the girls. Gwen smiled to herself, she too, had lived for those days and remembered them long after she'd left the family and returned home.

Charlie and Justine carried the pizzas over to the table.

'I'm going to sit next to Gwen,' Ferdie announced.

Justine glanced at Gwen. 'It's a bit late in the day to ask, but do you mind him calling you Gwen? You wouldn't rather he called you, I don't know, Auntie Gwen? Mrs Ellis?'

'Gwen is fine. We're friends aren't we, Ferdie?'

Ferdie nodded, his mouth too full of pizza to answer.

'My mother would think it was disrespectful, she's a bit old-school about names and manners. I always had to call her friends Tante when I was growing up.'

'Where did you grow up?'

'St Malo. My dad was based there for work. Actually, he was based in Paris, but after Mum's family home in Montmartre was sold they decided they'd prefer to live in Brittany and just keep a pied-à-terre in town.'

'I spent a short time in Paris when I was young,' Gwen said. 'I loved it, especially Montmartre.'

'Mum and I prefer the countryside; that's something we both have in common at least.'

'Mummy, is Gangan coming for my birthday? And will she bring Buddy?'

'The answer to both those questions is no. You'll see her soon though, I promise.'

'Can I have a puppy for my birthday?' Ferdie asked.

Justine sighed. 'I'm thinking about it. But I don't think there are any puppies available at the moment.'

'Lola's mummy knows a farmer who has some. You could ask her.'

'I could, I even might, if you stop talking and eat your pizza.'

Charlie poured Ferdie some water before picking up the rosé bottle and offering it to Gwen and Justine, both of whom shook their heads. 'You won't have heard about Pixie's plans for this place,' Charlie said. 'She's decided not to sell but to run it as a retreat and asked if I'd like to be a partner and to be in charge of the cooking.'

'That's wonderful news. You get to cook just like you wanted,' Justine said. 'I don't suppose she's said anything about me staying on in the cottage, has she? She did say Ferdie and I could stay and not to worry about moving out for now, but I can't help worrying.'

33

'There you go, Ferdie, the beach. Now all we need to do is find you a bucket and spade,' Charlie said as the three of them walked along the esplanade at Plage Trez, the main beach at Bénodet down on the south coast of Finistère on Sunday afternoon. 'And this looks like just the place,' he added, stopping by a shop with a display of beach paraphernalia overflowing onto the pavement.

With Ferdie happily carrying his new bucket and spade, they wandered along the beach to find a less crowded spot, where Justine spread out the rug she'd brought for them to sit on.

Time passed quickly for the next hour or two as the three of them paddled in the sea, built an impressive sandcastle, decorated it with seashells and ate the crisps and drank the lemonade Justine had brought. It was gone five o'clock when they packed everything away, shook the sand off their feet and began to head back to the car, Charlie carrying a tired Ferdie.

Once Ferdie was strapped in his car seat safely and they'd joined the traffic heading for the main road, Charlie glanced at Justine. 'I enjoyed this afternoon. Ferdie's a great kid.'

Justine glanced behind and smiled. 'He's asleep already. I can't thank you enough for this afternoon. You're very good with him.' Her phone pinged, indicating a text message, and she pulled it out of her bag where she'd stuffed it. 'Oh. Not sure whether that's a good thing or not.' She sighed and closed her phone. 'You know how desperate Ferdie is for a dog?' Justine lowered her voice in case Ferdie wasn't in a deep sleep. 'I asked Carole, my friend, to find out if the farmer she knew still had any puppies left. Secretly, I was hoping the answer would be no and that would be the end of it, but apparently there is one female pup left. It was the runt of the litter, but the farmer's wife has brought her on and she's ready for a new home. It's mine if I want it.'

'Coming from a farm I'm guessing it's a collie?'

Justine nodded. 'Which coincidentally is my favourite breed, so you can see I'm torn.'

Charlie glanced in his rear-view mirror, checking that Ferdie was asleep. 'May I give it to him for his birthday? I promise to help him train her and look after her. And we can all go on walks together.'

'It's expensive, Charlie. And what happens if Pixie tells me I still have to move out of the cottage.'

'That's not going to happen,' Charlie said confidently.

'You don't know that.'

'I know my Aunt Pixie and I'd place money on the fact that she isn't about to turn away a blood relative of her dead husband whom she adored. She'll also want the chance to be a grandma to Ferdie.'

'I wish I had your confidence. How was she when you talked to her?'

'Angry with Frank, which I suppose was only natural, and desperate to know who your mother is, which again is only natural.'

'And I've promised my mum I won't say. So stalemate.'

'Do you think your mum will tell Pixie herself now Pixie knows who you are?'

Justine was silent for several seconds. 'The thing is I haven't told her yet. It's not something I feel I can tell her over the phone. I know she'll be absolutely furious with me. I'll tell her on our next visit. But I hope you're right about Pixie not asking me to leave the cottage, I really love living there.'

'I am right, so stop worrying. So, how about it? Can I buy the puppy for Ferdie's birthday?'

'No. I can't let you do that. It's far too much for you to spend on a child you barely know.'

'A child I am already very fond of,' Charlie said. 'And I hope to get to know him and his mum better, if she'll let me.' He gave her a quick, hopeful glance.

Justine stared straight ahead and didn't answer immediately. Her resolve to keep her friendship with Charlie at arm's-length was disintegrating rapidly the more time she spent with him. This afternoon had been lovely and down on the beach she'd found herself wishing that just maybe she and Charlie could become a couple. After that confession it was clear that he was thinking that way too.

'We could go halves if you like?' she offered.

'Great. It can be our first joint present from us to him.' Charlie looked at her with a smile on his face. 'The first of many, I hope. Oh, and by the way, I'm making his cake.'

'He'll be thrilled about that, thank you.' Justine smiled back. Inwardly she gave herself a stern warning to take things carefully, not to rush things. She couldn't risk Ferdie being hurt if it all ended in tears and Charlie vanished out of their lives as quickly as he'd entered.

'I'll just text Carole and ask her to tell the farmer's wife we'd like the puppy.'

They drove several kilometres in a companionable silence before Charlie spoke again. 'May I ask you something? You don't have to answer if you don't want to.'

'Okay.'

'What happened with Ferdie's dad? Does he ever see him?'

Justine shook her head. 'I'd been with Patrice for about eighteen months when I fell pregnant, which came as a huge shock to both of us. Me probably more than Patrice as I'd decided I needed more in my life than a guy with no ambition and was about to break off the relationship. Apparently, the course of antibiotics I had to take for a bacterial infection knocked the pill off course. Patrice blamed me, decided he didn't want the responsibility and took off. I've no idea where he is and, no, he doesn't see Ferdie.'

'More fool him.'

'In a way, but I'm not sure he would have made a good father, so it's better he's not around,' Justine said and decided to change the subject. 'Tell me more about the plans Pixie has for the château and particularly, how you're going to be involved.'

'As far as I can gather, she's returning to the UK in September to start selling her house – and Grandma's. I think they're both planning on being back here again by the middle of October and we'll spend the winter formalising and organising Château Quiltu Retreats, ready to open next spring.

'The plans are pretty vague still, but basically, I'll be in charge of the kitchen,' Charlie said. 'Pixie will decide which courses to run and organise guest speakers. She's hoping Gwen will play a part too. Hey, maybe you can give a course on basket making.'

'I'd like that. Doing the markets is going to become more difficult as Ferdie gets older, but I've still got to earn a living.'

'Don't forget I'm more than happy to look after Ferdie if you need a hand anytime.'

'Thanks. I might have to take you up on that during the school holidays.'

'Are we nearly home yet, Mummy?' a small voice from the back said.

Justine turned round and smiled at Ferdie. 'Yes. Look, Charlie is about to turn into the drive.'

'Looks like Pixie's got surprise visitors,' Charlie said, drawing up alongside a smart Mercedes before stopping the car and looking across to where Pixie and Gwen were standing with an elegant woman and a man. A sharp intake of breath from Justine made him turn and look at her. 'Are you OK? You've gone a ghostly white.'

'Oh god, I don't believe this. Pixie's visitors? They're my mum and dad.' Justine looked at Charlie. 'All hell is about to break out, so be warned. How could she just turn up without any warning?'

Charlie was silent as he got out to reach in and undo Ferdie's straps and lift him out.

Seeing him, Pixie called out, 'You're back just in time to meet Brigitte, a lovely old friend of mine and her husband. We haven't seen each other for years. I can't believe she's managed to track me down here. Justine, why don't you come and meet them too.'

Charlie lifted Ferdie out of the car and set him down gently on the drive, in time to hear Justine swear under her breath before saying in a loud voice. 'Ferdie, come and hold my hand now, please.'

But Ferdie ignored her and ran straight across to the visitors. 'Gangan. Gramps. I've been to the beach with Charlie and Mummy. Have you brought Buddy? Are you staying for my birthday?'

The loud silence that greeted his words as he ran up to Brigitte resonated in strident, hurtful echoing waves around the group as the four of them froze and all eyes turned to look at Brigitte.

34

Pixie found her voice first and glared at Brigitte. 'You're Justine's mother?'

Brigitte nodded. 'I'm afraid so. We go somewhere private. I think we 'ave the need to talk.'

Pixie shook her head vehemently. 'Not me. You need to talk and answer a lot of questions. We'll go down to the lake.' Pixie turned and walked quickly away.

'Why, so you can push me in?'

'Don't tempt me.'

'Pixie, you're killing me here, slow down, I can't keep up.'

'You always did wear ridiculously high heels.' As Pixie altered her pace marginally, Brigitte tried to catch her breath enough to keep up.

'Justine, she say this was a beautiful place. She adores living here.'

Pixie didn't answer. Reaching the bench by the willow tree, she sat down and looked at Brigitte. 'Right, I'm waiting. Start talking.'

Brigitte sat down and took several deep breaths. 'First, Justine didn't mention that you were living 'ere for the summer. If I'd known, I promise you I wouldn't 'ave turned up like this causing a scene.'

'There would have been a scene whenever you came.'

'That's probably true.'

'So why now? Why not years ago? When Justine was born.'

'Because we were friends? Because I knew how 'urt you would be. Because... Oh, lots of reasons, including the fact that I was too ashamed to tell you at the time.'

'Ashamed that you'd had an affair with my husband or ashamed you were pregnant?'

'I didn't 'ave an affair with Frank.'

'But you obviously slept with him.'

Brigitte nodded. 'Remember your last IVF attempt? Of course you do. You talked to me about how if it failed, you and Frank 'ad both agreed to accept that you weren't meant to have a baby and you'd both put it behind you and get on with your lives as a couple. I 'ave the memory of you crying for days when it did fail and it was several months before you resigned yourself to the knowledge you would never have a child.'

'It was so hard,' Pixie whispered. 'I'd longed to be a mother, to have a family, to say I was devastated when I had to accept it would never happen is to understate my feelings. At the time I felt like giving up, that I didn't have anything to live for.'

'You had Frank. A man who was also suffering, but his main concern was for you. He came to see me a few times, asking me to try and 'elp you and did I think there was anything more he could do. One evening, he broke down, said you'd screamed at him when he'd suggested maybe some time away together would 'elp you both to heal. That night, he said he didn't know what to do, nothing seemed to be right.'

'I screamed at him a lot, I was a regular fishwife at the time,'

Pixie said. 'I remember him suggesting we got away from it all, had a long holiday. I couldn't believe how he felt a holiday would cure anything.'

Brigitte hesitated. 'The evening when he broke down he was already in a terrible state when he arrived on my doorstep asking if he could stay. He was my friend too, so of course I said he could. I made up the bed in the spare room. In the end we both slept there. That was the night Justine was conceived. It was also the one and only night I slept with Frank. I never set out to sleep with him.'

'Not an affair then – a one-night stand.'

'Frank rang me the next day to apologise. Said he wasn't in the 'abit of sleeping with his wife's friends and certainly not her best friend. He also said he planned on telling you, he felt so guilty.' Brigitte smiled ruefully. 'Took me some time to talk him out of that, but eventually he agreed not to tell you. On a "need-to-know basis", I didn't think it was fair to burden you with the knowledge. I'd 'ad a couple of glasses of wine before he arrived that evening and Frank also drowned 'is sorrows with a couple of glasses. We didn't love each other, it had just been sex between two consenting adults, and we both knew the chances of it happening again were nil. It 'appened once and once only.'

'Did you think of telling him when you discovered you were pregnant?'

'No, not at first. To find myself pregnant in my late thirties was unexpected but thrilling. Like you I'd spent most of my adult life longing for a baby but had never met anyone to settle down with. Remember, I'm a few years older than you – I admit to three, no more – and the ticking of my biological clock was getting fainter. The thought that I was actually 'aving a baby blew my mind. There was no way on this earth that I would terminate the pregnancy, which left me with few choices.' Brigitte took a deep breath. 'I could tell Frank and you and see if you wanted to adopt the baby when it was born. Two big problems with that. I didn't know how you would react to the news. You might 'ave kicked Frank out for being unfaithful and I would have broken up a good marriage and still been left 'olding the baby. Secondly, deep down, I knew that I wouldn't be able to part with a baby I'd given birth to. So I decided the easiest thing by far would be for me to keep the baby, disappear out of your life without saying anything and become a single mum. Selfish in one way, but I still think it was the right thing for me to do.'

'I never really understood why you disappeared the way you did. One moment you and I were meeting up for lunch every week and the next you'd vanished without a word. Even Frank was surprised when HR told everyone in the office you'd returned to France because of a family emergency.'

'Well, technically it was a family emergency – mine. I decided it was better to go quickly rather than prolong things. Also, I couldn't face seeing you because a, you would be upset that I was pregnant so easily while you kept failing, and b, you would quiz me as to who the father was and I wouldn't be able to tell you.'

'So you ran away with your sordid guilty secret.'

Brigitte pulled a face. 'You could say that, and I guess from your point of view it was sordid, but it never felt like that to me. I really felt unexpectedly blessed to being 'aving a baby. Oh look,' Brigitte pointed to the far edge of the lake. 'There's a heron, isn't he beautiful?'

The two of them watched the large bird for a minute before he slowly took off and flew gracefully away, then Pixie turned to look at Brigitte.

'Justine tells me Frank came to see you in St Malo after she'd contacted him.'

'Did she also tell you how furious he was with me for not

telling him I was pregnant? I warned Justine before she contacted him that it wasn't all about her, that other people's emotions were involved and there was more at stake than first appeared.'

'I still don't understand why Frank didn't tell me about the château viager scheme finishing or confide in me about letting Justine and Ferdie live in the cottage. I thought we were so secure in our marriage and told each other everything.'

Brigitte looked at her. 'Even all these years later he was terrified of losing you when you heard about Justine. Keeping quiet about Justine once he'd learnt of her existence was so hard for him. He wanted to tell you but was scared of the consequences. He knew that initially you'd be hurt, and furious with him, not to mention with me, and he desperately hoped that when you did meet Justine you would be forgiving enough to accept her as part of your family. He made both me and Justine promise not to tell you the truth until he was ready and felt the time was right.

'Which would have been when?' Pixie's voice was curt. 'Justine says she made contact with him four years ago and came to live here in the last fourteen months. Surely in all that time he could have found a way to tell me?'

'I think he was planning on finally bringing you 'ere this year and introducing you to Justine and Ferdie. I know Justine tried several times to get him to tell you. He tried so hard for so long to avoid hurting you that sadly, fate took it out of his hands and in the end he never got the opportunity to do the right thing and you've been 'urt even more by his secrecy.' Brigitte tentatively reached out for Pixie's hand and squeezed it. 'I am so sorry for everything. You and I used to be such friends, I hope you can forgive me and we can enjoy watching Ferdie growing up together. The one thing you have to remember above everything else is that you were the love of Frank's life until the day he died.

He tried to do everything he could to protect you from being hurt.'

Pixie slowly removed her hand from Brigitte's and stood up. 'Thank you for finally telling me the truth. At the moment I'm finding it hard to forgive Frank for keeping "his family" a secret from me for so long. As for us being friends again, maybe.' She shrugged and began to walk away. 'We'll have to wait and see.'

35

Gwen was in the kitchen when Pixie walked in and looked up anxiously.

'Where is everyone?'

'Justine and Brigitte have gone over to the cottage, William has taken Ferdie and Buddy for a walk around the grounds. Charlie is... I'm not actually sure where Charlie is. Are you all right? Cup of coffee?' Gwen moved towards the machine and switched it on, popping a capsule in and placing a cup under the spout.

'Please. As for me, I think stunned is the word. It never occurred to me that my best friend all those years ago would be the mother of Frank's daughter. At least I know the truth now.' Pixie pulled a chair out and sat down. 'When she got out of the car, I recognised her instantly and I was genuinely thrilled to see her. I missed her so much when she just vanished all those years ago.' Pixie shrugged. 'But now, now I don't know how I feel about her.'

'Did she tell you how long the affair went on?' Gwen asked quietly.

'She insists it wasn't an affair. It was just the once when Frank broke down.'

Pixie stood up and pushed her chair back under the table. 'Mum, do you mind if I take my coffee upstairs? I think I'd like to be alone for a bit. My mind has gone blank. I need to let things sink in.'

'Of course not,' and Gwen handed her the cup of coffee.

Once upstairs in her writing room, Pixie stood looking out of the window and sipping her coffee for a few moments before sitting down and placing her cup on the floor. She really must get a temporary table or desk of some sort up here until the furniture from her study at home came over. To think in a few months this would be home.

Home. Was she ready to call this place home? Did she really want a new beginning in a foreign country without Frank at her side? It would be easier to stay in England and carry on with her life there as normal. Only it wasn't normal any more, was it? It had turned empty and lonely the day Frank died. The last few months here had shown her that there was still a life out there for her to live if she was brave enough to grasp it. And a life here would include the ready-made family that another of life's curveballs had thrown at her.

Justine and Ferdie. The thought flashed through her mind that if Jean-Yves was correct, and there was no reason to doubt him, the château would belong to them at some point in the future, perhaps she should hand it over now and return to England. She could visit regularly and get to know them, but would they see enough of each other to become close in the way Brigitte was with them both?

Brigitte. Another problem, although a small smile played around Pixie's lips at the thought of her old friend. Could they ever regain the friendship they'd had in the past? It had been an unlikely friendship from the beginning – Brigitte, a few years older (and it was more than the three she'd admitted to earlier, more like five, even six), typically French in manners and dress, while Pixie, in those days, had been an impulse buyer of clothes and often threw mismatched items together without a thought until Brigitte had taken her in hand.

She'd believed Brigitte earlier when she'd said she'd never set out to sleep with Frank and it had only happened the once. She'd realised a long time ago that French women definitely did have a different perspective on sex – 'it's just sex'. Maybe they were the ones responsible for the whole idea of 'friends with benefits' these days. Pixie could imagine how distressed Brigitte must have been when she realised she was pregnant and her life was about to fall apart. Unable to confide in her best friend, returning home to France and facing her family alone must have been more than difficult.

Pixie swallowed hard, remembering the times Brigitte had been there for her every time she miscarried or the IVF treatment failed.

And then there was Frank. No, he shouldn't have slept with her best friend, and he shouldn't have compounded the mistake all these years later by not telling her the moment he'd learnt of Justine's existence. But deep down she did understand why he'd been so reluctant to tell her.

Pixie took a deep breath, picked up her cup from the floor and stood up. She stood for several minutes looking out of the window, putting thoughts in place. She would move here and make a new life for herself, and included in that new life would be Frank's daughter and grandson. The château would once again have a family living within its walls.

As she turned to leave, she was conscious of a sudden definite waft of perfume in the air. Frank's citrus aftershave. She stopped.

'Eavesdroppers rarely hear good of themselves,' she said quietly. 'But thank you for Justine and Ferdie.'

The familiar ruffle of her hair and then the air cleared.

Going downstairs, Pixie smiled. Things would work out.

* * *

'I am so furieux with you for not telling me Pixie is here,' Brigitte glared at Justine.

'That is fine because I'm furious with you too, for turning up without warning.'

Brigitte shrugged. 'I wanted it to be a surprise for Ferdie.'

'Well, you certainly achieved that.'

The two of them were in the spare bedroom at the cottage, making up the bed for William and Brigitte.

'What did you say to Pixie when you were talking?' Justine asked.

'I told her the facts about why it 'appened and afterwards said I hoped she could forgive me and we could become friends again. She didn't immediately fling her arms around me and cry all is forgiven. In fact, I'm not sure she will ever forgive me.'

'I think Ferdie will turn out to be the key in all this,' Justine said thoughtfully. 'Frank's grandson is a new generation. Every time Pixie sees him, she'll see Frank in him and in time it will become immaterial who is his mother or who his grandmother was. He will simply be Frank's grandson whom she loves irrespective of who gave birth to him.'

Brigitte brushed a tear away. 'When did you get so wise? Let's 'ope you're right, and also that it doesn't take too long to 'appen.'

'I hope I'm right too,' Justine said. 'I like it here. I like Pixie too.'

'How do the two of you get on?' Brigitte picked up a pillow and squashed it into a case.

'Warily at the moment. We sort of skate around each other. She says she wants to talk to me and the two of us to get to know each other, so at least the threat of eviction has been removed, but I don't know how long for now she's met you. I suspect it depends on how much she dislikes you and the fact you're the woman who gave birth to me.'

'She told you to leave before she knew who you were?'

Justine nodded. 'She was pretty upset to find Ferdie and me living in the cottage, but once I'd screamed at her I hadn't had an affair with Frank, she seemed to thaw a little towards me and definitely towards Ferdie. Now she knows you're my mother, how she reacts is anyone's guess. Charlie was saying only this afternoon that she wouldn't make us leave, but now, I don't know what to expect. Anyway, Mum, how long are you planning on staying?'

'No definite plans. We want to see Ferdie on 'is birthday and to spend some time with you both. We were 'oping we could take Ferdie out if you were busy. I suspect we'll have to see how Pixie is tomorrow. She might want us off her property. If she does, we'll find somewhere local to stay and you and Ferdie can see us there.'

'Whatever happens tomorrow, if you could look after him for the morning that would be good. I can go and collect his present then.'

'You have a party planned for the afternoon?'

'Lola, his best friend, and her mum are coming for tea, so not really a party, although Charlie is baking a cake.'

'Charlie, he is nice, no?'

'Yes, Ferdie adores him already.' To Justine's relief, she heard the cottage door slam shut, saving her from any more of Brigitte's probing questions. 'Dad and Ferdie are back. I'd better get Ferdie something to eat. You can bathe him if you want while I do that. He'll be tired after all the sea air this afternoon. I'll fix us some supper once he's in bed.'

36

The next morning, Justine waved Ferdie off with Brigitte and William before going across to the château to look for Charlie.

He was in the kitchen putting the finishing touches to an intricate chocolate fortress cake under the admiring eyes of Pixie and Gwen.

'Wow. That's brilliant. Ferdie is going to love it,' Justine said. 'I came across to see if you wanted to come to the farm this morning and pick up the puppy with me? But I guess you're busy, so no worries.'

'Give me ten minutes and I'll be ready,' Charlie said. 'I'm not going to miss out on that.'

'Have a coffee while you wait,' Pixie said, moving across to the machine and popping a capsule in. 'How is Brigitte this morning?'

Justine looked at her, surprised. 'A bit subdued, but she seems fine. Whether she will be when they return is anyone's guess. Ferdie is a bit hyper this morning, so I suspect she and Dad are going to have their hands full.'

Pixie handed Justine her cup of coffee. 'When Ferdie knows me better I hope you'll let me take him out?'

'Of course. What do you want him to call you? I've not told him that Frank was his grandad yet. I know Frank planned on you being with him when he told him so that he'd know you were both another pair of grandparents like my mum and dad.'

'I'll settle for grandma,' Pixie said quietly. 'It's not something I ever thought I'd be called, even if it's not strictly true.'

'Grandma it is. We'll tell him together soon. Knowing Ferdie, he'll take it all in his stride.' Justine hesitated. 'Can I ask you something? You said you wanted to talk about my staying on in the cottage so you could get to know Ferdie and me better. Does the fact that my mother turns out to be an old friend who made a mistake, shall we say, make any difference to you letting me stay here?'

'No. I heard Ferdie say that Frank promised he could live here forever, so I intend to keep his word,' Pixie said. 'But we do have to have a talk at some stage. Probably after Brigitte has left.'

'Do you mind her and Dad staying in the cottage? I think Mum is convinced you're going to insist she gets off your property.'

'Your parents are welcome to stay with you any time.'

'Thank you,' Justine said, giving Pixie a puzzled look. Something was different about her this morning. She was about to make a comment when Charlie called out.

'Right, I'm ready. Cake's in the pantry ready for this afternoon. Let's go collect a puppy.' And he caught hold of her hand and led her out of the kitchen towards her car. 'See, I told you she wouldn't throw you out on the street.'

'You did, but—'

'Stop worrying, one of your problems has been solved. Let's go and collect a new one. Do you need to set the satnav?'

Justine shook her head. 'No, we go past Camping dans La Forêt for two hundred metres and take the left turn. Carole says it's a terrible track full of potholes and seems to go on forever down into the valley.'

Ten minutes later, they were bouncing down the nightmare track with Justine doing her best to miss the worst of the potholes and ruts. The farmhouse though, at the end of the lane, was beautiful and well maintained. 'Maybe the drive is next on their list to receive some TLC,' Charlie said.

The farmer's wife came out to greet them and invited them into the kitchen, where they found the puppy snuggled up in a basket with a couple of kittens.

'I don't suppose you'd like a kitten as well?' she asked hopefully.

Justine shook her head at the same time as Charlie said, 'Yes. Good idea. We'll take them both.'

'Does the puppy have a name yet?' Justine asked.

'No, you get to choose.'

'Ferdie will love that,' Justine said.

The kittens were boxed and put in the car, the basket they were all in was given as a gift and the puppy with no name had a collar and lead on and was sitting on Charlie's lap happily in the front seat.

'I'll have to get a car harness,' Justine said. 'Or maybe a cage for the back of the car.'

'We'll go shopping tomorrow morning and buy everything we need.'

As they drove back up the rough track, Justine looked at Charlie, stroking the puppy and whispering endearments to him.

'I can't believe you wanted the kittens too.'

'I like kittens. Besides, they'll keep the mice down at the château. Grandma likes cats too.'

'We'd better stop in the village and buy some dog and cat food,' Justine said. 'And then decide where we're going to hide the puppy. I think maybe the locked barn until Ferdie gets back. There's a box in there and I've got a blanket she can have, that way the kittens can keep the basket.'

Pixie and Gwen were in the kitchen when they walked in with both the puppy and the kittens.

'Grandma, Pixie, I've got you both a present. You can decide amongst yourselves who has which,' and Charlie opened the cat box and handed one kitten to Gwen and the other to Pixie. 'They need names. And this is no-name puppy. He's going in the barn for now until Ferdie comes home.'

The afternoon of Ferdie's birthday was a fun-filled one. Ferdie's gentleness and delight with the puppy was wonderful to see. The moment Lola arrived he showed her the puppy and the two of them played all afternoon until the puppy fell asleep exhausted.

Ferdie's face when Charlie carried out his fort birthday cake, with a candle in each of the four towers, was a picture. Justine managed to catch a photograph on her iPad, which she promised herself she'd print out, he looked so happy.

Pixie was at her side as Ferdie blew out the candles. 'May I have a copy of that photo?'

'Of course. I'll print one out for you.'

'Thanks. If only Frank could have been here with us to celebrate.'

Justine smiled sadly. 'At least the three most important women in Ferdie's life are here together,' she said quietly, looking across to where her mum was standing with William. 'His mum and his two grandmothers, not to mention a great-grandmother,' she added as a smiling Gwen joined them.

'True,' Pixie said. 'I need to have a word with Brigitte,' and she made to move away, when Gwen stopped her.

'When you've had your word, will you invite her and William to lunch with us tomorrow. Charlie is doing a barbecue.'

'I'm not sure they'll still be here for lunch tomorrow,' Justine said. 'I think they may be leaving about midday.'

'Lunch can be at midday and they can leave at two,' Gwen said. 'Or stay another night. Go,' she indicated to Pixie, 'and make sure they agree.'

Pixie looked at her mother, her brow creased. 'Mum, I don't know what you're planning, but—'

'Not planning anything, just giving you more time to kiss and make up with a friend. Now go.' Once Pixie was out of range, Gwen turned to Justine. 'Do you tap your feet like Ferdie does when he's happy?'

'No, that's a pure Brigitte trait – only she does it when she's impatient as well.'

'Oh, that's interesting,' and Gwen wandered away, leaving a puzzled Justine.

'How's one of my favourite people then?' Charlie said, appearing at her side.

'I'm good and very grateful to one of my new favourite friends for making a certain little boy very happy this afternoon.'

'Happy to be of service, but why are you staring after my grandma like that?'

Justine shook herself. 'Just something she said. Anyway, I hear you're doing a barbecue lunch tomorrow and my parents are invited. Do you need a sous chef to help in the morning?'

'If you're not busy, that would be great.'

37

Gwen was on edge the next morning when she got up. If Pixie knew what she had planned, she would be cross, there was no doubt about it. But if her suspicions turned out to be correct, then at least she would have 'closure', as modern speak would have it.

Pausing in front of the mirror in her bedroom, Gwen stared at herself critically. She hadn't let herself go as so many women did as the big birthdays mounted up. Admittedly, she weighed more than she had at twenty, and her hair was grey these days, but all in all, she didn't look too bad. Of course, there were some mornings when she struggled to get out of bed, although since living in France that particular struggle seemed to have disappeared. She and Anouk both agreed a positive attitude helped to get rid of a lot of negativity that modern life threw at the elderly.

Anouk, now there was a woman after her own heart. She was looking forward to the two of them doing things together once living at the château was a permanent thing.

Carefully, she pinned her lighthouse brooch to her cardigan and gave it a gentle genie like rub for good luck, before going downstairs.

Pixie was already in the kitchen, playing with the kittens, a cup of coffee on the table and toast in the toaster. 'These are adorable, aren't they? I love black cats. What are we going to call them?'

'If we had three, we could go for Milly, Molly, Mandy, you adored those books when you were a child,' Gwen said, laughing.

'Trust you to remember those books. We could have Milly and Molly? Hopefully they'll both come to either name.'

Gwen put a pod in the coffee machine and pressed the button. 'You were talking to Brigitte a lot yesterday.'

Pixie heard the unasked question in her mother's voice and decided to ignore it. 'I'm getting used to the fact that she is Justine's mother, so as Justine and Ferdie are going to be living here forever, we're probably going to see a lot of them in the future. We need to get over our differences,' she added quietly. 'Anyway, what brought on this barbecue lunch today?'

Gwen hesitated. Should she tell Pixie why she'd impulsively organised a lunch? She took a deep breath. 'We've never really talked about my very first time in Brittany, have we? Other than to acknowledge that I was an au pair for one summer season when I was twenty.' She paused. 'I know it was a long time ago, but Brigitte reminds me of someone I met then.'

'Are you planning to interrogate her over the beef burgers?'

'I'm hoping I can get her to tell us a bit about her childhood. You were friends before – do you know anything?'

Pixie shook her head. 'I might have done, but I certainly can't remember anything right now other than she grew up in Paris. She had a sister, I think, whom she didn't get on with terribly well, and a couple of brothers. But you can't possibly remember Brigitte. She's only five or six years older than me, she would have been a mere child.'

Gwen shook her head. 'I didn't say I remembered her, she

simply reminds me of someone I knew then. There's something familiar about her, that's all. It could just be that she reminds me of an actor off the telly. I don't know, but I would like to find out.'

Before Pixie could say any more, Charlie arrived with a large bag containing meat, baguettes, salad ingredients and a couple of bottles of wine.

'Morning. You're both looking a bit serious. What's up?'

'Nothing is up,' Gwen said. 'Coffee?'

'Thanks. I thought I'd do some jacket potatoes in the pizza oven and I've bought steaks, pork chops and burgers. Just normal barbecue stuff. Justine said she'd come and give a hand prepping salad. There's plenty of cake left over for dessert and there's some ice cream in the freezer. So we're super organised.'

'Mum and I will make sure the table is set and the terrace is tidy,' Pixie said.

* * *

As everyone drifted out onto the terrace for an aperitif before lunch, Gwen was relieved to sense a friendly atmosphere. After talking to Pixie earlier, she'd decided that she wasn't going to probe too hard or too deep into Brigitte's childhood or family in case it caused more problems between Pixie and her new family.

William and Ferdie were the last to arrive, having walked both Buddy and the puppy down to the lake.

'Have you decided on a name for your puppy yet?' Gwen asked. 'We've decided to call the kittens Milly and Molly, so how about Mandy as they all grew up together?' She smiled, knowing the grown-ups would know why she was suggesting that name.

Ferdie screwed up his face. 'I think Mandy is a bit silly. Gramps says the name will come as we get to know her. She slept on my bed last night. Mummy said she had to stay on the floor, but she crept up.'

'Barbecue meat is ready,' Charlie called and within minutes everyone was sat around the table happily tucking in.

'Eating with friends and family is definitely one of the pleasures of life,' Brigitte said. 'I never really appreciated it growing up, it wasn't until my family unit began to disperse to all corners of Europe and family gatherings became a rare treat that I realised 'ow much I missed them.'

'Where did you grow up?' Gwen asked.

'Paris. And every year we'd decamp to Roscoff for the whole of the summer to the family holiday cottage. I was lucky, I had a wonderful childhood, well, the three of us did.' She glanced at Pixie. 'Did you know my father had a son with his first wife? So, technically, there were four of us, but my half-brother was considerably older than us. He's just moved back into our cottage in Roscoff.' She turned to Justine. 'I know he's hoping to see more of you and Ferdie now he's living closer.'

'I was an au pair when I was twenty for a French family,' Gwen said quietly. 'They were lovely, treated me like family from the day I arrived to...' her voice faltered, 'to the day I left. They also had a holiday home in Brittany, inherited from their grandparents, I understood.' Gwen picked up her glass of water and took a sip. 'I looked after three children very close in age. Their father also had an older son from a previous marriage.'

Brigitte put her knife and fork down on her plate and looked at Gwen who returned her gaze as she continued.

'The children were sweet – Odette, eight, Thomas, five and little three-year-old Brigitte.' Gwen paused. 'Your big brother's name wasn't Augustus Dubois by any chance, was it?'

Brigitte nodded slowly. 'Yes. And I know who you are now. You're English Gwen. The love of my brother's life. All these years, he's never stopped talking about you or wondering where you were.'

There was a sudden silence as everyone looked at Gwen, who simply sat there looking at Brigitte. 'I've never forgotten him either.'

'Grandma, are you all right?' Charlie asked, getting up and going to her. 'You've gone deathly white.'

Gwen stood up, shaking. 'If you'll all excuse me, I think I'll go for a lie-down.'

'I'll come with you,' Charlie said, putting his arm around her shoulders and leading her indoors.

'Please you 'ave to excuse me.' Brigitte stood up and left the table and made for the cottage with an anxious William following her.

'I have an uncle called Augustus. You have a brother called Gus – an unusual name in this day and age,' Justine said as they sat looking at each other. 'I hope Gwen is okay. It must have been a shock for her,' she added.

Pixie shook her head. 'Somehow, I don't think it was as big a shock for her as it was for the rest of us. I think she suspected that Brigitte was "her" Brigitte from long ago and wanted confirmation. Charlie will make sure she's all right.' She shook her head. 'Such a small world and it just got a lot smaller.'

Pixie gestured in the direction of the cottage. Brigitte and William were getting into their car and driving off.

Justine felt Ferdie tug on her leg from under the table, where he'd disappeared earlier to play with the puppy.

'Mummy, I think I'm going to call my puppy Trouble. She's just peed over my shoes.'

38

Pixie was in the process of clearing the lunch things away when Charlie came downstairs. 'How is she?'

'She's stopped shaking. I gave her a small medicinal brandy and tucked her up in bed.'

'Good. I think she's going to need all her strength in the next few hours.'

Charlie raised his eyebrows. 'Why?'

'Brigitte and William have disappeared off somewhere in the car. I suspect they're on their way to Roscoff with the intention of bringing Augustus back with them.'

'Where are Justine and Ferdie?'

'They'll be back in a moment. Ferdie needed to change his shoes because the puppy peed over them. By the way, she's now got a name: Trouble. I don't doubt for one moment that she's going to live up to it.'

Pixie looked at Charlie. 'When Justine gets back, could you take Ferdie for a dog walk or something? I'd quite like to talk to Justine on her own and this might be a good time.'

'Sure. Talk of the devil. Hello, Trouble. Ready for a walk, Ferdie? Come on then.'

'That looked suspiciously like my son and puppy being hijacked out of here,' Justine said as they left.

Pixie nodded. 'I want to talk to you. We'll leave this. I'll do it later, let's go into the sitting room. I've done a lot of thinking recently,' Pixie said, sitting down and indicating that Justine should do the same. 'And Jean-Yves pointed something out that complicates everything in one way and yet in another simplifies it. Has Brigitte ever talked to you about French inheritance laws?'

'No.'

'Well, as I understand it, French parents cannot disinherit their children. Sadly, as you know, I don't have any children – either with Frank or with another man. But Frank does: You. Which means you have a legitimate claim on this château and will inherit it eventually, as will Ferdie after you.'

'But you bought it with Frank.'

'Doesn't make any difference to you inheriting it. Anyway, I don't have a problem with that side of things. You're family, you inherit. But not yet,' Pixie said. 'I plan on enjoying living here for as long as possible. But first I have to ask, are you happy living in the cottage or would you prefer to move into the château with Gwen and me?'

'I can't think straight, this is all so unexpected. I never dreamed for a single moment,' Justine shook her head in bewilderment. 'Ferdie and I are fine in the cottage.'

'Okay. Which brings us on to my plan to run retreats et cetera here. I'm hoping very much that you will want to be involved.'

Justine nodded. 'Yes, I would like that.'

Pixie smiled. 'Good. Now a bit of a personal question. Do you have anything of Frank's as a keepsake?'

'Not really. He did give me my car as a Christmas present and letting me live in the cottage rent-free was wonderful.'

Pixie slipped the signet ring off her finger and held it out. 'In that case I'd like you to have this as a reminder of the father you never really had the chance to get to know properly.'

Justine slipped the ring onto her finger. 'Thank you. This means so much to have something like this that belonged to him. I'll keep it safe and hand it on to Ferdie when he's older.' She brushed the tears away and gave Pixie a watery smile.

'There is one more thing and I will have to talk to Jean-Yves about this, but I do intend to make sure that some of the money that Frank left me is shared with you via some sort of trust or something. He'd like to know that you and Ferdie had some security. It's something I know he would have had every intention of doing if... if the accident hadn't happened.'

There was a short silence as Justine fiddled with the ring and Pixie became lost in her thoughts before pulling herself together.

Pixie stood up. 'Phew. I'm glad that's sorted. Now we can both start to build a future here. I think I can hear Charlie and Ferdie. By the way, you do realise that my nephew is really smitten with you, don't you? He's changed from the footloose, fancy-free man of the last few years since he's been here and met you. I wouldn't be surprised if he isn't planning on settling down soon, becoming a family man.'

* * *

Pixie was upstairs in her writing room adding some more thoughts to the plan of her next book later that same afternoon when she heard a car on the drive. Quickly she stood by the window and watched as Brigitte and William got out and walked over to the cottage. To Pixie's surprise and inner relief, they were alone. She'd been wrong then in assuming that Brigitte had rushed off to drive the seventy-odd kilometres to Roscoff to break the news of 'English Gwen' being alive and well and to bring Augustus back here.

A creak on the landing below and a bedroom door being closed alerted Pixie to Gwen being up and about. There hadn't been sight or sound of her since Charlie had helped her to her room nearly three hours ago.

By the time Pixie got downstairs, Gwen was in the kitchen waiting for the kettle to boil.

'How do you feel?' Pixie asked. 'At least you've got some colour now.'

'I feel fine. Better than fine actually. And I'm thrilled that my hunch about Brigitte being who I suspected has proved to be right.'

'What made you really suspect the connection anyway?'

Gwen shrugged. 'I'm not sure. There was something about her that resonated with me, made me think even more back to that time in my life. Really it was just a gut reaction, nothing definite to go on.'

'So what happens now?'

'Well, of course in my dreams, we'd both be thirty years younger and Augustus would appear on a white horse, scoop me up and whisk me away to live happily ever after. If only.' Gwen spooned tea into the teapot and filled it with boiling water from the kettle. 'In truth, I don't know what will happen. I do know though, that I am happy he is still alive and we might get the chance to meet again.' Gwen bent down and picked up Milly and Molly from their basket and sat down, settling them on her lap.

There was a gentle tap on the kitchen terrace door. 'May I come in?' Brigitte called.

'Of course,' Pixie answered.

'We went to see Augustus this afternoon,' Brigitte said, looking at Gwen. 'He was so happy to hear about you and sends his regards.'

Gwen smiled. 'I hope you gave him mine.'

'I did. I thought you'd want me to.'

'Does he want to meet?'

'Yes. He wondered if you'd like to go for lunch tomorrow. William and I are happy to take you, disappear for a couple of hours, and then bring you back. Augustus is happy to come here, or take you for lunch in a restaurant, whatever you wish, but he thought you might like to see the cottage – and also meet up in private for the first time again.'

'I think lunch together at the cottage would be perfect.'

'Do you remember where in Roscoff the cottage is?' Pixie asked.

'Oh yes.'

'In that case, I'll take you. No need for you and William to worry,' Pixie said, turning to Brigitte.

'It's my brother she's going to see.' Brigitte glared at her.

'And "she" is my mother. I want to meet this long-lost friend.'

The two of them glared at each other for several seconds before Brigitte burst out laughing. 'D'accord. You and I take your mother to see my brother. We 'ave lunch together – like old times.'

39

The following morning, Pixie left Charlie in charge of things at the château and joined Gwen in Brigitte's car for the journey to Roscoff.

With Radio Bonheur playing softly in the background on the car radio as they drove through the countryside, conversation between the three of them was desultory. Waiting for the traffic lights in the village of Pleyber-Christ to change to green, Gwen turned to Brigitte. 'I should take something. I can't go to lunch empty-handed.'

'There's a big supermarche up the road, we can pull in there or we can find something in Roscoff,' Brigitte said. 'Although Augustus will not be expecting anything.'

'Roscoff will be fine,' Gwen said.

The nearer they got to the town itself, traffic slowed to a crawl as tractors and trailers harvesting the artichokes and the world-famous pink Roscoff onions crawled to and from the fields with their bounty. Traffic thinned out once they'd passed the turn-off for the ferry port and they were soon parking the car and making their way down towards the town.

Pixie had expected Gwen to buy a bottle of wine or maybe chocolates to take for Augustus, but Gwen stopped outside a souvenir gift shop and after studying their window display walked in. Reappearing five minutes later, she was smiling.

'I feel better about not arriving empty-handed. Come on, I know the way from here.'

As they turned away from the harbour to walk down a narrow street, Gwen stopped on the corner.

'Right, girls. The cottage is in sight, so I'd appreciate you two disappearing now.'

When Pixie went to say something, Gwen held up her hand.

'You can meet Augustus later when you come to collect me. I'd like to do this on my own without an audience,' she added quietly.

'Fair enough,' Pixie said, realising how emotional Gwen was and not wanting to have an argument with her in the street, even if she personally was struggling to get her head around the fact that her eighty-three-year-old mother was meeting up with an old lover she'd never mentioned before. 'We'll see you this afternoon, about three, okay? I've got my mobile, call if you want us to come earlier.'

'The front door will be on the latch, ring the bell and walk in. Augustus will be waiting,' Brigitte said quietly.

The two of them watched as Gwen walked swiftly down the street, waited until they saw her reach the cottage with its brightly painted blue door, ringing the bell as Brigitte had instructed before disappearing inside.

Brigitte sighed and looked at Pixie. 'It's a good job Gwen is the type of woman she is, the next few minutes will be difficult for her.'

'Why?'

'Let's find somewhere for a coffee,' Brigitte said. 'And I'll explain.

* * *

Gwen took a deep breath as she rang the bell before pushing open the front door of the cottage; even that simple act brought back so many memories. Always called the holiday cottage by the Dubois family, it was in fact a large terraced house, two rooms downstairs, a large kitchen at the back, two floors above with bedrooms and bathrooms. Gwen remembered smiling the first time she realised the size of it – a Devonshire cottage would have fitted into it three times.

Today as she walked into the hallway, the terrazzo tiles were the same but the decor had lightened. All those years ago, it had been cluttered with a dark dresser, a mirrored coat and hat stand, a bookcase down the length of one wall and children's bikes piled around. Now it was an empty space. Except for the wheelchair.

'Augustus, it's Gwen,' she called as she walked slowly through the hall, looking around and wondering.

'I'm in the garden, come on through.'

The kitchen had been modernised into a bland functional modern one that Gwen barely glanced at as she made her way out into the garden. The garden too, had changed. Gone was the gnarled apple tree with the swing hanging from one of its sturdy branches, gone were the flowerbeds in front of the fences, gone too were the hydrangea bushes that Gwen remembered edging the lawn where the children had played. The whole garden area had been crazy-paved. A fishpond with water tumbling over strategically placed rocks and water lilies covering the surface was the centrepiece. An open-sided loggia had been attached to the back of the house with several jasmine plants climbing its pillars and forming a natural roof protection over the teak table and chairs underneath. The table was already set for lunch, a bottle of champagne and a bottle of water nestled together in the ice bucket.

Augustus was making his way towards her from a gazebo built down by the bottom fence. With a subconscious jolt, Gwen registered the cane he was holding in his left hand and leaning on slightly, but her main gaze was centred on his face as she walked towards him. The face of the man who had filled her dreams for over half a century.

Of course, the face she remembered had weathered and lost its youthful luminosity, how could it not? Her own had done the same. Life had aged his face, leaving its grief, stress and laughter marks etched into lines and creases on the once smooth surface. But it was still the face of the man she'd fallen in love with.

As they both reached the fishpond in the middle of the garden and stopped inches apart, the look in Augustus's eyes told her all she needed to know and when she reached out to take the hand he was holding out to her, it felt like coming home. And if she was any judge, he felt the same way.

'Gwen, ma chérie. Today my 'eart and 'ead are filled with much joy. You 'ave no idea how I've longed for this,' Augustus said. 'Or peut-être you 'ave?'

Gwen smiled at him. 'More than you'll ever know. From the moment I left France all those years ago, I've wondered what happened. Why I was sent away so ruthlessly, why you disappeared like a pantomime genie in a puff of smoke, after everything I thought we meant to each other. Charlie would say you ghosted me.'

'Not me. My parents. Come, we sit under the loggia and I tell you everything.' Still holding her hand, Augustus led her back up the garden. 'The garden it is different, no? After the tenant left last year and I decided I settle here, I engaged a garden designer. It is all new and low maintenance so I can just potter without any heavy work but still a tranquil place to sit.'

'I love the sound of running water and the lilies are wonderful. Shame about the old apple tree though.' Gwen thought about the black and white photo in her bag.

Augustus glanced at his watch. 'Lunch will arrive in about five minutes from a local traiteur so we will 'ave a champagne aperitif while we wait.' He lent his cane against the wall out of the way and opened the bottle expertly with a gentle pop and poured some of the sparking liquid into the two waiting glasses. Handing Gwen one, he raised his own and said, 'Here's to the future.'

'The future,' Gwen echoed.

'But first we 'ave the need to talk about the past,' Augustus said. 'And why it all went wrong for us. Were you ill when you returned to England?'

When Gwen shook her head and said, 'No,' Augustus gave a sigh of relief.

'That is good. I explain why you were dismissed in such a cursory manner. I was ill and my parents panicked. They sent you away because I 'ad contracted polio. They feared for my life and it was many months before they even told me you 'ad gone.'

Gwen gazed at him, horrified, but before she could say anything the doorbell buzzed and a voice called out.

'Monsieur Dubois, j'arrive,' and seconds later the traiteur arrived in the garden and placed a large box on the table. 'You like me to unpack?'

'Non merci,' Augustus answered. 'We can do it.'

'Bon appétit,' and the traiteur left.

Together the two of them unpacked the box. As they placed

plates of charcuterie, salad, couscous, a crisp baguette, fromage and finally a tarte Tatin on the table, Augustus looked at Gwen.

'It was years before I learnt the truth about your departure and even longer until I was told about the letters you'd written to me.'

'You didn't receive them?'

August shook his head. 'Non. My father he burnt them without showing them to me.'

'That is awful,' Gwen burst out. 'All of it. The illness and what your father did.' She wiped a tear away as the realisation hit her of the damage that had been done to both their lives. 'I thought your parents liked me.'

'They did while you looked after the children, but as it became clear I would survive, they were terrified that I would leave them and move to England to be with you.'

Gwen gave a rueful smile. 'If only they'd asked you. That was never our plan, was it?'

Augustus shook his head. 'Non, we had the youthful daydreams of making the world a better place from here in Brittany.' He placed a round of Brie next to a piece of cantel on the platter. 'Voilà. Lunch is ready. We eat.'

Sitting there eating lunch with Augustus and reminiscing about a long-ago summer, Gwen felt her world had come full circle. This was where she'd longed to be for most of her life. At Augustus's side.

'I've just realised you are wearing the brooch I bought you all those years ago,' Augustus said.

'Which reminds me.' Gwen reached around for her bag which she'd placed on another chair. 'I bought this for you earlier. I wanted to bring you something. I'm not sure whether it's the kind of thing you would wear these days, but you can always put it in a pocket.' She held out a small brown paper bag.

'The assistant offered to gift-wrap it, but I was too impatient to wait.'

Augustus had opened the bag whilst she was speaking and was looking at the rope bracelet with its metal whale secured through a loop.

'It's a friendship bracelet. I thought if they'd been around when we were young, you and I would both have worn one, or even several. And the whale motif was perfect for you. You are still crazy over les baleine?'

'Oh yes. They've played a large part in my life.' Augustus slipped the bracelet over his hand. 'Thank you. It will most definitely not go in a pocket.' He poured himself a drink of water and took a sip before continuing. 'So, Gwen, tell me about you. Has life been kind to you?'

Gwen hesitated. 'The biggest unkindness life has thrown my way was taking me away from you. When I finally accepted that and got on with life as best I could, I have to say, yes, life since then has been kind, if lonely because it did not include you. I've two wonderful children, I've supported them and myself by making and painting garden gnomes. Do not laugh,' she wagged a finger at him as she saw the suspicion of a smile lurking on his lips. 'They're very fond of gnomes where I live. In fact, I'll bring one over for the edge of the pond when Pixie and I move here in October.' She picked up a knife and cut the tarte Tatin into slices before offering the plate to Augustus.

'We are going to see each other again?' Augustus asked. 'I would like nothing more than for us to be back in each other's lives, but...' he sighed. 'We've been a long time apart, although sitting here with you now it seems like only yesterday when you and I fell in love.'

Gwen reached out for his hand and he grasped hers, giving it a hard squeeze. 'Of course we're going to see each other again.

We've been given an unexpected second chance – and I can assure you, Augustus Dubois, that nobody is going to keep us apart this time. D'accord?'

'D'accord,' he echoed, before raising the hand he was still holding to his lips and placing a gentle kiss on it.

40

Pixie forced herself to stop thinking and worrying about Gwen and Augustus as she and Brigitte made their silent way to a pavement cafe near the harbour. Once they'd ordered their coffees, Pixie looked at Brigitte and waited.

'What has Gwen told you about that long-ago summer she spent here?'

'It was only this year that she even mentioned it to me, so basically nothing. Certainly no mention of your brother.'

'I was too young to have any real memories of that summer, so all I know is what has passed down from the annals of family history, and from Augustus himself. Although I do have vague recollections of Gwen reading us bedtime stories every night, something our parents had never done.'

'That sounds like Mum.' Pixie smiled. 'So what happened all those years ago?

'D'accord,' Brigitte took a deep breath. 'The bare facts are these. Gwen 'ad been looking after the three of us for a few weeks in Paris before we all decamped 'ere as normal for the whole of summer. Augustus was already 'ere as his university term had finished: he 'ad a summer job here working on one of the farms.'

The waiter arrived at that moment with their coffees and Brigitte waited until she'd moved away before continuing. 'Augustus has always maintained the summer he met Gwen was one of the best, if not the best, summer of his life. Even though he almost died and he lost Gwen. Something for which he blamed our parents, particularly our father.'

'What happened?'

'Augustus contracted polio.'

Pixie gave a horrified gasp.

'Our parents apparently "lost the plot". Gwen was given her fare home and told to leave immediately, with no reason given. And no chance to say goodbye to Augustus, who'd been whisked away to 'ospital.'

Pixie fiddled with her coffee cup. 'Did he make a complete recovery?'

'Yes, eventually. It took several years though, but he led a very full life afterwards. Unfortunately, he had a stroke in his late sixties, from which he has recovered, but he now suffers from post-polio syndrome. He gets tired really easily and has problems with the muscles in his legs, which means these days he struggles with walking very far.'

'And you didn't think to tell Mum about any of this as we were driving here? Given her some time to prepare herself?'

'Augustus asked me not to. He needed to tell her 'imself and to say sorry for breaking his promise.'

Pixie looked at Brigitte. 'Promise?'

'They'd only known each other a month, but they both recognised what they felt for each other was special. They planned to marry as soon as Augustus finished university and had a job.'

'Poor Mum.' Pixie shook her head. 'I can't get my head around how she's had to live all these years without closure, not knowing the truth about what happened to the man she'd loved.'

'Well, she'll know by now, so don't get too maudlin,' Brigitte said, standing up. 'I do know that he never forgot Gwen, and she was the reason he never married. No woman ever matched up to his first love. Come on, we need to find somewhere for lunch. And I fancy a spot of retail therapy. There are some very tempting shops here.'

Brigitte took charge, deciding that lunch would be in one of the town's hotels that had a dining room overlooking the sea. 'It won't be quite so touristy as the restaurants on the harbour.'

Pixie, still digesting the things she had learnt about Augustus in the past half-hour and wondering what effect the reunion would have on Gwen, was happy to have the decision made for her. Sitting there as the waiter placed the obligatory bread basket on the table, followed by their aperitifs, Pixie hoped her mum's meeting with Augustus was panning out the way she expected. A rueful smile touched her lips.

'A centime for them?' Brigitte offered. 'You think about Gwen?'

'Yes, but also about how life changes and careers off in unexpected directions. Wasn't it John Lennon who said, life is what happens to you while you're busy making other plans?'

The waiter arrived with their main course as she finished speaking, placing a plat du jour of sole meunière in front of them both. The two of them concentrated on their food for several moments before Pixie looked up and glanced at her friend.

'Brigitte,' she hesitated. 'I do understand how you came to sleep with Frank all those years ago and I'm sorry it changed your life so dramatically and I lost your friendship. But thank you for keeping the baby and allowing her to grow up into being Justine. You and William between you have raised a beautiful woman.'

'William adores her, he's always regarded her as his own daughter. We did plan on 'aving a baby together, but sadly les oeufs were past their use-by date,' Brigitte shrugged. 'C'est la vie. Incidentally, has Justine ever told you her second name?'

Pixie shook her head. 'No, why should she?'

'It's Francesca. The nearest I could get to a female version of Frank.' It was Brigitte's turn to hesitate. 'So, we can be friends again, yes?'

Pixie gave her a quizzical look. 'You think I can be friends again with the woman who slept with my husband?'

Brigitte pulled a face. 'It was a long time ago and only the once. I 'ave apologised. We move on, yes, for the sake of Justine and Ferdie and in Frank's memory? You know you were the only woman for 'im. What else can I do apart from repeating je suis désolé, je suis désolé over and over?'

'Sackcloth and ashes come to mind,' Pixie said.

Startled, Brigitte looked at her and registered the half-smile. 'Phat – you English and your sense of humour.'

'Tch, you French with your laissez-faire attitude to sex,' Pixie retorted before relenting and smiling at her. 'Yes, we can be friends again. Because in truth I can't thank you enough for bringing Justine into the world.'

Brigitte gave a relieved sigh. 'Good. Next time we come, I sleep in the château – the bed in Justine's spare room is very uncomfortable.'

Pixie laughed. 'Yes, you can sleep in any bedroom you choose.' Pixie took a drink of her wine before looking at Brigitte. 'After Frank died, I was in the depths of despair, wondering how I was going to survive without him. I still miss him, but his unexpected legacy of a stepdaughter and a grandson has given me the family we always wanted. And a reason to carry on,' she added quietly.

'And you 'ave me back in your life, that is good too, no?' Brigitte said. 'We 'ave good times together again.'

* * *

After lunch, they lingered over coffee on the hotel's terrace and it was gone three o'clock when they made their way to Augustus's cottage.

Brigitte pushed open the door and walked straight in, calling out as she did so. 'Augustus, it's me and I've brought Gwen's daughter to meet you.'

Pixie, following behind, caught her breath as she saw Gwen standing next to Augustus, with happiness clearly shining from her face. The two of them might have been apart for over sixty years, but standing there together they were a true couple. Pixie sensed that in this moment Gwen was the perfect example of the old French saying *Bien dans sa peau* – she was truly happy in her skin.

41

It was early evening when they arrived back at the château. Charlie was in the kitchen prepping vegetables for their evening meal with Trouble curled up in the basket with Milly and Molly.

'All well, Grandma?' Charlie asked, looking at Gwen, and receiving a beaming smile.

'Oh yes. Everything is coming up roses, as they used to say. Do they still say that?' She turned to look at Pixie and back to Charlie, who looked nonplussed. 'Well, I'm saying it again: everything is coming up roses.'

Charlie laughed and mouthed, 'What is she on?' to Pixie. 'That's good. I've got dinner organised for eight o'clock. William has taken Justine and Ferdie swimming at the Aqua Parc in Carhaix. They'll be back soon.'

'I'm going to have a lovely soak in the bath in that case,' Brigitte said. 'I'll see you all at dinner,' and she disappeared over to the cottage.

'Pixie and I are going to have a talk in the sitting room,' Gwen announced. 'I promised Augustus I would do what I should have done years ago.'

'We could have talked in the car on the way back,' Pixie protested.

'This is family stuff that I need to tell you. I didn't want to spring it on you in front of Brigitte.'

'I was going to go upstairs and get some writing done before dinner. Won't it wait until tomorrow morning?'

'What I've got to say won't take long. Come on.'

Realising that Gwen was determined, Pixie followed her into the sitting room.

The evening sun had already passed the windows but the room still held some warmth from its rays and Gwen sat on the settee to the side of the huge fireplace and patted the seat beside her.

'What's this all about, Mum?'

'This afternoon you have learnt that Augustus was the love of my life, but for circumstances beyond our control we were parted and never married like we'd planned to.'

'Brigitte told me Augustus contracting polio was the cause of your break-up. I'm so sorry.'

'It was more a severing apart rather than a simple break-up. I left France and returned to England heartbroken. For the next couple of years, I lived in hope that somehow he would come to find me. I wrote to him a couple of times with my address just in case.' Gwen paused. 'It was a long time before he completely recovered and nearly five years before he was fit enough to get on with his life again independently. That was when his mother told him she'd tried to stop his father destroying some letters from England, but he'd burnt them anyway.'

'Why?'

'Such a silly reason. He didn't want his son marrying an English girl and moving away. It was my parents who would have had to deal with me moving to France.' Gwen sighed. 'By the time

I was twenty-two, it was the sixties, the era of hippies, flower power and free love. I hadn't heard from Augustus, so in an effort to get over him, I threw myself into everything that was on offer. Not that I slept around, I found it difficult shaking off the dictum that your grandmother had instilled in me – nice girls don't, but I did drift into a relationship with Colin Fabien, your father. Falling pregnant with you and your brother was bad enough in the eyes of the world and your grandparents, but when I turned down Colin's offer to marry me, to make an honest woman of me, nobody understood.'

Gwen paused. 'We did move in together and I did adopt the name Mrs Fabien for a time to convince the neighbours we were legally married. It worked until Colin got drunk one night and started shouting the odds in the local pub. He could be quite volatile when drunk. Things went rapidly downhill after that and he just took off one day when you were three and I haven't heard from him since.' Gwen looked at Pixie with tears in her eyes. 'The only man I've ever loved enough to want to marry is Augustus. He is my soulmate.'

'That's quite a secret to have lived with for sixty years,' Pixie said quietly. 'I don't remember Colin ever being in our lives and I'm sorry I've never asked you more about your early life, simply accepting you as my mum and forgetting that you had a life before you had me and Gus.'

'That is the one thing I would never change, having you two.'

Pixie smiled. 'You've been a wonderful mother to us both,' and she reached out and squeezed her mother's hand.

'Now back to the present,' Gwen said, a determined note in her voice. 'I know we can't ever make up for lost time, but both Augustus and I want to have the pleasure of each other's company for the rest of our lives – however long that turns out to be. So when we get back to Devon at the end of September, I intend to organise the estate agents and everything else like we planned, but I'm not coming to live with you in the château. I'm going to live in Roscoff with Augustus. I hope when you move over permanently, we can come and stay here with you from time to time.'

'Mum I want you to be happy, but are you sure about this? It's such a quick decision. You only met up again today. Augustus is a lovely man, but he obviously has health problems, you'll more than likely end up as his carer. That wheelchair in the hall isn't an ornament.'

Gwen turned to look at her. 'Yes, I do realise there is every likelihood of that happening, but if our lives had panned out the way we planned, I would have been at his side through every-thing. The least I can do is to be there now. And that is what I intend to do.'

Pixie took a deep breath and stood up, holding out her hand to Gwen and pulling her up. Once she was on her feet, Pixie enveloped her in a tight hug.

'If that is what you want to do, I'm not going to try and stop you. You looked so happy this afternoon, standing at Augustus's side. You, of all people, deserve to be happy.'

* * *

There was a mood of quiet contentment out on the terrace as everyone met up for dinner that evening. Gwen was excited, telling Brigitte and William the plans she and Augustus had talked about that afternoon. Brigitte, for her part, wasn't in the least bit surprised and gave Gwen a hug.

'I'm so happy for you both. Augustus is a good man who deserved better from our parents, God rest their souls.'

Justine walked across from the cottage carrying a gift bag,

with Ferdie running alongside her with Trouble. When Pixie had stopped handing nibbles around, Justine gave Ferdie the bag, took hold of Trouble's lead, and instructed Ferdie to do and say what she had told him earlier. Everybody watched as he marched over to Pixie and thrust the bag out to her.

'Mummy said I was to give this to you because you wanted a picture of me on my birthday. There is one of me and Frank too. Mummy says you'll be very happy to receive them because you loved Frank and you love me and you're going to be my grandma. Thank you,' and Ferdie gave a little bow and ran back to Justine. 'Did I do that right, Mummy?'

'Perfect.' Justine beamed.

'Can I have some crisps now?'

'Help yourself, but don't be greedy.'

'Justine, these are beautiful. Thank you so much for both of them, but the one of Ferdie with Frank is extra special,' Pixie said, standing there with the two photos in the silver frames that Justine had found in an antique shop.

'I thought we could take one of you and Ferdie too, sometime this summer,' Justine suggested.

'And maybe we can get Charlie to take one of the three of us?' Pixie looked at Justine hopefully.

'If you would like one, we can do that.'

Charlie came out of the kitchen with a leg of roast lamb on a platter and called across to William. 'Can you carve this please while I get the vegetables and potatoes? Thanks.'

Pixie waited until everyone had a plate of food in front of them and conversation was subdued before she asked Brigitte when she and William were leaving. 'I'm not asking you to leave, by the way. I was just wondering when you were planning on going home as there is something I'd like to do before you do go.'

'I was thinking about midday tomorrow,' William answered.

'Perfect.' Pixie glanced along the table to where Ferdie and Charlie were busy talking together. She lowered her voice just in case. 'I thought I'd scatter Frank's ashes down by the willow tree while everyone is here.'

William nodded and looked across at Justine. 'Would you like me to look after Ferdie while that happens? He's probably a bit young to realise what's going on but...'

'Sure you wouldn't mind, Dad?' Justine said.

'I've had very little involvement with Frank, whereas the rest of you...' he shrugged. 'That's sorted then. Ferdie and I will walk to the village and then play a game with Trouble and Buddy while you all say goodbye to Frank.'

* * *

That night, before she went to bed, Pixie opened the wardrobe doors in her bedroom and reached in to pull out the box that contained Frank's ashes. Carefully, she placed them on the bedside table so she could see them as she lay in bed and talked to Frank.

'I was unbelievably hurt and angry when I first heard about Justine and then the news that my friend, Brigitte, was her mother. But Brigitte has explained what happened at the time and how twenty-six years later you were scared about telling me, even though you were thrilled to have an unexpected daughter. I do wish you had felt able to tell me yourself, instead of waiting until you judged the moment to be right, which sadly was destined never to arrive.' She paused. 'Yes, I would have been upset, hurt and angry, but together we would have weathered the storm, like we always managed to somehow. Tomorrow I'm going to scatter your ashes down by the willow and the lake – one of our favourite places in the grounds, so I hope you'll find it a peaceful place. The people who loved you and who you loved in this world will all be there – me, Justine, Gwen, Charlie and Brigitte. No, I know you didn't love, love her, but she was a very dear friend and gave you Justine. Ferdie is too little to be there or understand, but he will grow up knowing his granddad is under the willow tree. Goodnight, my darling, and thank you for the gift of Justine and Ferdie.' Pixie reached out and turned off the bedside light and was asleep in minutes.

42

The next morning, Pixie was up early as usual, but instead of making for her writing room, she showered and dressed before picking up the urn and going downstairs to make coffee and think about the day ahead.

Downstairs, she placed the urn out of harm's way on the dresser and switched the coffee machine on. Minutes later, as she sat nursing her first mug of coffee, Gwen came into the kitchen.

'Thought I could smell coffee.' She helped herself to one before sitting down at the table with Pixie. 'I'm glad I've caught you alone,' she said. 'There are a couple of things I want to say. I know Justine is happy to be involved with helping run retreats at the château, but I think you need to give her more responsibility and put her in charge of front of house. I'm probably not going to be here that much.'

Pixie nodded. 'You're right. I'll talk to her about it. And?' She looked at Gwen.

'I want to go and stay with Augustus today. I'm going to ask Brigitte and William to give me a lift to Roscoff when they leave. It's not far out of their way, I'm sure they won't mind. We've so much catching up to do, and plans to make. I've packed my case with a few things ready. You don't mind, do you? You've got Charlie, Justine and Ferdie here. The three of you can start to make proper plans.'

'I'll miss you, Mum, but no, I don't mind. So long as you aren't rushing into something you'll regret?'

Gwen shook her head. 'At our age we have to seize the moment, *carpe diem* and all that. We can't be sure how many moments we've got left.'

'I can understand that. If William and Brigitte can't take you, I will,' Pixie said. 'But may I come and pick you both up next week and have Augustus stay here for a while? Give me a chance to get to know him too.'

'That would be good.'

Charlie appeared just then and soon the kitchen was filled with the smell of eggs and bacon and toast.

* * *

It was ten o'clock when Justine and Brigitte arrived, Justine carrying a yellow rose in a pot and Brigitte with a bouquet of lilies and white gardenias mixed with some colourful Gerber daisies. William had left with Ferdie and the two dogs on a walk to the village.

Pixie stood up, fetched the urn from the dresser and took a deep breath. 'Come on then. Let's send Frank on his way.'

The five of them wandered down through the grounds to the lake and the willow tree in silence.

Pixie looked at the bench and turned round to face the others. 'Would anyone like to say anything? Mum? Justine?'

Gwen shook her head, but Justine gave a small start and looked at Pixie. 'Would you mind?'

When Pixie gestured to her to go ahead, Justine moved forward and placed the rose at the side of the bench.

'You weren't in my life for very long, Frank, neither did we get to know each other as well as most fathers and daughters do and I'm sad about that. But I'm glad we did at least get to know each other a little and you met Ferdie. Letting Ferdie and I live in the cottage has changed our lives in so many ways, for which I shall be eternally grateful. A yellow rose is the symbol of gratitude, so I shall plant this down here by the willow tree where it will always remind me of you. Thank you for everything.' Justine brushed a tear away as she stepped back to stand at Brigitte's side.

'Brigitte?' Pixie asked quietly.

Brigitte shook her head. 'No words from me, just these flowers,' and she placed the bouquet on the ground by the potted rose before straightening up and smiling at Pixie.

Pixie took a deep breath. 'Standing here in the grounds of the château saying a final goodbye to you, my darling husband, is not something I ever thought I'd be doing,' she said quietly. 'Ten years ago, we made so many plans, the two of us sitting down here in your favourite place. The life I'll live here without you will be different to the one we planned together and I know I shall miss you forever, but thank you for the gift of the family I always wanted. I promise you've left them in safe hands. I love you.' Carefully Pixie took the lid of the urn and looked at Justine, 'Shall we do this together?' And she gently shook some of the ashes out before handing the urn to Justine.

The two of them walked around the willow tree, taking it in turn to shake the urn until it was empty.

'There you go, Frank, you're free to enjoy the ever after now.' As she and Justine turned to rejoin the others, Pixie stopped. 'One thing I forget to say, Frank, I'm going to have a bronze plaque made for the bench, dedicating it to you, so feel free to sit on it and enjoy the view any time you get tired of floating around.'

Walking back up to the château, Pixie felt that a great weight had been lifted, that she too, was free now to get on with the rest of her life in Brittany.

'You okay, Pixie?' Charlie asked, falling into step alongside her.

'Yes, thanks. I feel it's another step forward, drawing me closer to a new life here. I must admit I'm looking forward to a quiet few days once Brigitte and William leave for home and Gwen goes to spend time with Augustus.'

* * *

William was loading luggage into the car and had happily agreed when Gwen had asked him earlier for a lift to Roscoff. Charlie volunteered to fetch her case and ran back into the château.

Pixie gathered Gwen into a tight hug. 'Mum, you're the bravest woman I know. Be happy. I'll see you next week.'

William slammed the boot shut, Gwen and Brigitte kissed everyone goodbye and, within minutes, Pixie, Charlie, Justine and Ferdie, holding Trouble on her lead, were standing on the drive waving goodbye. As the car turned out of the drive and disappeared, the three adults let out deep sighs.

'It's going to be quiet around here for a few days,' Pixie said. 'Which is just as well, the three of us have got a lot of planning to do if we're going to get Château Quiltu Retreats up and running for next spring.' Her mobile buzzed and she pulled it out of her jeans pocket. 'Morning, Jean-Yves. I was going to ring you and make a rendezvous. That would be lovely. Okay, I'll see you later.' She ended the call and turned to Charlie and Justine. 'You two can cope without me, can't you? Jean-Yves wants to take me out for lunch. He's picking me up at 12.30.'

'I'm sure we can amuse ourselves and Ferdie for a couple of hours,' Charlie said, putting his arm around Justine. 'Shall we take a picnic lunch down to the lake?'

'Yes,' shouted Ferdie. 'Can we have crisps and can I fish?'

'You'll have to help me get it all ready first,' Charlie answered.

'If we have boiled eggs, can I peel them? I'm good at doing that, Mummy says,' Ferdie babbled excitedly.

'Today we're going to have cheese and tomato baguettes. Reckon you can butter the baguettes?'

Ferdie nodded happily. 'I can spread the mayonnaise too.'

* * *

A quarter of an hour later, the three of them were making their way down to the lake. Ferdie running ahead with his bamboo rod, Trouble bounding alongside and Charlie and Justine carrying the picnic hamper between them.

'So, you and I are going to be working together,' Charlie said. 'Think we'll manage to cope with mixing business with pleasure?'

Justine glanced across at him. 'Depends. I've heard some chefs are very temperamental, are you one of them?'

'No. The main thing you need to remember is, in the kitchen I'm the boss.' Charlie grinned at her.

'Okay, I'll remember that. So where does the pleasure come in?' Justine raised her eyebrows at him.

'Well, I'm sure working with you with be a real pleasure, but I'm looking forward to extending that pleasure to outside working hours. I would very much like us to be more than friends,' Charlie said seriously.

They reached the bench at that moment, where Ferdie was waiting for them, and Justine didn't have time to reply.

'Let's get your fishing rod ready and you can have a go while Mum and I set up the picnic things,' Charlie said, helping Ferdie to hook a piece of bread onto the line. He watched as Ferdie carefully cast the line before returning to Justine, who gave him a serious look.

'I've got Ferdie to think about as well as me. He likes you a lot and I know you like him too, you're so good with him. The thing is, as you've probably realised, we come as a package. I can cope with being hurt if we become more than friends and it doesn't work, but I can't risk Ferdie being hurt.'

Charlie held up his hand. 'Stop. Let's get a certain question out of the way. I know how I feel about you and Ferdie, but how do you feel about me?'

'I like you a lot,' Justine said. 'Probably even more than Ferdie does,' she confessed with a smile.

Charlie's face lit up. 'That's it then. We are definitely going to mix business with pleasure in a wonderful way. Everything will work out and I promise you that I will never hurt either of you.' And Charlie leant forward and placed a fleeting kiss on her lips. 'Right, let's get this picnic underway. Ferdie, come and eat,' he called.

Sitting there with Ferdie between her and Charlie, Trouble sitting in front of them all watching every mouthful they took, Justine realised she was happy and looking forward to the future. She watched as Ferdie leaned in closer to Charlie to whisper something.

'Charlie, if you married Mummy would you be my daddy?'

'Ferdie!'

Charlie smiled and whispered back. 'Yes, I would be.'

'So we would be a proper family?' Ferdie asked, looking at

Charlie seriously. 'You'd live with us in the cottage and everything? Read me bedtime stories?'

Charlie nodded. 'Yes.'

'That would be cool. So when will you ask Mummy to marry you?'

Charlie looked at Justine over the top of Ferdie's head, smiling. 'I plan on doing that when the time is right, but it may be sooner than you think.'

Justine, sitting there in a state of peaceful happiness, knowing what her answer would be when he did ask her, returned his smile and sighed contentedly. Life was good.

43

Pixie sat out on the terrace, deep in thought, watching Charlie, Justine and Ferdie down by the lake enjoying their picnic. Already it seemed to her that they were forging themselves into a family unit. Ferdie would be a lucky little boy if that was to happen officially and she had a funny feeling it was well on the way to happening. Charlie had grown into a good man and she was looking forward to him playing a part in the future of Château Quiltu. Justine too, was a lovely young woman and a good mother who deserved to be happy. Now she'd recovered from the initial shock of learning Justine was Frank's daughter, she felt that the two of them were forging a close and loving friendship. As for little Ferdie, he'd already crept into her heart and she was looking forward to having him in her life.

'There you are,' Jean-Yves said, coming around the side of the château.

Pixie jumped up. 'I'm so sorry, I didn't hear you arrive, I was miles away.'

'Pas de probléme,' Jean-Yves said, greeting her with a kiss on the cheek. 'But I do 'ave a slight problem. I must return to the office earlier than I expect. I do not 'ave the time to drive to the restaurant I wanted in Huelgoat.' He looked at her, a worried expression on his face, unsure of her reaction. 'We could eat at the bar in the village if you like?'

'If you don't mind what I call a thrown-together fridge lunch, we could eat here,' Pixie offered.

'That would be wonderful, if it's not a bother,' Jean-Yves said, visibly relaxing.

'Come on then, let's see what we can find in the kitchen.'

Pixie quickly scrubbed a few new potatoes and put them on to boil, took lettuce, tomatoes, cucumber and hard-boiled eggs out of the fridge, cut them up and tossed them together, opened a jar of tuna chunks and added them into the mix.

'There, that's my version of a Niçoise salad,' she said, laughing. 'Should really have anchovies, but I'm not a fan. Now, I know Charlie always has a decent dressing somewhere in the fridge – ah, here it is. We're good to go. I'll just toss the potatoes in some butter.'

While she'd made the salad, Jean-Yves had taken plates, cutlery, glasses, water and wine out to the terrace.

'So, tell me what were you thinking about when I arrived?' he asked as they sat companionably together eating.

'Mainly I was hoping that Charlie, Justine and Ferdie would become a family,' Pixie said. 'A lot has happened in the last few days, including my mother disappearing off to live in Roscoff with an old boyfriend.' She glanced at Jean-Yves. 'I know you offered to help with the official things regarding Château Quiltu retreats, but there is something else I need your help with. A private matter.'

Jean-Yves looked at her and waited.

'I want to make sure Justine and Ferdie are secure. I know Frank would have made provision for them if he'd lived. I was

thinking maybe some sort of trust fund for Ferdie when he's eighteen and some money for Justine now.'

'There's a lot to discuss there. I think it best for my secretary
to ring you and make a rendezvous for you to come to the office,'
Jean-Yves said.

'Thank you.'

'Pixie,' he hesitated. 'When my wife died unexpectedly, I was
blown off course and it took me a long time to recover. In fact, it's
really only been in the last year or so that things 'ave improved.
Your loss is so much more recent, but you will come through the
grief eventually, and when that 'appens, I hope our friendship
can grow.'

Pixie smiled at him. 'I already value our friendship, but you're
right, it is going to take time to get used to being without Frank in
my life. I still miss him terribly. But I'm looking forward to
building a future with my new family,' she said, looking down
towards the lake, from where laughter was drifting up on the
breeze. 'One thing I'm sure of though, is the next few months are
going to be busy ones.'

Jean-Yves glanced at his watch and stood up. 'I am sorry, but I
'ave to leave. Thank you for a delicious lunch. Next time, I
promise we will get to Huelgoat. And remember, I'm always on
the end of the phone if you need me for anything.' He leant in
and kissed her cheek in farewell before getting into his car.

'See you soon.' Pixie watched him drive away before clearing
the table and wandering into the château. Whether he would
ever become more than a good friend, only time would tell, but
she did like Jean-Yves. For the moment though, she intended to
focus on her family and turning Château Quiltu into the retreat
she and Frank had dreamed of running.

Walking slowly through the château, she climbed the stairs to
her writing den. She'd promised herself earlier that today would

be the day she sent the synopsis and the first three chapters of her new book to her editor. The book she'd had the germ of an idea for all those weeks ago had somehow taken off in an unexpected direction. She could only hope her editor would like and approve it.

Pixie opened her email program where the letter to her editor sat together with the attached manuscript ready to be sent. Her finger hovered over the send button as she read the title again, 'Life at the Château'. With a smile, she pressed the button and heard the whoosh as the email went on its way.

Thoughtfully, she closed the laptop down. Nobody ever knew what the future held. The only certainty she could hold on to at the moment was the fact that she had two new people in her life, courtesy of Frank; a family she already loved and wanted to be a part of. Whatever had happened in the past, Pixie knew she was ready to move on and enjoy the rest of her life here in France with her ready-made family in Château Quiltu.

ACKNOWLEDGMENTS

As always, my first thanks have to go to 'Team Boldwood' and in particular my editor, Caroline Ridding, who somehow knows how to get me to dig that little bit deeper to improve the story. She also has the patience of a saint! Thanks to Amanda and Nia for all the marketing and the work they do behind the scenes. Huge thanks to copyeditor Jade for her patience on this one and to Rose the proofreader.

Thanks to all my online friends who this year were needed more than ever, and the Boldwood Girls (and Boys) who are so supportive of their fellow authors. Thanks guys!

And, of course, I must thank my readers, the people who enable me to carry on doing a job I love. I've had so many letters from readers this year, thanking me for providing some escapism and helping them through a difficult time.

Love,

Jennie.

MORE FROM JENNIFER BOHNET

We hope you enjoyed reading *Summer at the Château*. If you did, please leave a review.

If you'd like to gift a copy, this book is also available as an ebook, digital audio download and audiobook CD.

Sign up to Jennifer Bohnet's mailing list for news, competitions and updates on future books.

http://bit.ly/JenniferBohnetNewsletter

Explore more gloriously escapist reads from Jennifer Bohnet.

 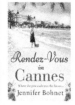

ABOUT THE AUTHOR

Jennifer Bohnet is the bestselling author of over 10 women's fiction novels, including *Villa of Sun and Secrets* and *The Little Kiosk By The Sea*. She is originally from the West Country but now lives in the wilds of rural Brittany, France.

Visit Jennifer's website: http://www.jenniferbohnet.com/

Follow Jennifer on social media:

- facebook.com/Jennifer-Bohnet-170217789709356
- twitter.com/jenniewriter
- instagram.com/jenniebohnet
- bookbub.com/authors/jennifer-bohnet

ABOUT BOLDWOOD BOOKS

Boldwood Books is a fiction publishing company seeking out the best stories from around the world.

Find out more at www.boldwoodbooks.com

Sign up to the Book and Tonic newsletter for news, offers and competitions from Boldwood Books!

http://www.bit.ly/bookandtonic

We'd love to hear from you, follow us on social media:

facebook.com/BookandTonic
twitter.com/BoldwoodBooks
instagram.com/BookandTonic

Printed in Great Britain
by Amazon